LEGACY
OF
STARS

TYLER
BOWMAN

DEDICATION

This book is dedicated to family and friends, whose
support in achieving this dream saved my humanity.

PROLOGUE

We have always believed that we were not alone, that others existed and thrived out there among the stars. Based on this assumption, humanity undertook an interstellar search the likes of which would propel its advancement into the final frontier. Centuries of technological breakthroughs coupled with the mass fertilization of planets and asteroids would ultimately result in the vast and rapid growth of the human race known as The Great Expansion.

Humanity realized this quest through the combined effort of all countries, cultures, and eventually, civilizations. It was this singular objective that would put an end to war and our nature for senseless killing. Intelligent life gained the prestige that it rightly deserved. All people would be given a role and contribute. The purpose-driven life thrived.

Through unimaginable cooperation, human life expectancy would spike (in large part due to *Turritepsis Dohrnii,* a species of jellyfish), humans and mechs would peacefully coexist, genetic engineering would be used for the greater good, and our greatest limitation—ourselves— would cease to limit us.

Eventually reasonable space travel would be conceived, though it would take another 250 years from the onset of that task. It was discovered that if a miniature black hole could exist in a stable and controlled environment, then its gravity could be used to create spatial distortions.

1

Only through pure serendipity, as if fate had truly played a role, was the ability to detect and capture dark matter made a reality. A pulsing combination of both high and low frequencies led to the success of this long-theorized feat. Applicable space travel was no longer inconceivable. A four light-year trek was now similar to a stroll down to the mini-mart.

It was at this time humanity began introducing itself to foreign solar systems, then naturally, galaxies. The hope that extraterrestrial life would finally be confirmed grew astoundingly large. The climax to the seemingly impossible, and the answer to our greatest question, had finally arrived—or so we thought.

Among the exoplanets and stars explored, countless discoveries in the form of abandoned megastructures, previously terraformed surfaces, and unnaturally created poisonous gases were made. Interstellar archaeology, as it would become known, showed that sentient civilization after sentient civilization, for known and unknown reasons, all eventually collapsed.

Centuries of encountering Dyson spheres, real and artificial planets, and once-inhabited asteroids would all result in the absence of intelligent life. It would be a full millennia before the hope of finding other living creatures who shared our universe would start to wane. Humanity as a whole, from galaxy to galaxy, believed for so long in this common goal. Now, without their singular purpose, what would become of them?

So much had been achieved during this initiative, and although the result was not expected, the benefits to the survival of humankind were infinite. The search for alien life ended up ensuring the survival of human life. Although the universe had claimed a multitude of other species, humans would prevail; at least, that was the justification to such unsavory findings.

The realization that we were actually alone was in its own way unfathomable. What is a civilization to do once it believes it has advanced as far as it can advance, and discovered all there is to discover? What effects are there when there is no longer a higher purpose, a greater cause?

Galactic wars eventually broke out. System against system; galaxy against galaxy. Weapons for killing, and methods thereof, were nightmarish in nature. Communication among civilizations and colonies fractured. Alliances were created and betrayed in the flash of a shooting star. After a time, no one knew which galaxy was fighting who and when, or even why.

The universe became a free-for-all. Gangs of space bandits formed, roving from system to system, preying on those who could not protect themselves. Humanity had cycled full circle, once again actively contributing to its own demise.

If ever there was an end of times this would surely be it; at least for this once rare, sentient species . . .

CHAPTER 1
NOCTURNE GALAXY

They'd reached the part of the trip that Joxy dreaded the most. Nocturne Galaxy's nearly impenetrable gaseous barrier surrounded *The Legacy*. These ever-shifting walls of corrosive clouds have been the demise of many seasoned captains. Joxy swore as she manipulated her ship's controls, summoning all of her focus and the skills necessary to keep her crew, and their home, safe.

The idea of venturing all the way out to this reclusive galaxy was never appealing, and as beads of sweat burned her eyes, it became even less so. At the edge of the known universe, Nocturne stood sentinel to the ever-expanding unknown. Considered one of the most fortified galaxies in existence, most would-be privateers knew to keep well away.

"Hang on!" Joxy grunted through gritted teeth as she banked sharply to avoid a fast-emerging cloud.

A clear view of the Nocturne Galaxy opened before them, filling the entirety of *The Legacy*'s view-port. A few sighs of relief escaped the bridge. Joxy wiped the back of her hand across her face. The strain at the corners of her eyes and mouth faded into a stubborn smirk. Her sharp features shifted into an air of confidence as she threw her thick, dark braid back over a shoulder.

"Raygo, upload docking procedures and bring up the mission display before ghosting. You know they don't take too kindly to your kind this far out from the civilized universe." With all the maneuvering she just performed, there was no way their presence wasn't lighting up every proximity scanner in a two light-year radius.

"Aye, aye, Captain, but procedures appear standard with no further mission updates. The Nocturians are remaining vague. I don't like it."

"Me neither," Joxy said.

"I'll be keeping an eye on things." Raygo, more or less the ship's first mate, de-atomized right in his seat. Molecules broke down to their component atoms before scattering throughout the ship's environment.

Dragging over a holo, Joxy expanded it with her fingertips, reexamining what little information they had. They were supposed to be docking in the orbit of a planet known as Hawaii 5 in the Pepsi system. *Whose bright idea was it to name everything in this quadrant of the universe after ancient Earth culture,* she mused while scanning the screen. She paused the feed in the section describing how two NG S-14 warships would escort *The Legacy* upon its entrance to the system. It went on to explicitly state that BAIs were forbidden, all weapon systems must be shut down, and ships will maintain a speed no greater than one light-year per hour inside of Nocturne. After handing over controls to Tano, her second, Joxy double-checked that weapons were down, then ran a quick scan to ensure no other bio-signature but her own registered. Although the data showed her as the only organic life form on the ship, she knew that somewhere on the quantum level, Raygo watched over her.

BAIs were a relatively new advancement for mankind, though a monopolized one. Even humble critics would admit that they were the next link in our evolutionary chain. Created in combination of human drive and alien matter typically found at the sites of extinct civilizations, what would be questioningly termed Biological Artificial Intelligence came into existence. This label became very misleading in the sense that the intelligence wasn't all that artificial.

The lack of mission details wasn't unexpected in Joxy's line of work. It was the fact that Nocturne command was hiring an outsider, someone unofficial, that bothered her. The variables were sketchy at best. As it currently stood, their mission objective was to simply travel into the Void (the new, unknown part of the expanding universe) and observe. The fact that they had not yet been informed of what it was they were to observe had all of her instinctive alarms blaring.

This wouldn't be Joxy's first venture into the unknown. She'd used the Void plenty of times in the past to escape from other galactic authorities. Few pursuers ever followed for long because things tended to get a little funny out there. Throughout all of her escapades, she had never witnessed a single tangible thing in the Void.

"Tano, how are we looking, anyone yet?" she asked, sliding the holo displays to the side, revealing the ship's bull's-eye window beyond.

"Negative, Cap, no sign yet. We're almost to the Pepsi sys—wait, yeah we got action. Two S-14s fast approaching."

"Maintain speed, but be prepared for evasive maneuvers," she said. "They haven't paid yet, and I sure don't trust the bastards. They could be after the bounty so let's stay on our toes."

Two warships popped into view. Each one ominously circling *The Legacy*.

"They're scanning the ship," Tano said. "I'm reading multiple bio and mech scans, and some I've never seen before."

Joxy's chest tightened. Surely, they haven't figured out a way to detect BAI sigs in the quantum realms. If the Nocturians were to locate Raygo, the two warships would open fire without hesitation. They would be deemed too much of a threat.

"They're requesting we shut down our drives and that they be permitted to come aboard," Tano said.

Joxy breathed a sigh of relief.

"Acknowledge the request. I'm powering down the drives now," she said. "Assemble The Devils in the cargo hold and prepare to be boarded."

Tano shot a quick salute before turning to run down the bridge, his heavy footfalls fading into the hull. A voice, not her own, resonated in Joxy's mind: *"Don't worry, I'm still around. Now let's go see exactly what we've gotten ourselves into this time."*

Reassured, Joxy put on her stern captain's face. The one she used only on special occasions. Plucking from the back of her chair the black-and-lime jacket that matched the colors of her ship, she started after Tano. Joxy loved this jacket. It was fashioned after a pre-expansion design that made her appear a little slimmer. There was no mistaking the authority it held.

Joxy could barely make out Tano's steps above the shrill whine of the G-drives powering down. She didn't like being exposed like this. Let alone having strangers aboard her craft and around her crew. *The Legacy* held many secrets, and she preferred to keep them, well, secret. Posturing up, the captain within her sauntered into the cargo hold, her jacket fluttering against the heel of her boots.

Elite members of her crew stood at attention. Alert, patient, and ready for whatever may come. Each of them seasoned in their own way, with glorious tales of battles and loot. Their loyalty to the captain was unwavering, forged through tribulations that most others would collapse under. Joxy earned her respect the hard way. The only way. Humans were stubborn, and mechs even more so, both believing themselves invincible. It was a rare thing to find such camaraderie as that found aboard *The Legacy*.

Steps measured, chest out, and eyes forward, Joxy strode through the hold toward the awaiting assembly of Nocturian soldiers. Their pearl and garnet armor appeared to be give off its own light. Shields, state-of-the-art stuff, but her crew had toys of their own.

The modest detail parted down the middle for an ornately dressed, paunchy man whose taste seemed to match his size. Decked out head to toe in a gold-trimmed Enhancement skin (commonly called Eskin), which was a necessity for a man of such heft, he made his way forward. Throwing his hands wide into the air with dramatic flair, he addressed his audience.

"Ahh, Captain Joxy, you do not disappoint. Tales of your beauty have reached even our far-flung galaxy. Though I'd be willing to wager more have heard of your exceptional prowess."

Joxy tilted her head, humbly accepting the man's flattery. He spun around, hands still raised, refocusing his attention on the ship.

"And such a lovely vessel. If you return, we must talk price."

"If we return," echoed Raygo.

The man stepped past her to admire her crew, a sour stench trailing in his wake. Pacing in front, he examined them closely as though he were a buyer at an auction.

"I, of course, would be interested in the crew as well, given their familiarity with the ship. They appear well equipped, their upgrades worth every drop of dark matter, I'm sure. Never can be too careful though, especially for someone as notorious as yourself."

Joxy didn't like how this conversation was going.

"Sir," she started.

"I am Kurd!" the large man blurted. "Personal Emissary to the Lord Emperor himself."

Face flushed, Joxy swallowed her anger.

"Forgive me, Kurd. I meant no disrespect," she said. Then, her voice darkened with seriousness, "The brief I received did not mention who I was to meet, only that I show. As a matter of fact, your galaxy was not very forthcoming with information at all. Now would be a good time to elaborate Emissary, or must we continue with these dramatic formalities and propositions any longer?"

His robustness faltered a fraction, eyes darting around. He appeared nervous about how to respond to such bluntness, such disrespect. Joxy smiled inwardly at his discomfort. She surmised that the emissary could not afford to compromise the mission, and she was gambling that the emperor had made this point abundantly clear. In what she imagined was only an effort to save face, Kurd plastered an exaggerated smile on his face, feigning ignorance to any slight.

"Of course, good Captain," Kurd bowed, "please forgive our vagueness and taste for extravagance. You have traveled far and are eager to get down to business. Perhaps we could retreat to quarters more suitable for such discussions. There I would be honored to unburden the details with which I have been entrusted."

Joxy eyed the man warily.

"Follow me," she said, turning away.

Kurd chased after her, guards in tow.

"Leave your men," she instructed without stopping. "My crew will keep them company." A smirk lined her face.

The emissary struggled to keep up. If not for his Eskin he would never have made it. Even with its assistance, Kurd was panting hard by the time he reached her side. The two ascended further into the ship, where she led her guest to a small, unassuming room. The Nocturian seemed to be trembling as he entered.

The room was eerily black save for a faint green hue emanating from some unknown source. The furniture, just as black, consisted of a few suspension chairs and a table secured to the floor. This was *The Legacy's* equivalent to a war room. An impenetrable, silent chamber where elaborate schemes could be contrived in absolute secrecy. "Here your message will be received in confidence, I assure you," Joxy said. "Please, take a seat." She motioned toward one of the odd-looking chairs.

Joxy knew her guest was uncomfortable. The suspension chairs were a creation of Raygo and Tano, designed to interpret the radiation emitted by one's thoughts. No one outside of the crew had ever seen one before. To get things moving, she slid into one of the chairs and gave Kurd an expectant look. Awkwardly, he rolled into one himself. In unison both chairs tilted back.

A cool, metal apparatus pressed itself against the base of their skulls. Kurd flinched at the touch, but remained seated. The green light of the room pulsed gently as suspension was engaged.

"Why were we intercepted before docking at Hawaii 5? The brief indicated an escort, not a boarding," Joxy thought.

Kurd all but fell out of his chair at the sound of Joxy's voice inside of his head. He grabbed at his chest, gasping. He would have sworn that the captain's lips didn't move, yet he heard her as clear as though she had spoken.

"Wah-wah, what's going on?" he mouthed, but the words never filled the room. Instead, they were sent directly to Joxy's mind, through suspension. *"Have I been drugged?"*

"Relax Kurd, you have not been drugged." She tried to sound soothing. *"Just think what you wish to say, and I will hear it. No one will be able to intercept our conversation this way. Now tell me, what's going on?"*

He inhaled a deep breath, taking a moment to collect himself. The astonishment never left his eyes. Focusing his thoughts, he tried his luck at the nifty tech.

"Please forgive the change of plans, Captain, it was the Lord Emperor's intent all along." He cleared his throat even though he was speaking mentally now. *"We could not afford to have you seen. There are those who would have inquired about—uhm—your presence. These are challenging times for any galaxy, and ours is not spared from division. We must be careful with this information. You were sought out due to your discretion and familiarity with the Void."*

"And what information is that?"

Kurd shifted his bulk around in a fruitless effort to find a more comfortable position. The faux-leather upholstery protested in the process.

"If what we believe to have discovered is true, then the universe, and Humanity itself, will change forever. The purpose for The Great Expansion potentially realized."

"Go on," she said, circling her hand in the air for him to get to the point. So far, she was skeptical.

"Roughly twenty years ago our scanners detected an anomaly far out in the Void. Imagine our surprise. We believed it to be a glitch in our systems somewhere. Nothing is supposed to be out there, Captain. Our scanners only indicate a physical distortion, no other readings. For years the anomaly would be there one minute, gone the next. Coming and going with no decipherable pattern as of yet."

Joxy's mind raced at the possibilities. What was this Nocturian saying? Was something magically popping up where nothing was supposed to be? During her many escapades into the Void, nothing—absolutely nothing—was ever out there. *Unusual instances had occurred there though, hadn't they,* she asked herself. Visions, hallucinations, whatever you wanted to call them. Her ship sometimes responded oddly.

Moments when things like that would happen, she always chalked it up to the never-ending nothingness playing tricks on her mind. Her main concern at the time had always been escaping the pursuing authorities. Was there something more to it? It was possible.

"What is believed to be the significance of the anomaly other than its obvious peculiarity?" she asked, feigning indifference. She would keep the abnormal experiences of the Void to herself. *"Are you actually suggesting that there may be someone or something out there, Emissary? After all, that was the goal of expansion, was it not? To end speculation and determine who our neighbors were once and for all."*

"It sounds incredulous, I know, because I struggle with it myself. However, the emperor believes very passionately that the time has come. Thousands of years, countless expeditions, and every fallen civilization absent the presence of intelligent life. It has to mean something; they have to be somewhere!"

Joxy had the feeling she was about to be sent on a wild goose chase. Albeit a lucrative one.

"But it doesn't make sense for that somewhere to be the Void," she pointed out. *"That's new universe."*

"We agree, it doesn't make sense. That's why we believe it's important. This close to the Void, we're the only ones whose scanners have detected it. Something the size of either an extremely large ship or a small planet is sitting out there, stationary. No orbital or propellant motion at all, none."

"What is Nocturne's true purpose behind making contact?" Raygo asked Joxy.

"Who the hell is that?" Kurd's voice shouted in Joxy's head. *"Is someone else here? You assured me our conversation here would be confidential."* He flailed in his chair, attempting to get out, unable to gain purchase.

Joxy recognized what happened, but she did not allow her body to telegraph the revelation. Being in suspension allowed Kurd to hear what Raygo had said to her. It wasn't all that surprising given Raygo had modeled the tech after his own abilities. She would have to convince him it was nothing; otherwise, she would be forced to kill him and his men and attempt to flee the galaxy.

"Kurd, get ahold of yourself," she yelled into his mind. *"All I asked you was what the Nocturians' true intent is with making contact with whatever might be out there."*

"You—you asked me?" he stammered.

"Yes, me, who else? I told you this room was completely safe. No interference in or out. Do you not trust me? Are you accusing me of lying?" she said.

"No! No, of course not. An infinite apology, Captain. This method of communication seems to be taking its toll on me." He wiped away a bead of sweat at his brow. *"How about we continue in the more traditional way,"* he grunted, finally able to roll himself free of the chair.

Joxy observed the emissary cautiously, looking for any sign of doubt from the man. Her kager blade was nestled at the small of her back. *It would be a swift and easy kill,* she thought as she leapt from the chair to her feet.

"Ah, much better," Kurd announced, stretching to his full volume.

"Are you okay?" Her hand reached back, poised atop the blade.

"Yes, I'm fine, thank you. We are not familiar with this tech out here at Nocturne. We'll be sure to look into it. It's fascinating. The emperor will be envious to hear of my experience."

"I'm sure," she said, her lips drawing to a line. "Now if you don't mind, would you please answer the question? What is the plan if we do encounter something out there, something . . . sentient?"

Kurd hesitated before responding in trite, political fashion.

"This has been humanity's greatest goal, and we of the Nocturne Galaxy continue to uphold the old values. However, due to the divisive nature of such a discovery, we could not possibly send a delegation of our own. Instead, it must be someone unofficial, not easily traced back to us. Given your evasive reputation, it would make sense for you to be out there, possibly stumbling across such a discovery."

Joxy folded her arms. "I see, and once we've *stumbled* upon whatever's out there, what exactly are me and my crew tasked with doing?"

"Your mission is to simply observe and report. Take *The Legacy* to the provided coordinates and put eyes on this anomaly. You are not to engage. Report back any observations, then await further instructions."

"And if whatever we find proves hostile?"

A pensive look came over him as his eyes swept the dimly lit room.

"Avoid altercation, if at all possible, but if the situation does turn hostile, then do what you must to protect yourselves. Just make your way back to Nocturne as quickly as possible for debriefing."

Joxy wasn't too worried about a scuffle, if that's what it came to. Her ship was equipped with the latest in weapons and G-drive tech. They had the options of fight or flight. What she worried about were the laws of physics and whether whatever was out there fought with the same ones they did.

"How far?" she asked, dreading the response.

"Three months, give or take."

Joxy's shoulders dropped.

"The good news is that it's not moving any farther away. The bad news is that it's not getting any closer."

That's a bit of a mission commitment, she thought. Usually they try to stick with the routine grab-and-go jobs. Those were safer and more predictable. This job would require more in the way of logistics.

"I'll require half the payment up front," Joxy stated matter-of-factly. "With the stipulation that no matter what we do or do not find out there that the remaining half will be paid upon our return."

Being the good bandit that she was, she added: "The price has doubled. Take it or leave it. This is not a negotiation. These are my terms."

She knew she was taking advantage of the situation. It was not in her privateer nature to do otherwise. Her crew would be proud.

Kurd reacted as she imagined he would. A gasp escaping his drooping mouth with a look of hilarious awe painted upon his chubby face. Joxy watched as the emissary's eyes darkened briefly, only guessing at the intricacy of betrayal that he was surely plotting.

"That is a substantial amount of dark matter. What makes you think our modest empire has such riches?" he asked with disdain.

"Nocturne lies on the fringes of the Void, where dark matter tends to accumulate more frequently. No one is blind to the wealth of the *modest* Nocturians."

"Your wit is ceaseless, Captain Joxy." Kurd exhaled. "On behalf of the Lord Emperor and the Nocturne Empire, I accept your terms. I dare not engage negotiations for I fear your price would only rise."

"My reputation has in fact preceded me." Joxy said, a jovial smile spreading across her lips. "Shall we return to our men? Let's hope they've played nicely in our absence."

* * *

The two of them arrived at the cargo hold to a cacophony of laughter and merriment. Crew from both sides were participating in acts of strength and skill, creating a light mood all around. Barrels of skid were stacked to the side, a steady flow pouring into the soldiers' cups.

Skid was an intoxicating drink with universal appeal. The concoction affected both humans and mechs alike, having effects similar to that of alcohol. Matter of fact, it was the bioengineering of Earth grains and a revolutionized, low-gravity method of fermentation that created such a brew.

"It appears as though my crew has tapped into the ship's private stock." Joxy gestured to the barrels. "Would you care for some quality skid before your departure, Emissary Kurd?" She couldn't hide her amusement.

Kurd took in the scene with rage, the folds in his neck turning red. This was against protocol, Joxy knew, and the soldiers would pay dearly for their lapse in discipline. A Nocturian soldier came rushing up, fear in his eyes. He snapped a sloppy salute before addressing Kurd.

"Sir, the crew has been exceptionally hospitable. We felt it rude to reject their offer of a drink." He licked his lips. "Quite the vintage."

For appearances sake, Kurd did not lash out. He didn't have to, his tone said it all.

"Sergeant," he hissed, "I can see quite clearly that you and your men have partaken of more than just one drink." Kurd's eyes narrowed as the soldier swayed on his feet. He grabbed the bridge of his nose before turning official. "Organize the men. Our business here is done," he ordered.

The sergeant turned on his heels and started to walk away when Kurd addressed him again.

"Sergeant, I want you to personally oversee the transfer of the dark matter. Can you handle that?"

"Yes, sir!" he saluted, a little sharper this time.

"Good, because as of this moment your reputation cannot afford anymore mishaps," Kurd said icily.

The sergeant scurried away. Kurd turned back to Captain Joxy. *Good, let him wonder at my trickery. Maybe it'll serve to keep him in check when we next meet,* she thought

He bowed at the waist, so it wasn't much of a bow. "Thank you for your kindness, Captain. It's been a pleasure to have met, and I truly hope this is not our last encounter. Maybe next time I will take you up on your offer of skid. Until then, may the stars be with you on your journey."

"Give your emperor my regards," she said sarcastically. "Next time I'm in his galaxy I'd like to make his acquaintance."

Joxy strolled away, her jacket billowing behind. She could feel the emissary staring daggers at her back.

* * *

Back at the bridge Joxy watched her holos as she oversaw the transfer of dark matter. She was surprised the Nocturians had agreed to such a ransom. It only added to her unease about this mission. *Wealth meant nothing when dead,* a memory of her father's voice echoed.

"Great work, Tano. Did they let slip anything useful?" she asked.

"Skid would make a mute mech talk," Tano said with a laugh. "They have orders to tail us, to ensure that we leave the galaxy. The emissary kept them in the dark. No one seemed to know more than that."

There's no telling how the universe would respond to the knowledge of the anomaly. Joxy understood the need for such discretion. She wondered if the emperor was withholding further information.

"Captain," Tano shouted. "The Nocturians are running another scan of our ship. Any idea why they'd do that?"

It appears the emissary was more suspicious than he let on, she mused. Maybe I should have taken him out when I had the chance. Her hand reflexively inched its way to her back.

"Just routine I'm sure," Joxy said. "Now crank up the drives and get us the hell out of here."

"Aye, aye, Cap."

CHAPTER 2
SEGA CITY

Five years earlier ...

Propped up on his elbow, Jim leaned over, watching Joxy's eyelids flutter, wondering what she was dreaming about. He could have scanned her neural network with his holo to find out, but the mystery was more stimulating. Her dreams were her own; he just hoped that he was a part of them.

Easing down, Jim brushed his lips against hers with a playful, gentle nudge. He was always the first of the two to rise and loved watching Joxy as she slept, entranced by the way her dark hair framed her face against the pillow and the slight pulses from the veins in her slender neck. *No artist in history could have replicated such beauty,* he thought.

* * *

Joxy began to stir, a smile already forming on her lips as she stretched her arms and legs, the muscles contracting.

"Uh, it's too early," she groaned, covering her face with a pillow. Jim tugged the pillow away, his eyes hovering right above hers. A mischievous grin lit her face. Swinging her arms around his neck, she pulled him back down. They locked tongues passionately for a few moments before Jim reluctantly resurfaced for air.

"Would you – *muah* – like some – *muah* – stim?" Jim asked in between pecks.

"That would be lovely, honey," she cooed.

Blue sunlight poured in through the open veranda doors. A soft breeze stirred the shades, caressing the sheets against her lithe body. Shouts could be heard from vendors selling their wares down below.

Jim slid from the bed and into the bottom half of his Eskin. Some days were better for him than others. Today he needed the assistance. Walking out of the room he stopped at the doorway. "I bought you a gift down at the markets," he said grinning. "It's from one of the seedier shops that you love. The merchant said it was rare, if he can be believed." He shot her a wink. "I'll see you downstairs."

"I got you a gift, too," she said, edging the sheet up her thighs.

"Then we'll exchange gifts in the kitchen." He shook his head, then slapped the wall before walking out.

Joxy could tell from the naughty look on his face that he was up to no good. Two of his legs were failing him, but so far his third one still worked just fine. She could hear Jim chuckling as he made his way down the hall. After one last stretch, she hopped from the bed and threw on a robe. Its plush fibers began filtering the toxins from her body. After all the skid they had indulged in the night before, she needed it.

Stepping onto the veranda, she took in the city's ecosystem down below. Their suite offered a spectacular view. Sega City—actually a planet—was terraformed centuries ago to accommodate a variety of exotic plants and animals from all over the universe. An unusual combination of oxygen, helium, and nitrogen made up the planet's atmosphere to allow for the survival of these different life forms, resulting in what humans found to be a notoriously potent tang to the air. That said, in many circles off planet, the distinct odor was worn as a perfume among the most distinguished of the higher classes.

Sega City was caught in the orbit of two battling neutron stars. Their close proximity in combination with the artificially created atmosphere resulted in the most stunning skies this half of the universe had to offer.

Joxy remembered vivid stories that her father had told her growing up. Tales of exotic planets, crowded systems, and far-flung galaxies so immense and colorful you just had to see them for yourself to believe. And so, see for herself, she did.

Sega City was near the top of any tourist's list. She knew Jim had brought her there not only to experience the planet's beauty but also because he had an ulterior motive that both frightened and excited her. She'd been anticipating his proposal for a while.

Joxy pulled the warm robe closer as another breeze whirled by. She watched as one sun set while another rose, considering it a blessing to witness such a sight. She loved it here, and she'd loved Jim since they met as teenagers. Maybe they could finally settle down, raise some children, and put an end to their adventurous ways. Though the crew would be disappointed, wouldn't they?

Hers was a lifestyle she was forced to adapt to at a young age, though she came to love it and the crew she put together along the way. Joxy had always felt that her and her crew's actions were righteously justified, though that didn't make them any less dangerous in nature. Helping prevent corporate takeovers of planets, taking reclaimed foods back to the people whose planet was harvested, and pocketing a thing or two, here and there, from the wealthy galaxies to support her humanitarian efforts. Her love for Jim outweighed it all.

But who was to tell her, Captain Joxy of *The Legacy Starborn*, that she couldn't have both? Their union didn't have to change anything, not if they didn't want it to. She would leave it up to Jim. That's how much she loved the man of her dreams. She'd do anything for him. She would have done anything for him even before he became ill, but now that he was, she was even more eager to do so.

Jim was sick, very sick. On a job to a little-known, remote system, he had contracted something. Something that caused his body to deteriorate right out from underneath him. Nanos, elixirs, transfusions, nothing would touch it. It was as though his body was doing this to itself naturally, and so far it hadn't proved contagious. If something didn't change soon, it could end fatally. Because of this, Jim and Joxy lived every day as if it were their last. Taking on more daring jobs and experiencing extravagant trips. The universe was their playground, and nothing short of death would stop them.

Smiling, she walked back into their suite. She shed her robe, letting it fall to the floor before sliding into her own custom Eskin. Her jacket lay across the arm of a chair by the door; she scooped it up on her way out and made her way to the lift.

The sweet smell of freshly brewed stim permeated the lower level. This enhanced version of coffee provided all the kick—and then some—with none of the jitters. The perfect pick-me-up after a long night of drink. Some things would never change.

Two steaming cups sat ready for consumption on the kitchen's floating island. A slender purple box with a frilly blue ribbon nestled between them. Joxy stood there and eyed the box. It wasn't the proper dimensions to hold a ring, but maybe a necklace. Where was Jim?

She cocked her head to the side; a faint shuffling noise came from the next room. Panic rose. Without wasting another second, she dashed from the kitchen.

Jim lay sprawled on the floor. Soft, wet sounds emanated from his throat as foamy saliva escaped from the corners of his mouth. She rolled him onto his side and pressed her forehead against his shoulder, praying a quick prayer to whichever god would listen. Tears poured forth as she rocked on her knees.

"Come on, baby. Don't do this. Stay with me," she moaned.

Her head shot up.

"Emergency medical!" she screamed to the suite's AI.

"A request for immediate medical assistance has already been made," the emotionless voice stated. "Estimated arrival time is three minutes."

CHAPTER 3
BOUNTY HUNTERS

The two Nocturian warships drifted away after escorting *The Legacy* out of their galaxy via a less treacherous route of toxicity. Scanners no longer registered the NGS-14s, but Tano assumed they were maintaining pace right outside of their range. He wondered what the extent of their orders were. Did they plan to tail them all the way to the Void, or even perhaps into the Void itself?

"Cap, our weapons are back up," Tano reported. "I'm setting them to auto-op. With the addition of all that dark matter, our drives are performing at maximum efficiency." He pumped a fist in the air. "*The Legacy* is back, baby!"

"Thank you, Tano. I'll take the helm for a while. Go make sure the crew didn't drink all of the skid. Keep an eye on the scanners. I want to know immediately if the Nocturians come back into range."

Tano took off to round up the crew. He wanted everyone sobered up and ready for action. The captain's unease was almost palpable. She had fully disclosed the mission to him so he knew of the possibilities and their ramifications.

At some point there was bound to be trouble. It was unavoidable and, further, predictable. Tano planned for any and all scenarios. Ever vigilant, he was a huge factor in their success and reputation. The mech was dispersing orders on his augmented holo vision as he walked through the ship. His unique upgrades allowed him to synchronize with the ship, enabling him to monitor her every aspect. Tano was a mech. As a matter of fact, every crew member aboard *The Legacy* was a mech with the exception of Joxy and Raygo.

The first mechs typically consisted of both human and robotic components. In general, the term simply meant that a human endured some type of synthetic upgrade to the body. These procedures were all the rage for centuries. What ultimately transpired was the ability to emulate—transfer—the human consciousness into a mechanized counterpart. The kinks in the science were disastrous initially. But the trend continued. To many, the reward was worth the risk, and after a time the process was perfected.

Most of the humans who became mechs made the decision for the money and power that came with having special abilities; others chose to do so because their natural bodies were on the fringes of death. Someone who could transform an arm or a leg into a weapon or tool was a valuable asset, especially aboard a bandit vessel.

Over the years Tano became more and more at one with the ship. His specialty parts allowed him to scrutinize the ship's vitals and make constant adjustments that no one else knew to make. Everyone, that is, except for the captain. Her intuition and familiarity with the vessel allowed her to pick up on most of his tailoring.

While touring the ship, he was pleased to find that the crew had already maneuvered into their positions and were alert. There were crew whose job it was to manage the drives, shields, weapons, freight, along with the basics such as cooking and cleaning. Joxy ran her ship like a well-oiled machine. She couldn't afford not to. Everyone's role was vital.

Tano observed the remaining skid barrels that had been returned to inventory when a distinct red symbol flashed across the center of his holo vision. After acknowledging the warning it disappeared, replaced by three red figures that the scanners picked up. The details panning across the bottom of his holo indicated that these were not ships from Nocturne, but rather the Sega System. These were stardusters, rapidly approaching *The Legacy's* flanks.

"Oh, shit," Tano blurted. "Bounty hunters!"

He signaled the alarms.

* * *

"It should be safe to come back now, Raygo," Joxy said into the empty bridge.

While she waited, the atmosphere on the bridge came alive with energy, her loose hair rising on its roots, the air reeking of charged particles. She always thought this part was the coolest, the re-atomization. Before you knew what was happening a figure would materialize right in front of you.

Joxy clapped in amusement. "Bravo, bravo," she said. "Hell of an entrance and one that will never grow old."

Raygo smiled his perfect smile with his extra-white teeth. He looked as though he had been designed in a lab, and justifiably so.

"If I can be candid, Captain, it's entertaining for me as well."

She lounged in her worn leather captain's seat, some patchwork here and there. One leg dangled over an armrest, her kager blade mindlessly twirling between her fingers, she stared into Raygo's eyes, intently, like a panther, watching for some indication.

He acknowledged the blade with a smirk and a tilt of his head. A gleam formed in his eyes.

"The Nocturians are suspicious of your presence," Joxy said as she sat up. "While in suspension, Kurd was able to hear you speaking to me. I'm sure your presence aboard this vessel is old news among the gossip circles. In fact, I'm surprised that Kurd had the composure not to hint around to it. Now I'm sure he knows. They ran more scans before leaving."

"Suspicions are all they have. Like most people, they simply fear what they do not understand."

Raygo walked to the circular window at the front of the bridge. He stared out at the billions of stars, seemingly lost in thought for a moment.

"Our scanners are top of the line," he said. "As long as they're out of our range we should be out of theirs. However, if you'd prefer, I can remain in a de-atomized state."

Joxy stood. After holstering her blade, she massaged her temples.

"No, we should be fine especially while we're on a mission for them. We'll have to be cunning once this is all over, getting the rest of our payment while also making a clean get away may prove challenging." She flashed him a knowing smile. "It wouldn't be the first time though, would it?"

"You're right. The Nocturians distrust us as much as we distrust them. It makes sense that they called on us, considering they deem us disposable."

"But not easily disposed of."

She walked up beside him, and they both stared into space. The urge to touch his hand was overwhelming. Her fingers gave a slight twitch.

"What do you think we'll find out there?" she whispered. "Whatever it is, it was put there for a reason. I'm not sure if I can just stand down and stand by."

"Let's err on the side of caution," he said turning to face her. "Until we know exactly what that reason is, we'll play it safe."

He cupped her face in his hands as he leaned forward, placing a kiss on her forehead. A reassuring kiss like a phantom from the past. Her body let loose a shiver. Tilting her head back, she looked into his eyes. The gleam was still there.

"How many of you are in there? I've never asked."

"Seventy-three is we," he said, amused by his own wit. Joxy responded with a burst of incredulous laughter, leaning into his chest for support. It was hard for her to wrap her mind around what it meant to be a BAI. How could so many coexist as a single entity?

Caught in Raygo's embrace, Joxy was about to say more when suddenly the ship's alarms erupted. Tano exploded onto the bridge. He hesitated only for a fraction of a second at the sight of them. They quickly broke apart.

"Captain, we've got three Segan stardusters fast approaching. It seems they knew we'd be here."

"A Nocturian must have tipped them off for a portion of the reward money," she said, gaining her composure. "I don't blame them. We are a tempting prize."

"The crew are in position," Tano stated.

Joxy plopped back into her seat, swiveling toward the window. Her fingers flew among the controls as she caught glimpses from her holos at the trajectories of the incoming ships. She prepared to evade.

"I don't want to be the first to fire. Let's see if we can outrun these little guys," she said.

Tano unleashed a torrent of commands to the crew while simultaneously evaluating a flight plan that would most likely evade pursuit and enemy fire. "Raygo, help manage the weapons system," Joxy barked. "If fired upon, retaliate with unrestrained hostility."

Raygo dispersed, leaving behind the familiar aroma of charged particles; his exits were a little less grandiose than his entrances. Holos hovering in front of the captain showed that multiple plasma cannons now traced the three enemy ships. Typically passive, violence only being a last resort, Raygo was a dead shot when it came to protecting those he loved.

"Captain, one of the ships is reaching out," Tano announced.

"Pull them up."

An elaborately decorated man materialized into view, his entire body projected onto the bridge.

"This is Captain Vaughn, Commander of the Segan Armada," the holoed figure said in a stiff way. "I have orders to detain you and your crew, to repossess your vessel, and bring you back to Sega City."

This was by no means their first encounter with bounty hunters. But these were Segan fighter vessels, stardusters, a class of their own. Not some space pale necks, but tried-and-true warriors.

"And on whose authority are those orders?" Joxy asked.

An evil smile spread across Captain Vaughn's lips. "Oh, I think you already know the answer to that," he hissed.

Joxy flinched, knuckles turning white as she gripped her chair.

"Veruna," she breathed.

"Captain Joxy of *The Legacy*, I am officially ordering you to power down your weapons and shields. Failure to comply will result in our engagement," he said, waving a hand dismissively. "To be honest it doesn't matter to me either way, your bounty is good dead or alive."

The holo faded out as the commander was last seen laughing to himself.

"They're splitting up," Tano said. "I'm uploading a flight plan that should get us to the Void before they are able to engage. Orders, Cap?" He looked up expectantly.

Stardusters were fast, very fast. It would be close, but if they could reach the Void, it may just level the battlefield.

"Full power to drives. Raygo, keep an eye on our rear, these guys are fast."

The force pressed Joxy into her seat as they accelerated. Because of the design of the ship and its drives, she typically didn't feel accelerations. But these speeds weren't typical, so she wasn't surprised to be feeling it now. A specially designed AI kept the ship on its flight path. Small asteroids and chunks of ice disintegrated against the shields. It was impossible to avoid all space debris when traveling this fast.

Scanners indicated that the three pursuant ships were maintaining pace. Joxy assumed they were outfitted for the specific task of hunting them down. Not many vessels could reach, let alone handle, such high velocity.

Plasma cannons erupted overhead, the energy from their recoil quivered through the ship. Crew members operated smaller arms along the sides, top, and bottom. Multicolored munitions flew through space. A stray round going this fast could wipe out an entire planet.

The Legacy pitched to one side, shields taking the brunt of an impact. A separate set of alarms blared. Tano ordered crew here and there, in an attempt to combat the damage. Some of the men were sucked through a torso-size hole into the vacuum before that section of the ship could be sealed off.

"Not a lot of damage, but we can't afford too many of those," Tano warned.

The stardusters shouldn't have the ability to target-lock at this speed. They're either firing blindly, extremely lucky, or . . .

"They must have worked out our trajectory. Tano, disengage the AI, and hand over manual controls. If we continue on our current route, they'll have us before we can reach the Void."

"But Cap, that's suicide. There's a high likelihood of us crashing into something our shields can't handle."

He sounded scared, but Joxy set her jaw and braced herself.

"Do it. Raygo, concentrate fire to our bow. Tano, have the men do likewise. I'm redirecting all power to our shields up front. If they don't know where we're going, they shouldn't be able to hit us."

The Legacy came tearing through galaxies like a rogue comet on stim. Joxy kept to an unpredictable route, and it was all the Segans could do to stay in range. She monitored incoming planets, careful to avoid any that were inhabited. Others, she simply paved through, creating deadly debris fields in their wake. It's not something they would be able to maintain for long, with their weapons' power stores rapidly depleting.

The Segan ships continued to fall back. One of the stardusters flickered on the holo, then disappeared. Scans registered no sign of life amongst the wreckage. Two to go.

Breaking free from the last of the universe's detritus, *The Legacy* plunged into the Void. Space was dark, but the Void was even darker. There was zero light pollution and no gravity interference.

Joxy slowed the drives, not wanting to overwork them or exhaust their resources. If she wasn't careful, they could implode. Displayed on the weapon's feed, in a deep red, was "15% Power." Not nearly enough for a drawn-out dogfight. She was sure that Captain Vaughn would follow them into the Void. His ego wouldn't allow him to do otherwise.

As if on cue . . .

"Cap, two stardusters to starboard. Drives are still cooling. I don't think we'll get far on them."

Joxy wracked her brain, using her mind's eye to run through the ship's manifest. For bandit reasons, she never recorded it. Weapons, ammo, strange doohickeys whose purpose even she could only guess at.

Then, in a eureka moment, she slapped her armrest.

"What about the net array? The one we picked up at that Little Caesars system for heavy asteroid belts. We haven't had a chance to try it out yet, but our small arms are pretty much useless, and the cannons wouldn't last long enough to matter. Picking up what I'm laying down, you guys?"

The net array had been recently installed at the top of the ship. It was essentially a laser net, cast in strong pulses to obliterate asteroids. A convenient acquisition given their current situation.

"It's risky," Tano said.

Raygo agreed. "It would require us to get dangerously close with virtually no weapons and only minor shield protection." He sighed and then chuckled. "Short odds, but we've had shorter."

"All right, I'm shutting down the drives completely. Let's kill the weapons and shields," she ordered as her hands flew across her screens. "I'm diverting all available power to the net. On my command, Tano, you'll initiate."

The remaining Segan ships homed in on their prey. They smelled blood. Commander Vaughn reached out, once again appearing on the bridge.

"Your careless actions have cost the lives of twelve Segan Astros!" His smug look was replaced with one of rage, and holographic spittle flew from his lips. If he was standing there, Joxy would have needed a towel. "I should eradicate you and your crew from this universe." His hands talked as much as his mouth. "Out here, no one would discover the smallest of debris for millennia."

Joxy straightened her posture.

"Commander Vaughn, we of *The Legacy* no longer pose a threat. Under Universal Law we are entitled to a peaceful surrender. Let the ship's record show that—"

"Do not preach to me of law, you bandit," he shouted. He wiped a sleeve across his lips as he collected himself. "Your bounty negates any entitlement you may feel that you have."

Joxy's eyes occasionally darted to her holos during this tirade as she monitored the Segan's reckless approach. No doubt their own scanners indicated an exposed and defenseless ship. That was the idea, and it seemed to be working. *Just a little closer.*

"But what about Veruna?" she asked in an innocent tone. "I'm sure there's a big bonus for bringing us in alive and not destroying this ship."

Vaughn's anger faltered; his shoulders dropped. Joxy knew she had him. Veruna would have his head if she were to somehow discover that the Segan Commander opted to kill them when given the opportunity to bring them in alive. Vaughn couldn't risk it. One of his astros would talk.

He threw back his shoulders and raised his head.

"Captain Joxy, prepare to be boarded. Any sign of hostility, and I will gladly turn you to slag."

The holo cut out.

On the display, two blue icons proceeded toward a likeness of *The Legacy*. A green circle around the ship indicated the effective kill zone. Stronger at its source, the net array grew weaker as it expanded. The first starduster entered into range, its color changing from blue to purple.

"Easy . . . " Joxy whispered, the atmosphere on the bridge tense with nervous energy. Tano had the net controls poised, ready to commence. Joxy watched as the second ship turned purple. Waiting the span of a few breaths, she then gave the order to fire.

He selected the command for the net to start pulsing.

Two purple figures continued their approach.

"Tano, fire the net now," Joxy ordered.

Nothing happened.

"It's not responding. My controls are not responding," Tano shouted as he frantically pressed buttons.

She pulled up the net controls. There was no indication of a malfunction, but they weren't working for her either.

"Raygo, can you make your way to the net's control box? Our equipment down here is glitching."

His response was almost immediate.

"Nothing up here's operating. I think the Void is interfering with some of our systems. Looks like one of their ships is pulling back a little. The other is positioning itself for docking."

"Fucking void," she said through a huff. "Tano, get The Devils down to the cargo hold. We'll have to improvise. This asshole is not taking over my ship."

Joxy threw on her jacket, then left the bridge to link up with her tactical forces unit. "Over my dead body," she grumbled to herself. "Keep trying the net. Let's hope I can buy us enough time for it to start working. Either way, we're not going out without a fight."

Turning a corner, she entered the ship's hold.

Standing at the ready were five of her fiercest crew outfitted with some nasty weaponry.

"Jones, Lily, you're with me. You other three, spread out and find cover. I'm not sure how diplomatic this is going to be."

The mechs fanned out, anxious for a fight. These were the moments they were designed for.

"They've docked," Tano said over her comm. "Commander Vaughn is demanding we open the doors."

"Open them. Let's grant this man his death wish."

An air-lock sat beside the massive cargo door, its yellow lights flashing in a cautious cadence. Hissing could be heard as seals broke and pressure equalized. The air-lock door swung open on its well-oiled hinges, coming to a stop before slamming into the hull behind it.

On the other side stood Vaughn in all his decorative glory. Six astros flanked him, each in armored suits, each handling assault rifles. The arrogant commander wore only his uniform and officer's pistol.

"*Don't let him fool you,*" Raygo cautioned. "*He's rockin' some unusual mech tech.*"

Vaughn sauntered through the door into the hold. His trailing soldiers fanned out.

"Captain Joxy, I wish I could say that it was a pleasure to finally meet you. In some ways I can respect what you represent, but in others I simply begrudge you. I've dedicated a lot of my time scouring the universe in search of you and Veruna's favorite pet."

Joxy's two mechs stepped forward, but a clipped wave of her hand held them back.

"That's right," Vaughn said with a laugh. Keep your dogs at bay, or I'll be forced to put them down. Except I don't think I can refer to you as captain anymore, being that you no longer have a ship."

"And what is to become of us once we've been taken captive?" she asked, stalling.

"Your ship will be placed under my control." His eyes lit up, already imagining how celebrated he'll be. "You and your men will be put into the cooler until we arrive at Sega City, where you and this magnificent vessel will be handed over to your old benefactor, Veruna."

She had to keep him talking, buy more time. The astros prowled around her, making her uneasy. She hoped that the other three Devils were well hidden. This bounty of theirs may have finally caught up to them, but she held no regrets because she always followed her heart. Their odds here were slim and getting slimmer by the second. If Tano or Raygo couldn't get the array back online, like now, then the cargo hold was about to turn into a slaughterhouse.

CHAPTER 4
VORG

Five years earlier . . .

Milk-colored lightrails traced Sega City like a network of veins. There were apartments and offices so tall that the tips of their buildings scraped along the planet's stratosphere. Joxy had been overwhelmed the first time she laid eyes on the Sega System's royal jewel from orbit, for it was both beautiful and terrifying. Even though she lived on a ship, the thought of living in a building that tall petrified her to her core. Joxy didn't enjoy taking the lightrails, but she had to admit they were convenient. Being able to travel anywhere on a planet at near the speed of light—without turning into mush—was definitely a luxury. The stations were usually crowded, as this one was today, that it felt like forever before she finally reached an exit.

The medical hub Jim had been rushed to wasn't far from the station. The mechs had wored quickly to stabilize him for transport and had also refused to allow Joxy to accompany them. It was only when their emergency transport vehicle was about to take off that her personal holo received the coordinates to where they were taking him.

The hub was one of the buildings that stretched impossibly high into the sky. Her neck hurt as she craned it in an attempt to find where it ended. She couldn't. When she walked in, she immediately noticed how well organized and sterile the place was. She might have felt comfortable here except for the eerie silence that gave the hub an unsettling vibe.

A sharp, flowery scent that tickled her nose permeated the lobby. A welcome holo sprang up close by and Joxy rushed toward it. Frantically searching the patient directory, she located Jim's name and found where he'd been deposited. Pod 104, condition listed as critical.

Preoccupied with worrying over Jim's present state, she didn't notice when one of the facility's robots appeared next to her.

"I am ROB 1267568. If you would like, I can escort you to pod 104. Most unaccompanied visitors tend to get lost. I can address any questions or concerns as well."

Hands buried deep inside her jacket pockets; her index finger anxiously twirled at the bow on Jim's gift. She hated places like this. They frightened her. Especially now. All she knew was that she couldn't lose Jim. She had promised herself to at least hold it together until she found him. Joxy pushed back the lump in her throat.

"Yes, that would be nice. Thank you," she said barely above a whisper.

With smooth features and big, round eyes, the menial AI bot was designed to appear comforting and friendly. Joxy kept her attention on it as she followed behind, keeping her eyes locked on its back. The fear of catching a glimpse of others suffering in the rooms to either side gnawed at her. It would be tough enough to endure seeing Jim.

One would think pod 104 was relatively close to the lobby, however this was not the case. The medical nerve center was a labyrinth of vast proportions. Pods and terraces stretched in every direction, farther than one would think possible. Joxy was too despondent to be awestruck as she made her way through the facility.

She was beginning to acknowledge that they had been walking for quite some time when the ROB stopped and turned toward a pod. Above the door, 104 appeared in black numbers. Joxy stopped short.

"What's his status?"

"The condition of pod 104 is currently critical," ROB fired off in algorithmic emotions. "Bio scans have indicated rapid organ deterioration resulting in the need for life support."

Joxy flinched, first at the fact that the ROB referred to Jim as a number, then at the diagnosis, which slammed her to her knees.

"But why?" she cried. "Why is his body doing this?"

ROB paused to process the question. AIs didn't typically pause.

"There are no identifiable symptomatic causes at this time. Further tests are currently being conducted."

She already knew the answer, or non-answer rather. It had been the same since Jim's trouble had started.

"Please . . . can you give us some time alone?" Joxy didn't have the nerve to ask how long Jim had left.

"Yes, but I must advise you not to stray down these halls and not to attempt to open the pod. The door is locked due to the patient's severity and possibility of contamination. When you are ready, press the call button beside the latch and a ROB will appear promptly."

The bot whirled around and sped toward the lobby. Joxy couldn't force herself to stand, instead she crawled over to the pod's door and leaned her back against it. She stretched her legs out, resting her chin on her heaving chest. Tears trickled off her cheeks, sopped up by her Eskin as memories flooded through her mind. Jim, *The Legacy*, Tano and the crew, that was her family, and she was about to lose a member.

Reaching into a pocket she extracted the box with the bow, placing it in her lap. She was fortunate to have had the foresight to pluck it from the kitchen's island before leaving. She didn't want to open it, not without him. But if she didn't do it now, she might never be able to. Pulling at one end of the bow, the blue ribbon untangled itself and slipped from the box. Joxy tilted the box to its side, and a compartment slid open. Using a finger, she persuaded it the rest of the way out.

Whatever the gift was lay in the tray wrapped in silk. The shiny green fabric caught and reflected the light with dazzling beauty. A single teardrop splattered, breaking the silk's spell. She took the contents in her hand, noting that it had some heft to it.

Gently moving the fabric aside, she uncovered an intricately carved knife, her golden eyes, hovering above, were mirrored in the blade. Picking it up, she clumsily maneuvered the weapon, not too sure how to hold it. It seemed to have good balance as far as she could tell. She loved it. It was just like Jim to give her a gift so unorthodox—laser cutters had replaced knives long ago.

Underneath was a card:

> *Joxy,*
>
> *This blade symbolizes our strong love for one another.*
>
> *Forged from rare Earth ore Titanium, just like us, it will never break. My love is yours, for eternity.*
>
> *Jim*

Joxy placed the blade back on the silk, her body quivering. So wrapped up in her grief she didn't notice the figure standing above her. Whoever it was let loose a sharp whistle.

"Wow, a kager blade." It was a woman, and Joxy jumped at the sudden intrusion. "Those things are rare and quite expensive, though I must admit, it's an unusual gift for such a beautiful young lady."

Joxy lifted her head as she wiped the tears from her eyes. She took in the smartly dressed woman. Turning her head to look down both ends of the hall, she wondered how in the hell this withered old lady managed to sneak up on her. The woman offered her hand.

"My name is Veruna, I'm on the board here at the med hub." Joxy accepted the woman's hand, surprised at its strength as it more or less lifted her to her feet. Collecting herself, Joxy closed the box and slid it back into her pocket.

"Joxy, I'm here visiting my—husband. He's very sick," she said, turning to look into the pod for the first time. Her breath caught. Jim was unrecognizably pale and withered. For a second, she thought the ROB might have brought her to the wrong place. It took all of her will not to collapse back to the floor as her knees began to buckle.

Veruna came up from behind and placed a reassuring hand on her back. Such intimacy from a stranger intimidated her, but she already felt herself trusting the woman for some reason.

Both of them watched as a team of ROBs hovered over Jim's body, preparing to conduct and analyze a multitude of tests.

"We're doing what we can for him, trying mostly to ease the pain. His condition is quite unique. It's not every day that we receive a patient we're unable to diagnose."

Joxy struggled to withhold her next question, then blurted it out anyway. "Is he going to die?" she asked.

Veruna faced Joxy with her icy blue eyes. The depths of knowledge Joxy found there made her feel as though she were a child far from home. Those cold, deep eyes seemed to be probing her, evaluating her.

"Here in Sega City, we have arguably the best medical facilities in the universe," the woman said, taking a professional tone. "Even with such power at our fingertips, I cannot wholeheartedly say I believe his body will make it through this ordeal."

Joxy felt as though she'd been gut punched. She stared at the floor.

"I would give my life for his," she said softly.

"Maybe you won't have to," Veruna said, shrugging her shoulders and pressing her lips together.

Joxy jolted internally. "What do you mean?"

"Outside of this facility, I head many other special-interest organizations, the kind that allow me to rub elbows with some very powerful people. One such organization comes directly to mind, and I believe they may just be able to save your dear Jim."

Joxy stood speechless as she tried to comprehend. Before she could respond, Veruna was instructing her to follow. Taking one last hopeful look at Jim, Joxy tagged along after this apparent godsend. After winding through the complex for a couple of minutes, they exited, popping out onto a crowded street.

Traffic was so intense that the tide threatened to swallow Joxy whole. Veruna reached out, clutching her by the collar of her jacket before she could be swept away. The oncoming throng parted, creating a tiny island of the two women amid a storm of bodies.

People rushed by, their glances darting back and forth. Looks of recognition and possibly even fear were present on many of their faces. Joxy knew she had a reputation, however, most of the stares rested on Veruna. *Who is this mysterious woman?*

"Stick close to me," Veruna ordered.

The sea of people parted for them the entire way, the wiry little woman taking point as she dragged Joxy along behind her. After a few blocks they managed to reach a rail station.

"We'll take the rail to my lab at the industrial quarter. It's a private sector, so there won't be any crowds to fight."

Fight what crowds? Joxy wondered. Everyone parted like we were bleeding from our eyes, or something. Veruna stepped up onto the station's platform, where she entered her destination on a control terminal.

"See you on the other side," she said before vanishing into the lightrail's wall of light.

Joxy dreaded this mode of transportation, which always made her feel queasy afterward. With a deep breath, she walked up onto the platform, closed her eyes, then stepped forward. The experience happened so fast that there was no time for any sensory input. It was simply like stepping from one room into another.

On the other side, Veruna stood waiting. After taking a single step, Joxy doubled over and dry heaved. She hadn't eaten all day, having rushed over to the med hub as soon as the emergency mechs whisked Jim away.

Veruna slid an arm under Joxy, helping her to right herself. "I'll get you something nourishing in just a bit. We're not far from my office. Bear with me a little longer."

Joxy didn't respond. She was too busy battling nausea as saliva pooled in her mouth. She welcomed the help, leaning heavily on the woman for support, not only of the physical kind.

Veruna was right; few people traveled the streets running along the private sector. Those who did seemed in a hurry and preoccupied. The posture of people with implanted holos were easy to identify. Stiff necks, awkward movements, and an open gaze as they stared at things only they could see. *Working on the go*, Joxy said to herself.

Buildings in this part of the sector were squat in shape, made from a material that looked like some kind of polished metal. Strangely, none of the structures appeared to have doors or windows. As Veruna escorted her along the sidewalk, Joxy reached out a hand, dragging it along one building's smooth surface. It was warm and soft, not at all what she'd expected.

A pedestrian approached one of the buildings up ahead. A section of the façade parted, opening to allow the person entry before sealing itself back. She saw no seams where the opening had just been. *Very odd,* she thought to herself, *but not the strangest thing I've ever seen.*

"What are these things?" Joxy asked, pointing to one nearby.

"Labs. Very important ones."

Due to the clipped tone of Veruna's answer, Joxy wondered at what kind of experiments were being conducted inside.

An edifice loomed ahead, even more impressive than those of its surrounding counterparts. Out in front was a meticulously designed courtyard crammed with what appeared to be original, pre-expansion statues and fountains. Joxy could only guess at their value, not to mention their legality. It was against the law to remove any artifacts or resources from Earth, and she was willing to bet that these museum-quality pieces dated back to the Roman Empire.

As the two of them neared the building, a section of the wall opened up to produce an entry. Joxy welcomed the opportunity to be back inside, away from the blue sunlight, and to her surprise, away from the planet's strange air. The air inside felt cool in her lungs; tasting and smelling natural, or at least not recycled or having a bitter tang. It was how she imagined the air on Earth would be like. And although they had stepped inside, the effect was that of walking outdoors, thanks to the decorative waterfalls and bright foliage that consumed this first floor like a jungle.

"Wow," Joxy said, stunned. "This is absolutely beautiful."

Veruna smiled, pleased with her reaction. "Each building is designed to be a self-sustaining ecosystem. The concept is old, but the science is new. There is absolutely no waste or byproduct. The only limitation is the material that we use to construct these buildings. It is extremely rare, and alien in nature. What you're seeing is the future."

Joxy gaped. If the resource used to build these environments were made available to all, then people could live comfortably even in the most inhospitable of zones. *What the hell were these buildings made of, and how do you find this stuff?* A million questions raced through her head. This material alone could end some of the galactic wars that were currently raging.

She took in as much as possible while Veruna led her through the overgrown lobby. One question above all still nagged at her: What could Veruna do for Jim?

"What kind of organization do you run here?" Joxy asked as they hopped onto a lift, its sudden acceleration planting both of her feet firmly as they shot up through the building.

"Mostly research and development. We have contracts with a diverse group of galaxies, corporations, and scavengers that allow us first dibs on many new discoveries. From those discoveries we develop applicable, specially tailored products. Our clientele is even more diverse," Veruna grinned without humor.

"So, you modify alien tech?"

"To put it simply, yes. Pretty much."

Joxy looked down at the lift's floor where she noticed the image of an abstract letter *V*. She thought that perhaps it stood for Veruna, but then laughed at the idea. She was about to make a joke of it when the lift pinged and its doors slid open.

Veruna led her into what could only be described as a palatial office. Scattered about were giant, ornate columns covered in moss, vines, and exotic flowers. The columns seemed to subdivide the room into smaller sections. Passing through several of these sections, the two of them made their way to the back. Veruna told her to take a seat on one of the crisp leather couches.

A bank of hovering holos clustered around them. Planets, stars, graphs, data, and other unintelligible images were projected on their screens.

"This organization sounds like it does some very important work. It must be expensive. I'm not sure if I could afford the research it would take to help Jim." What could she possibly offer this woman, this organization?

"Here at VOrg it's not all about profit margins," Veruna stated.

Now I know what the V is for, Joxy thought.

"We're more interested in real value, real results."

It sounded rehearsed.

"But why Jim, why us?" Joxy waited for the catch.

"Let's get you something to eat. You must be famished, and then I'll explain everything."

A gorgeous man dressed in a finely tailored suit appeared at Joxy's side, his unusually tanned features flawless. The man had an assured aura and radiated wisdom. Something about it appealed to her, which was intriguing but also alarming. *There is more than meets the eye with this one,* she thought.

Veruna pointed with her hand. "Joxy, meet Raygo. Raygo, Joxy. Her husband is Jim, the one I told you about earlier. Would you be a dear and grab our guest something to eat, then we'll all sit down together and talk business."

Joxy sat there wondering when Veruna could have spoken to Raygo about Jim. She'd been with her since they met. Her instincts tugged at her. Something was off about all of this, and for the first time, she wondered if Veruna could be trusted. But all the doubt vanished as a silver tray, crammed with an assortment of delicious foods, floated to a stop before her. Her stomach growled as she dug in, not caring in the slightest about her bad manners.

Veruna sat watching her in silence, an amused look on her face Joxy attempted a gracious smile at Raygo, but her mouth was so full that bits of food dribbled out. Raygo only smiled back without expressing a lick of judgment.

Joxy felt a lot better after eating. She could feel herself coming back as the nausea from the lightrail subsided. Mentally, she was still exhausted; the events of the day overwhelming to say the least. Veruna waved for a holo. One of the displays broke free from the nearby cluster and hovered over, settling between the two women.

"Show main lab," Veruna said.

The holo switched from showing a congregation of large asteroids to what appeared to be the inside of a lab. Humans and mechs could be seen standing around a man harnessed to a floating table. The lab was impressive, beyond state-of-the-art as far as Joxy could tell. She had made trips to other med units, but she didn't have a clue as to the purpose of the machines and equipment in this lab.

"Is this where you're planning to bring Jim?" she asked. If anywhere was capable of helping him, this placed looked it.

Her eyes skipped between Veruna and Raygo. Raygo's hands rested in his lap, legs stretched out and crossing at the ankles. He was at ease, as though this was all so casual. Veruna expanded her fingers, and the scene on the holo zoomed in, making the man at the center of attention now clearly observable. Joxy could count the freckles on his face even though she already knew how many were there.

Her eyes widened in shock.

Veruna spoke in a solemn tone. "He was rushed over here shortly after our departure from the hub. His condition is dramatically worsening." She reached over and grabbed Joxy's clammy hands. "We fear that he won't last another day."

"No, wait. What? Not last another—then why bring him here?" She jerked her hands back. "Why give me false hope? I thought you could help him, that there was something left you could do."

How could she have allowed herself to put so much faith in this stranger? Her face boiled in anger and shame as her emotions spiraled. She just wanted to leave this place, this nightmare, as quickly as possible. But she wasn't going anywhere. Not without Jim.

Suddenly she felt Raygo's warm presence sitting beside her. His solid arms wrapped tenderly around her as she let loose her emotions. She didn't care that it was a complete stranger embracing her. She didn't quite care about anything at that moment, other than Jim's life. A heavy feeling of hopelessness devoured her as she cried into her palms.

Veruna sat back and took in a deep breath.

"Not all hope is lost, my dear. We may not be able to save his body, but we may be able to save his mind. His consciousness, his memories, and what some might even consider to be his soul."

Joxy looked up from her palms in confusion. Tears wet her face, and she needed to blow her nose. She brushed away wet strands of hair as she tried to make sense out of what she just heard.

"You mean by turning him into a mech?" She shook her head. "No, he and I have talked about it. That's not what he wanted."

Veruna failed to stifle a laugh. "Mechs are a thing of the past. What we do at VOrg is the future." Her eyes burned with passion. "We are breaching the precipice of human evolution. Throughout time our mere existence has been balanced upon sheer luck. Our own sentience was the universe's gift to humanity. To explore, create, and put its vast resources to purpose.

"The goals of the universe have always been to create, destroy, and use energy. We are anthropic machines designed to achieve those goals efficiently. By being smarter, living longer, and exploiting our unlimited resources, humanity will thrive like no species before us. We will not be wiped away like our predecessors . . ."

Veins bulged from Veruna's neck and forehead; spittle dotted her lips and chin. Her obsession with this belief changed her entire demeanor. She became wild with energy.

" . . . I call them 'BAIs.' Biological Artificial Intelligence."

Joxy's mind swam with this information. She had tried her best to keep up. Had she understood correctly?

"Let's see if I'm following you," Joxy said, finally able to speak. "You want to emulate Jim's consciousness into one of your BAIs?"

Veruna snapped her fingers. "Precisely."

"And these BAIs are like some sort of evolved mech?"

"Oh, no. My gosh, no. They're so much more. In fact, we're not even sure of their full range of capabilities yet."

Joxy didn't want Jim becoming some lab rat. What if something went wrong? But something has gone wrong, terribly wrong. The love of her life was running out of time.

"What do these things look like?" she asked, fearing some hideous being.

Raygo stood and walked to the center of their section. He spun around, spreading his arms wide as though he were on display.

"They look like this," he said.

CHAPTER 5

THE VOID

"You know I'm not here just for you and the ship. So, where is he?" Commander Vaughn demanded as he poked his head around water barrels and in between crates of cargo, searching.

"And who are you referring to?" Joxy kept up the charade.

"Don't play games with me," he said. "Veruna has told me all about her pet that you've stolen. I don't agree with the existence of such a creature, but I have my orders for him as well. Now, where is Raygo?"

One of Vaughn's eyes was a different color than the other, and as it whirled around inside of its socket as though it had a mind of its own, Joxy assumed that it was some piece of fancy mech tech at work. The eye came to an abrupt stop, settling on her.

Joxy stuck out her chin, easing her hand behind her. "You may try to take my ship, but you'll never capture him," she said.

Vaughn drew his officer's pistol. It went from his hip to hands in the blink of an eye.

"Pause it! Keep your hands where I can see them, and tell your mechs to stand down, including those hiding in the cargo."

Vaughn kept his pistol trained on Joxy and her two guards. Two astros came running up from behind to help cover.

She didn't have time to ponder how he knew that. "Come on out boys, you've been made," she said.

A few moments later the other astros came forward, escorting the rest of The Devils at gun point.

"I can feel something tracking me here at quantum. You have to continue to stall. We can't afford to provoke them until we've destroyed the other starduster."

The situation was grim. Their fate rested on the Void.

Vaughn's eyes narrowed as they concentrated on Joxy. He pointed by her feet. "Set the box down there. I'm getting a lot of indicators."

An astro stepped up. He slung his rifle over his shoulder and clamped it to his back. Lifting his forearm, he removed a small cube from his armor.

"At her feet," Vaughn instructed impatiently.

Joxy was growing worried. *"Raygo, run!"* she urged.

Little did she know that the concept of running at the quantum level was absurd. He was in multiple places at once, with a small presence lingering even after he had left.

The astro knelt in front of her. The others shuffled forward, guns at the ready, motioning for her crew to step back. Reluctantly, they did. Through the astro's visor, Joxy noted beads of sweat pooling on his face as he gently placed the device on the floor. The VOrg logo was etched into the cube's sides. Looking around, it appeared that all of the astros were nervous, even their commander.

Vaughn holstered his pistol. The astro stepped back, pulling up a holo from the same armored forearm.

"The device is ready, commander," the astro said warily.

Vaughn took a few steps further back than the astro. "If you won't get Raygo to show, then we'll make him. Initiate."

The little machine thrummed to life, vibrating the air around it. Panic set in, sending Joxy's heart racing as the familiar coppery smell of charged particles hit her olfactory sensors. Her eyes widened in horror and disbelief when she realized what the contraption was for.

"*It's identifying and attracting my atomic code, forcing my atoms to reconstruct.*" Panic layered his words. "*I can't fight it, I'm being . . . absorbed.*"

"Please," Joxy said. "Leave him alone. Take me, take *The Legacy.*"

The look of enjoyment on Vaughn's face disgusted her. She knew that he was getting a kick out of watching her beg. His chest even seemed to swell, as though this conquest was all but complete.

"I believe we'll take you, your ship, and Raygo, but there's really no need for your crew," he said as he gave an almost imperceptible nod.

The Devils picked up on it.

The highly trained mechs dived for cover as their limbs transformed to weaponize. Assault rifles opened up, bullets sprayed all around Joxy, pock-marking her ship's hull and cargo.

Two of her warriors were clipped before reaching cover. One of them, shot in the shin, now dragged their foot behind while the other sprayed green fluid from their torso. Both mechs still functioned, returning fire from their positions.

The firefight wasn't directed at Joxy, not yet, so she took advantage of the mayhem and sprang into action, kicking the cube. It tumbled, edge over edge, like a rolling die. It came to a stop just inches from the astro's feet. Joxy crouched and rolled to the side, popping back up with her kager in hand. Flicking her arm, she threw the blade. It sang as it flew through the holo and penetrated the astro's armored forearm.

The astro let loose a howl of pain. The holo flickered out, and the air around them no longer seemed to vibrate.

"It's stopped." Raygo sounded relieved. *"But it managed to trap a small part of me."*

An explosion happened nearby that sent Joxy to her knees just in time as a wave of bullets flew over her head. Crates were flung into the air, ripped to pieces as munitions tore into them. She watched from her place on the floor while a vortex canon consumed one of the astros, then spit him back out in a mangle of pulp and gore with small chunks of armor sprinkled in.

Commander Vaughn took cover behind a small vessel latched to some tracks in the floor. Pistol in hand, he peeped over the top. "Everyone get back to the ship," he shouted, "and someone grab that damn cube!"

The Devils, all of them hunkered down pretty tight, were a little banged up, but their expressions burned with bloodlust. "Don't let them retreat," Joxy ordered.

All at once her men stood, leaning on each other for support. Their arms came together, began to entwine, then fused together. Their torsos reconfiguring into large, circular grenade launchers. Drawing power from one another, they each let loose a barrage of gravity grenades.

The astros were running, weaving in and out of cover as they fled for their ship. Grenades landed all around them, exploding into super-dense pockets of gravity that instantly smashed everything within their radius. Pools of blood and spatter dotted the hold.

Dodging lasers and grenades, the astro with the cube controls darted back to the device. He was in the process of bending over to scoop it up when the air around him began to stir, once again reeking of ozone. Raygo appeared behind him; half a hand missing. Sensing a presence, the astro quickly spun around.

With his good hand, Raygo withdrew the kager from the soldier's armor. Using surgical precision, he sliced through the armored suit's joints. Before the astro even knew what had hit him, he collapsed into a heap. Raygo bent down and plucked the cube from his fingers, then smiled up at Joxy as she came storming past, the agility and speed provided by her Eskin helping her to navigate the debris. He tossed her the kager blade as she raced to intercept Commander Vaughn before he could board his starduster.

She shouted into her comm for Tano to close the air-lock door. If Vaughn made it onto his ship, he would attack as soon as they were clear. At the other end of the room, yellow lights started to flash. Amongst the freight she spotted a bobbing head. Vaughn seemed to be running at upgraded speeds himself.

"Vaughn!" she screamed, hoping the sound of her voice would cause him to falter.

Vaughn slowed, then came to a stop just in front of the closing air-lock door. This was her chance. With all the momentum she could gather, Joxy launched her blade. Vaughn whirled around, firing off a single shot, before disappearing through the air-lock. The door latched and sealed behind him.

She sprinted over to where he'd stood just seconds before. Smoldering on the floor was her kager, at least what was left of it. Wisps of smoke trailed from the vaporized metal. Joxy could hear the clasp disengaging as the starduster prepared to separate on the other side of the hull.

She was as broken as her blade. She almost had him; she should have had him. Now they were doomed. Picking up the kager, she placed it back into its holster. The weight of it no longer so familiar. Was this an omen of what was soon to come?

Raygo came up behind her, tossing the cube up and down in his good hand.

"Well, I'll have to figure out how to crack this thing," he said. He waved half a hand in front of her face. "Thankfully, this is all I lost." He winked at her.

Even at such a perilous moment she couldn't help but bust out laughing, and he joined her.

"I thought I was going to lose you," she said with a snort.

"Veruna's been busy. This is some highly advanced tech." He paused. "You saved me, Joxy. Thank you." He leaned in toward her.

"Captain! Cap, can you hear me?"

Their moment interrupted.

"Go ahead, Tano."

"Net controls are back to operational. What are your orders?"

"Are both ships still in range?"

"Yes, Captain, but not for long."

Joxy took off through the hold, maneuvering through the blood and debris. Raygo trailed her. They passed The Devils, who were still collecting themselves, literally. Then Joxy bounded across the bridge and jumped into her seat. She spun around, pulling up her holos.

On the Universal Positioning System (what they called the "UPS"), a purple ship similar to a starduster joined another. Joxy swiped over and the controls for the net array appeared. The controls indicated that the net was primed and ready for use. She held her breath and without wasting another second, fired.

She didn't know if this plan would work. The net was designed for asteroids, not ships. But when the two ships vanished from inside the green circle, the bridge erupted with cheers.

She clenched both fists. "Woo-yeah!"

Using the ship-wide comms system, she addressed her crew.

"This is your Captain speaking. The Segans are no longer a threat. We have finished the bastards off." She let the good news sink in a moment. "I want everyone to rest up. We're going deeper into the Void than ever before."

She watched the screens as her crew celebrated the victory, jumping around hugging one another. They had all been in some close encounters, though they never took for granted escaping yet another one.

"Tano," she said, "let's get some guys down there to help Jones's team. They put up one helluva fight, but they're pretty banged up."

Joxy set a course for the anomaly once again. The unforeseen getaway had shaved a few days off their journey, but they still had a couple months left. Hopefully the rest of the trip would be uneventful, but luck rarely found *The Legacy* and her crew.

Tano looked up from his station. "Scans show that a badly damaged escape pod survived the attack. Do you want me to transmit another pulse?"

"No. Let their death drag out. Life support won't last long. Besides, they wouldn't have shown us the same mercy."

* * *

The Legacy's trajectory had them arriving at their destination in just under two months. The last twenty-one days had gone smoothly. Too smoothly, and it made Joxy anxious. Her ship had suffered only minor damage from the battle inside the cargo hold. And after the mechanics—jokingly referred to as the "mechy mechs"—had applied some patchwork where needed, the ship was back to fully operational. But the only thing that eased her anxiety in the slightest was the constant ship-wide diagnostics that she ran.

Time in space wasn't what it used to be. Everyone had heard the horror stories of early space exploration. In 3121, no one lost their minds or had to worry about bone density, not since the late second millennium. With the creation of Eskins, humans were easily able to cope with the varying degrees of gravity among the plethora of celestial objects. Whether it be ships or planets, the enhanced layer provided additional strength and agility to assist people through their daily rigors.

Over the centuries, ships became more like communities, some greatly larger than others, even equaling in population to some of the more impressive cities throughout the universe. No longer were their interiors spartan, all cold metals and hard plastics, outfitted with only what was essential to stay alive. Modern designs ranged from luxury to economical, modest to grand, with literal cities built into the hulls of some behemoths where polymer-paved streets zigged and zagged, their sidewalks lined with fancy restaurants and designer-brand stores. It'd been determined long ago that crew morale was just as vital as a stable G-drive.

Once this job ended, if they were able to cleanly break away from the Nocturians, Joxy would visit Earth. No one lived on the blue planet anymore. It was considered a Universe heritage site, protected by a long list of galactic treatises. Growing up, her father told stories of Earth. Hours of stories. He'd been there multiple times as a part of scientific expeditions. He raved of the natural beauty; gigantic bodies of water as far as the eye could see, mountains, waterfalls, and beaches. You might as well get comfortable when he dove into his Earth stories, as he would continue on and on about the wide variety of plant and animal life.

After one such expedition, her father, Bran, had presented her with a blue parrot feather that he had smuggled off the planet. During her childhood, it was her most valuable treasure, but she had to promise not to show any of her friends. Dad made her swear. Such paraphernalia was against the law. She grew up keeping the feather under her pillow, finally losing it during an attack as a child.

When she finally visited Earth herself, she would try and find another one. It was always a dream of hers to travel the planet and to experience the wonders her father had described. Now she had another reason to go. To find a feather *and* to collect some Earth titanium so that her kager blade might be fixed. It was a gigantic risk smuggling anything off of humanity's founding planet, but a risk she was willing to take. She had lost her father's gift, she wouldn't lose Jim's.

* * *

While hunched over the cube for hours, tinkering with its various components, Raygo made minor adjustments to the device's quantum control board and accidentally engaged a photon that turned the cube back on. Before he knew it, he found himself once again being absorbed into its interior containment field. He fought against the contraption's force with all of his strength to no avail. But because he had dug around its insides for the past few hours, he had a vague idea of its mechanics. Just before his left arm was entirely consumed, he managed to readjust that photon with his opposite hand in a manner that reversed the immersion process.

Raygo watched in relief as his arm, then his missing hand, rematerialized. The cube's power bordered the impossible, and based on his calculations-not to mention the two very personal encounters-he concluded that the device had to contain an equivalent amount of power to that of a supermassive black hole, similar to the ones found at the center of galaxies. It appeared to be designed to break matter down to its most basic parts and then reconfigure it again at will. Meaning a ship, planet, or theoretically an entire galaxy, could be targeted and absorbed, then carried around in a jacket pocket, undetected.

The implications were frightening. Used for nefarious purposes, it made VOrg and the Segans an even more formidable force. He'd make sure to add his own filters to the device to avoid accidentally absorbing himself again, or one of the crew. Or, even worse, just in case it ended up back in the wrong hands.

Commander Vaughn had been fairly intent on retrieving the cube, but that was before his forces were obliterated in front of his eyes and he went running to save his own life. All Raygo and the rest of *The Legacy's* crew could do was hope there wasn't more of this nasty kind of tech floating around out there.

For fear of it being activated remotely, Joxy had decided it would be best to work on it in the suspension chamber. She assigned Raygo the task of deciphering its capabilities; hell, he already figured out how to get his hand back, might as well find out what else it could do and if they could control it. Tano assisted him in this effort, trying to repair its holo controls that had been so badly speared while Raygo was busy on the cube.

"Everything Segan is created by VOrg!" Tano growled in frustration. He slammed the armored forearm piece onto the table. "Sega is just a front for them. Veruna rules that system. There's no telling how far her reach goes." He leaned back in the suspension chair, taking a break. "I know one thing, though, if she isn't aware already, she's going to be pissed when she finds out we have her little cube here."

Raygo smiled at the thought of Veruna's anger. Boy, did he know that temper all too well. "Oh, she'll be mad all right. Forget a few stardusters, next time it will be the entire armada." He shrugged his shoulders. "Maybe we'll be safe out here. It's this anomaly we're heading toward that worries me more than Veruna right now."

Raygo and Tano shared concerned looks. They each loved Joxy in their own way, and this mission made them uneasy about her safety. The possibility of running into other sentient life was their greatest threat. What if they proved hostile, or even more realistically, what if this was some elaborate ruse by the Nocturians to get them out of the picture for some reason they had yet to decipher?

Although the cargo hold had gone through hell, with much of the cargo utterly destroyed, the spare mech parts, tucked away in a corner far from the action, had survived the onslaught. Jones and the rest of his team of specialized mechs had made their necessary repairs by the time Raygo retrieved his missing digits. The ship and her crew were back in order.

* * *

Joxy exhaled loudly, relieved at the moment, not having to worry about Nocturian tails or bounty hunters. She seriously doubted that anyone would come looking for them this far out. Still, she continued to run scans, keeping an eye out for anything that might be lurking in the Void.

It was creepy, really, looking out the window and seeing absolute darkness. Not even a single star, no beacon of light, nothing. It baffled her how so much space could be empty. *What was its purpose?*

Lounging in her chair, Joxy assessed her holos, watching as their estimated time of arrival slowly ticked down. Brooding on the mission, she couldn't help but wonder what anything would be doing way out here. She thought it safe to assume that whatever they, or it, was, probably didn't want to be bothered. A chill ran through her as she imagined all the nightmare ways this shit show could play out.

Joxy jerked her head up. She thought she saw something moving behind the holos, over by the window. Tapping the control pad on her armrest, the screens vanished. She knew no one else was on the bridge. Raygo and Tano were working down in the suspension chamber. The rest of the crew were either resting or at their stations.

She hopped up and made her way over to the porthole. *Is something out there?* Craning her neck against the clear polymer, she scanned their surroundings as best she could. All she could see was a corner of the galley to her right. She didn't think she had imagined it, something had definitely floated by, but what would be out in the Void? All the patchwork was done, so it wasn't one of her mechy mechs goofing off out there.

The captain walked over to a side scuttle for a different view. This time all she could see was a large barrel from one of the cannons. She returned to her seat. Pulling up the holos, she ran a quick proximity check. Nothing. She bit her lip, narrowing her eyes back toward the porthole.

There it was again!

She jumped from her seat and darted back over to the window. Whatever it was had vanished again.

"Fucking Void," she grumbled.

Joxy knew the hallucinations would come; they always did. She just didn't know in what form they would manifest. Resting her chin in her palm, she patiently peered into the Void. There was no avoiding these delusions, and as sure as they arrived, they always went away, so she waited.

Once she learned to accept them, the visions no longer frightened her. They weren't a terrible price to pay in order to avoid capture. Staring out, the lack of stimuli became hypnotic. The darkness crept through the window, poured onto the bridge, and encased Joxy in a pitch-black shroud. The whine from the G-drives faded as it was replaced by a memory of absolute panic.

"Joxy . . . Joxy, wake up honey, we've got to go." Someone was shaking her, her body lolling back and forth.

Her eyes reluctantly drifted open. Her father was crouched over her. His long, brown beard hung inches from her face, eyes wrinkled in worry.

"That's my girl. Now, come on, we have to hurry."

She felt his warm breath on her face.

"But, Daddy," Joxy pleaded, "what about all my stuff? And I can't leave Mr. Fluffers, he'll get lonely." She pouted as she stared into her father's golden green eyes, just like her own.

Sorrow haunted his features. "We'll come back just as soon as we can." He lied.

"You promise?" She held out her pinky.

He grabbed it with his. "Promise."

Joxy would remember this moment as the only promise her father ever broke.

"We're going to move as fast as we can to *The Legacy*, honey. I need you to run, no matter what, run and don't look back. I'll be right behind you the whole time."

He had dutifully prepared his daughter for this scenario, knowing it was likely to happen at some point. Grabbing under her arms, he hoisted Joxy out of bed and carried her to the lift. Outside the walls of their building, screams rang out. Bran had booby-trapped their flat.

Floodlights lit the perimeter. Through a window, Joxy caught glimpses of people running around in metallic armored suits streaked with green-and-red insignias.

They rode the lift to the top of the building. Bran set his daughter down and unslung an arc rifle from his back, a cursive *V* etched into its stock. No sooner was his weapon in hand had a hunter climbed over the edge of the roof, followed by another, then another.

Bran stepped in front of Joxy, taking aim at the first bounty hunter. A bright blue laser beam blasted from his barrel, hitting the armored suit square in its chest. The beam then arced over, hitting the second hunter in the neck. The third hunter caught it in the torso, and all three launched from the roof.

Joxy never even knew that her father had such a thing. She was amazed by the pretty blue light display. Bran reached down and grabbed her hand, then they rushed over to the edge of the roof. Looking down over the ledge, Joxy saw a swarm of hunters scaling the building.

Bran fired.

Seven more fell to the ground. He pulled his head back just in time as return fire shot past him, into the night sky. Crouching, Bran pulled at a loose brick. Something clicked. Joxy stood by her father waiting to see what would happen next.

A light bridge sprang forth from the top of their building, stretching out and connecting to the next building over. Looking out over the city, she saw similar bridges popping up everywhere, creating an unhindered path to the city's outskirts. She felt her father's hands under her arms once again as he lifted her onto the bridge. She took off running. Bran followed closely on her heels, keeping stride as he fired at their pursuers below.

The two of them crossed bridge after bridge, running from building to building. The pedestrians on the streets below looked up in curiosity, pointing and murmuring in excitement as two figures made their way across. Bran kept an eye on their rear, occasionally firing back at any hunter within range.

On the streets, hunters fought against the crowds as they gave chase. Shots whizzed by from behind and below. Bran did his best to fight back, his arc rifle leveling the odds a little.

Miraculously, they reached the last bridge. They had lost the ones chasing them from down below, getting caught up in the maze of buildings and mass of people. There were still a few hunters firing aimlessly from a few bridges away.

The Legacy was stashed in the nearby Rajun Forest. Genetically altered five-hundred-foot trees provided a thick canopy that hindered scanners, making it difficult for anyone to locate a ship. They ran for the wood line, cutting between two of the monstrous trees.

The forest was dark. Little to no starlight filtered in. Bran had brought Joxy to these woods often. They didn't need light; the path to the ship was engraved in both their minds. Laser munitions blasted into trunks, spraying them with wood chips and dirt. The air filled with a charred odor. Tiny splinters lodged themselves into Joxy's soot-covered cheeks. Smoke stung her eyes.

Joxy kept running. She knew these people would stop at nothing to kill them. But Daddy won't let that happen.

Their ship was hidden just up ahead. With a burst from the last of her energy, she ran through the holo camouflaging the clearing where it sat. She crawled quickly up the ramp, allowing herself to collapse at the top.

"We made it, Daddy," she panted. "Let's get out of here."

Laser fire could still be heard off in the woods. An uneasy feeling crept into her stomach.

"Daddy!" she screamed into the darkness. "Where are you?" Tears cut tiny rivulets through the soot and dirt on her cheeks. Her tongue pushed at a small pool caught in the corner of her mouth. She tasted salt and grit.

The unknown was overwhelming. The firing had stopped minutes earlier. Joxy was torn between running back into the woods or finding a place to hide on *The Legacy*. Too frightened to go back, yet too stubborn to hide, she stood watching, waiting, straining her eyes and ears.

Something emerged through the leaves to her left. Cocking her head to the side, she tried to make sense in her mind's eye of what it could be.

"Joxy," Bran whispered in a strained voice.

She yelped, running down the ramp toward his voice. Almost tripping over one of his legs, she stumbled to the ground next to him. Bran let loose a muffled grunt.

"Help me up, honey. We've got to get into the ship and fast. The forest is full of hunters."

Legs trembling, she helped her father to his feet. A sticky wetness clung to her nightshirt and fingers. One painful step at a time, Bran made his way up the ramp. A crimson streak trailed behind them.

They reached the top. "*Legacy*, close cargo door and retract ramp."

"Yes, Captain," responded a feminine voice.

With a screech, the giant door started to close.

Metallic suits stumbled into the clearing, the ship's lights illuminating their armor. Bran dragged his daughter down behind the door just before rounds penetrated the all-but-empty hold.

"Get us in the air, *Legacy*. Let's get out of here." He struggled to get the words out, barely a murmur.

Bran wheezed. In the clear light of the cargo hold, Joxy could see where the blood oozed from his chest. Without hesitation she reached over and placed a hand on top of the wound like she had seen on her holo shows before. The blood continued to rise and spurt. Why wasn't it stopping?

Bran's shirt and pants were soaked. He locked eyes with his daughter. They wrapped their arms around one another. When she looked into his eyes once again, she could tell his pain was fading.

"Set course for emergency destination." He began to cough, his breath coming in labored gasps.

Joxy was afraid. Her father's limp body was too heavy for her to move to the ship's med bay. Even there, she doubted anything could be done for such grisly wounds.

Rocking her body back and forth, she said, "Tell me what to do, Daddy. You can't leave me, I need you!"

He brought his hand up, gently wiping away the tears.

"It's going to be all right, baby girl. You're going somewhere safe. The universe is dangerous. I need you to grow up strong, fierce. As long as you have *The Legacy*, you can carve your own path through the stars." He turned his head and spit out a mouthful of blood.

"*Legacy Starborn*," he spoke into the hold, "as your rightful captain, I hereby relinquish you from my authority and into that of my heir, Joxy. You will obey and protect her as you have done so for me all these years. *Legacy*, do you confirm?"

"Yes, Bran. It has been a pleasure. On the other side, follow the stars."

With the transfer of command accomplished, Bran let out his last breath.

Joxy screamed, "No!" Then desperately shook him, pounding at his chest with her small fists. Blood no longer leaked from his wounds. Her screams echoed throughout the hold. She laid her head against his neck, speaking into the soft tissue.

"But you promised . . . "

The vision faded along with the enveloping darkness. Joxy's cheeks were wet, her knuckles sore. Her control pad had cracked. She could still smell the blood.

"What the fuck?" Her chest heaved, heart pounding.

The Void had taken her down traumatic memory lane. It had all seemed so real. She wiped away the beads of sweat on her upper lip. Catching her breath, she looked back out the window.

Nothing but emptiness.

Joxy made her way to wobbling feet. Taking a few uneasy steps forward, she reached out and touched the polymer window, ensuring herself that it was still there. She needed assurance that the thin barrier between herself and the Void still existed.

Taking another deep breath, she turned. Raygo stood at the bridge entrance, not even bothering to conceal the worried look on his face.

"I heard screaming from down the hall." He took a couple of steps forward, looking around the room. "Are you okay?"

"Another hallucination, the Void playing its tricks again." She couldn't look him in the eye. She was still torn up inside. Instead, she shook her head and sat back down. "How's the cube coming along?"

Raygo knew better than to press. "Tano was able to reconfigure the cube's holo controls, and we have full access. It's dangerous tech. We need to be cautious."

VOrg was upping the ante. Would Veruna's quest of creating to destroy ever end? Joxy was tired of fighting, tired of having to look over her shoulder. Life was an uphill battle. Ever since she obtained her ship, people had tried to steal or con it from her.

The vision weighed heavily on her mind, but it made her think. She knew why bounty hunters were after her, but why had they been after her father all those years ago?

* * *

Two heavily gunned warships circled an escape pod. The small pod was charred black from flash fire. A tiny leak emitted just enough thrust to create a nausea-inducing spin. Scans indicated a signature coming from inside, human and mech. Out here in the Void such an encounter was unfathomable.

"Bring it in," Kurd ordered. "This should be interesting."

CHAPTER 6
EMULATION

Five years earlier . . .

Veruna had assured her gently, "He'll remember you. Memory retention averages 96 percent." It was the four missing percentage points that bothered Joxy.

Joxy sat there worrying herself with these thoughts while Veruna patiently looked on. Veruna's offer was the only option. If Joxy wished to save at least some part of the man she loved, then she would have to take the risk.

"All right." Joxy was staring hard at the floor, nodding her head. "Let's do it." She clapped her hands. She hoped she was making the right decision, for Jim's sake. She wondered how sharing a singular body would work. Would Jim's personality even shine through all those other personas? As a BAI, would Jim's consciousness be forced to watch life through someone else's eyes? Veruna had made it seem like all those minds worked in unison, creating a super-consciousness fit for controlling the BAI's elaborate capabilities.

As soon as she came to her decision, Veruna leapt into action.

"You're making the right decision." Veruna placed a hand on Joxy's shoulder, then told Raygo to "get everything prepared. We must move quickly. We'll follow shortly. Just one more important matter to discuss with the captain here."

Joxy flinched. She wondered if a catch was coming.

Raygo gave Joxy a warm smile before he left. "Jim and I will see you shortly."

"How did you know I was a captain?" Joxy asked. Had she mentioned it? She didn't think so.

Veruna motioned for another holo. It glided over. She scrolled through it as she spoke.

"I am well-informed on Captain Joxy of *The Legacy Starborn*, last remaining Starborn vessel. VOrg keeps close tabs on those who come in and out of Sega City. It was such a nice surprise to learn that you were a guest here on my lovely little planet." She continued scrolling.

Joxy didn't like the sound of that. Sure, Veruna had been the perfect host up to that point, and what she was offering would be incredibly hard to turn down, but something didn't sit right. Joxy was starting to feel like she'd been played somehow.

"We're not docked on planet. We didn't even enter orbit. How—"

"I know," Veruna cut in. "Your crew has her hidden in a glacier cave just outside of orbit."

Joxy straightened. All the alarm bells in her head blared.

"Once I discovered you were on planet, I knew that your ship wouldn't be far, so I sent out a team." Veruna motioned to the holo beside her.

The screen showed a live feed coming from someone's suit camera. Joxy saw her ship sitting in a giant cavern, its exterior lights dulled by the black ice. Her lips formed a thin line.

"So, what is this, huh? Are you trying to steal my ship? I'm sure you know that no one can pilot it without consensual authorization. It's pathetic you'd try to extort me by dangling Jim's life." She spat in disgust.

"I admit that this all seems rather opportunistic, but just hear me out. Please. I am proposing that you maintain your position as captain and that you and your crew come to work for VOrg. You'd be doing little different than you already are."

Joxy sat back and sighed. She eyed both holos: Jim on one, *The Legacy* on the other. The two things she held dearest in life. There wasn't much of a choice, she knew that. The terms weren't even bad, not if it saved Jim. She'd play along, for now.

Joxy closed her eyes, allowing her body to sink into the chair. A part of her wished it would swallow her whole. "You have a deal," she said softly.

"Wonderful," Veruna said, a little too cheerfully. "We'll talk details later. For now, let's go save Jim."

Veruna offered a hand, but Joxy brushed it away as she stood up on her own. Stepping through the holos, she walked across the office, avoiding miscellaneous furniture until reaching the lift. Joxy forced herself to be strong and optimistic as the two of them rode the lift in silence. They stopped a few floors down.

The gilded doors opened to a rather unremarkable lobby. Joxy imagined all the floors beneath Veruna's office must be bland by comparison. A sign with an arrow pointed down a hall. Stenciled in black it read "Main Lab." She assumed the building was crammed with labs, stacked upon one another. Only God knew what went on in them.

Joxy knew Veruna was playing God.

"This floor is where we run our brain emulations. Adding and subtracting from our BAI vessels, trying to find the best combinations of consciousness."

"There are more like Raygo?" For some reason this surprised Joxy.

"Our first batch had twelve. With each new consciousness, their limits would rise." Veruna cleared her throat. "Eight of them had to be terminated, leaving Raygo with three brilliant siblings. Their organic makeup, a part of which these buildings are constructed from as well, allows them to harness all those different thoughts. Each emulation is essentially adding another supercomputer to the mix, whereas a mech is limited to just one."

Veruna's words were tender, bordering on loving. She spoke as though they were her children, or a beloved pet. Joxy thought that in some demented way, Veruna probably believed she had birthed them or, rather, spawned them.

They walked through the lobby and started down the long stretch of hallway. There were no doors and no one in sight. It was an odd sensation, walking down a seemingly endless, empty hall. The metallic walls started to feel like they were closing in.

"So, he was part of the first batch. How many BAIs do you plan to make?" Joxy also wanted to know whose minds they were emulating. Had they been volunteers, or were some of them unwitting souls snatched from their deathbeds back at the med hub? She was terrified of the answer.

"I mentioned earlier how rare the material was. Our network is painstakingly scouring the universe for more. As of right now, very few people are aware of its existence. If we get desperate, then we'll simply tear down a lab and repurpose it. It's not the only ingredient in the cocktail, but it's definitely the hardest to come by."

"And what is 'it,' exactly?"

"We're calling it 'NH2I,' 'New Humans to Infinity,' or 'Humans 2.0,' whatever you prefer —and it's what makes the BAIs possible. To our knowledge, VOrg possesses all of what's been found. My BAIs will be humanity's ruling class, our own living gods. The epitome of myth and legend."

Joxy began to sweat at the way Veruna said, "my BAIs." This had all seemed like a good idea initially, but now that she knew more she was no longer sure. She didn't want her man turning into some modern-day god; she just wanted plain old Jim. People had been scared enough when mechs were first introduced, and this was far more extreme. She was on the verge of changing her mind when a seam appeared in the wall up ahead, parting to allow entry into the busy lab behind it.

Jim was there. She ran to his side, a gasp escaping her lips. Somehow his body had managed to deteriorate even more since watching him minutes before on the holo. He resembled a corpse, and the sight all but wrenched her heart in two.

Joxy picked up one of his cold, shriveled hands. She thought she saw his eyes flutter at the contact. Cables ran from some contraption mounted to his head. Small probes punctured his skull. The scene was terrifying to behold and reminded her of the horror shows that her father sometimes let her watch as a little girl. Tracing the cables she saw that they snaked only a short distance away, crossed over the spongy floor, up to another floating table to where Raygo lay. He rolled his head to the side, as best as the contraption would allow, and gave her a reassuring smile that seemed to say that everything would be all right.

Looking beyond him, she spotted Veruna conferring with what appeared to be two scientists. Veruna paused to flash Joxy a smile of her own. Hers seemed to say "I own your ass," before she returned to her conversation.

To Joxy, the room was spinning with battling emotions and uncertainty. She struggled to catch her breath. Leaning down, she choked back a sob and whispered "I love you" in Jim's ear. A tear fell and landed in the corner of his eye, creating the illusion that he, too, was crying. She wiped it away as more of her own tears fell in the process.

Veruna spoke from behind her. "Everyone is ready now. Are you, dear?"

Using both hands, Joxy wiped her face. She took a few steps back and straightened her posture. "Let's get this over with."

Doctors, scientists, and specialists all busied themselves by monitoring screens and ensuring everything was in place. Vitals and cable connections were checked, then checked again. VOrg couldn't afford any mishaps. Their greatest creation, Veruna's prized possession, was at stake.

A crowd of doctors and lab technicians in white coats spread out from the two tables. Not for any precautionary reason, but to better observe the scene. The process itself was rather uneventful. No flashing lights or dramatic noises, only status updates announced to the lab. Jim's limp body gave no indication of when his heart ceased beating, only the EKG's high-pitched beep let the room know that he had flatlined. Joxy's breath caught in her throat. Only the absurd fact that in order to save his life, she had to let him die, kept her from going completely unhinged and smashing that annoying machine. Somebody in the room declared the procedure complete. "Ninety-eight percent memory retention," someone else read from their data feed.

Veruna cheered along with everyone else in the lab. She wrapped her arms around Joxy and bounced excitedly in place. Joxy just stood there, numb and uncertain, unable to drag her eyes away from Jim's corpse. She knew that she needed to talk to Raygo—Jim—but she couldn't believe that the man of her dreams was gone. Not gone, gone, but all of his familiar hugs, kisses, smells, and gentle loving, gone.

"You made the right decision," Veruna said. "You saved Jim. You'll also enjoy working for me. I have so many great plans for you."

Joxy was too heartbroken to be annoyed by Veruna's snide comment. She also didn't dare kid herself with Raygo. He may appear physically perfect, and may even hold Jim's consciousness inside, but she would never allow him to touch her in the ways she let Jim. Nothing would ever be the same.

"Can—" She swallowed. "Can I go speak with Raygo, alone?"

"Of course, I'll clear everyone out and let you two have the room for a few minutes. Okay?"

"Thank you."

"All right, everyone get out!" Veruna ordered. "We'll get back at it in five."

Joxy slowly walked past Jim's body as a doctor pulled a rubber sheet over him. Raygo sat up on his table now while another doctor removed the contraption from his head, before scurrying out with the others. The BAI slouched, staring at the floor. He appeared dazed and pale. Small specks of blood dotted his scalp.

She reached out and grabbed him in fear that he would fall over. "Do you want me to tell the doctor to come back in?"

"No, it's okay." He waved a hand nonchalantly. "I'm fine, really, just takes a few minutes to get adjusted. It's frightening, at first, for the new addition. We've all welcomed Jim though, and he's calming down now."

Joxy tilted Raygo's chin back, their eyes locking. "Jim? Jim, it's okay baby. I'm here." She scanned his eyes and face for any sign. "Can you hear me?"

A few moments passed. A gleam came into Raygo's eyes. She knew that look all too well.

"There you are," she said softly, their faces but an inch apart. She wanted so badly to lean in and kiss him. It's not just Jim in there, she brutally reminded herself. She closed the small gap and kissed him anyway.

Joxy's eyes were closed as their lips parted. The taste and texture were so foreign that it scared her. Opening her eyes, she noticed that the gleam was gone. Quickly taking a step back, embarrassed, she stammered apologies.

Raygo laughed in an easy way. He held up a hand for her to stop. "It's OK. Jim's a part of us and we're a part of him. I know it must be complicated to understand, but we love you how Jim loves you, and he, we, love you a lot."

Joxy let loose a laugh of her own, partly because she was still embarrassed, but mostly because this was all just so crazy.

"I have so many questions."

"I can only imagine, and we'll get to them, but for now you must make good on your deal with Veruna. Do not let her fool you, she—"

The wall parted behind Joxy, and Raygo stopped talking. The doctors and technicians were making their way back into the lab. Veruna walked right up to them.

"Did you two have a good visit?" She gave Raygo a knowing look before turning the question to Joxy.

"It was good. I know that Jim's in there and that he's getting adjusted. I'd like to talk more with Raygo."

"That's wonderful, but for now let's leave Raygo with the doctors, let them do their doctor stuff, while we two ladies chat over a glass of skid." Veruna extended her arm, pointing the way out. "Shall we?"

Joxy darted a quick glance at Raygo, whose face was a blank canvas. As they left the lab she stopped by Jim's covered body. "When will you be incinerating him?"

Veruna responded matter-of-factly. "We won't. We'll be conducting a thorough autopsy and get to the bottom of whatever caused this. It may prove . . . beneficial."

Joxy almost chucked up the food she'd eaten earlier, and she would have if she didn't manage to swallow it back down with a grimace. She couldn't remove the image from her mind of Jim splayed out on a cold metal table. His organs resting beside him.

* * *

Back at Veruna's office, over a glass of exceptionally strong skid, the old woman laid out the details of a mission. But that wasn't saying much, as the details were rather lacking. Still, the task was simple. A vicious gang of bandits were holed up on a VOrg-owned asteroid. Joxy's job would be to remove the threat so that VOrg could continue mining operations.

Joxy let herself finally relax a little. If these were the kind of low-level tasks Veruna had in mind, then this deal would be cake. Maybe everything was going to work out fine.

"These bandits have been nothing but one big headache. Keep in mind that they're armed and extremely dangerous. I would advise a swift attack, and try not to venture too close." Veruna softened her voice. "I'm putting a lot of faith in you and your crew, Captain. Come back successful from this mission, and we'll make some time for you and Raygo to get better acquainted."

It was obvious to Joxy what Veruna was doing, dangling Raygo in front of her like some treat to be had, all in an effort to coax her into doing the hag's bidding.

"Don't worry, we'll take care of it. Right now, though, I need some sleep. I'm exhausted. It's been an . . . interesting day." She stood up to leave. "I'll be back bright and early—"

"Wait, we have plenty of rooms here. Take your pick," Veruna insisted.

"I appreciate the offer, but I prefer my own suite. And there're some things I need to collect," Joxy lied.

Veruna grinned. "How about an escort then. Sega City can be a dangerous place for a young lady."

"I can handle myself. Plus, by now I'm sure everyone will know that I'm working for you."

The two women appraised one another.

"This may be true."

Joxy made her way back to the lightrail station that she had arrived by earlier that day, even though it felt like it'd been weeks ago. Once again, the streets were all but empty. *Everyone holed up in their labs,* she figured. After hopping a couple of the rails, she arrived back at the hotel. Once she reached her suite, she headed straight for the lift, riding it up, not even looking in the direction of the kitchen, where two cups of cold stim still sat on the island. That still didn't prevent her mind's eye from betraying her and replaying images of Jim seizing up on the floor.

She walked into the bedroom, shaking those traumatic images from her head, and plopped herself onto the bed. Something poked at her ribs. Reaching into her jacket she removed the box holding the kager and placed it on the nightstand. Rolling over, she curled her body into a ball, pulling the sheets over her head. Burying her face in the pillow, she inhaled deeply. Jim's scent still lingered. The comforting aroma put her to sleep almost immediately.

* * *

A night of fitful sleep had Joxy feeling little rested. She wanted to hurry up and get this first job over with and make Veruna happy. Talking more with Raygo was all she could think about as she made her way to the hotel's hangar. Her light craft, a Wasp XX9, was a space and land vehicle—a souped-up shuttle—that she kept stashed in the cargo hold of *The Legacy.* The small vessel carried no weapons and provided only basic shielding, but damn if it wasn't fast.

The *Wasp* left Sega's atmosphere in a blur. The glacier, roaming just outside of the planet's gravitational influence, took but a few minutes to reach. Circling the giant block of ice, she spotted the entrance to the cavern. Joxy didn't even bother with trying to locate Veruna's cronies, she knew they were lurking around.

Tano had received her heads-up, along with a quick sit-rep of Jim. The cargo door opened as she flew up and parked in the hold. The *Wasp's* landing gear engaged the rails in the floor, pulling itself along and positioning out of the way. Most of the crew were there to welcome her back, but the mood was somber, the gist of Jim's fate having already made the rounds.

Her eyes watered, but she fought back the tears. She would not cry in front of them. "Men, a lot has changed in a short amount of time. Tano will update you all later with details on what's happened. Right now, we have a mission to execute. We're doing an eviction, and I want it pulled off without a hitch." Her eyes bore into the mechs as she growled out a sharp string of commands.

The crew scattered to their positions.

"Tano—the bridge, now."

Joxy and Tano walked through the ship together in silence. Their footfalls echoed behind them. She knew that he was containing his worry, along with what she was sure was a million questions, for her benefit, and she appreciated that.

Reaching the bridge, Joxy continued on past her captains' chair to stop at the bull's-eye window. Looking out the front of her ship at the dark glacial ice, it struck her how similar its lightless depth was to that of the Void. She allowed herself a few moments to collect her thoughts. *Be strong. Don't let the universe break you.*

Joxy spun around, holding onto a nearby bulkhead for support. "Jim's dead." The proclamation almost caused her knees to buckle.

Tano's jaw twitched as though he were having some sort of hardware malfunction. He seemed to finally regain some control of his functions and was able to eke out a simple question. "What the hell happened?"

Joxy knew that had his voice box been biological, it would have cracked. She wobbled over and collapsed into her chair, her fortified façade completely melting away. "I didn't have any other choice. I swear I didn't, Tano."

She could tell what Tano was thinking. That Jim seemed fine just days ago, when they had taken the *Wasp* and departed for Sega City. She was willing to bet that he probably knew of Jim's plans to propose. So, how could Jim be gone? He was just here.

He rushed over and knelt beside her. "It's okay, Joxy, tell me everything."

And so, she did. Filling him in on everything from finding Jim on the floor to the devilish deal she made with Veruna. How terrible it was seeing Jim's dead body and how they wanted to cut him open, study him. She told of Raygo and the BAIs. VOrg's plan of creating a ruling class. She spewed it all.

"So, this mission, this so-called 'eviction,' it's for Veruna, for VOrg? And once complete, you'll be allowed to speak with Jim, or this Raygo character, rather?" He paused there, a look of concern. "This woman is just using you to handle her dirty work. I don't like it one bit, and I'm not so sure Jim would approve, either."

He grabbed her hands, an apologetic softness in his eyes. "I shouldn't have said that. I understand why you did it. Obviously you didn't have much of a choice. Let's just get through this first mission and then go from there. We'll figure something out. We always do."

Joxy brightened, knowing Tano had her back. He would help her to make sense of it all.

She gave her friend a sad smile. "You're right. We'll figure it out. Now let's go handle some business." She removed her jacket and flung it over the back of her chair. Bringing up the holos, she entered the coordinates to the VOrg asteroid. "We'll do their dirty work, only until it's time for some dirty work of our own," she growled.

* * *

At the edge of some unimpressive galaxy, on the outskirts of an asteroid belt, roamed asteroid #59974. According to VOrg's database, the asteroid was unofficially named Golton. Initial scans indicated a few hundred life-forms, along with only a handful of small arms. *The scans aren't adding up to the bandit safe haven Veruna described,* she thought. Unless there were some stealth cannons somewhere, it appeared that Golton had no real way of defending itself from an assault.

It didn't feel right, so she warily approached the rock, going against Veruna's advice and deciding not to attack unless fired upon first.

"Tano, swing her around. Let's do a flyby. I'm seeing an ice shelf on the far side. That's where they'll be."

Joxy kept her eyes locked on the data feeds, searching for anything unusual, or remotely resembling hostility. With their shields up, they could risk a close sweep. As they flew in low, they spotted a few dozen environmental domes. A handful of them were torn open, exposed to vacuum.

Some of the bandits could be seen outside, seemingly collecting ice or mining the surface. All of them stopped what they were doing to look up and find *Legacy's* hull eclipsing the starry background. No one ran for cover or unleashed a barrage. They simply continued to stare in their patchy space suits, curious. Joxy decided to land

"Land her just outside the settlement, and organize Jones and his team. Have them meet me at the armory. We're suiting up and going out." She was already making her way from the bridge.

Tano relayed the captain's orders as he banked the ship left. Jones and his team of four took pride in their moniker, "The Devil's Asses," because they would always get the "shitty" jobs, but to them, those jobs were the best.

Joxy suited up in high-impact armor. A little bulky in the ship's gravity, it would provide perfect maneuverability on the low-gravity rocks. Holstered to one of her thigh plates was the kager blade. She was checking her battle rifle's cartridge, Teflon-coated slugs filling it to capacity, when her team of commandos filed in.

"Listen up! Something's off here. All the bandits I know would have been fighting to their last breath by now. Jones, you'll take Lily and Rome shelf side. I'll run point with Brigs and Rooney straight for that big dome in the center of town." She looked to each of them in turn. "Do not fire first. I want to speak to whoever is in charge. We all clear?"

"Hoo-ah!" they shouted in unison.

She lowered her faceplate. "Let's move out."

Their procession through the ship sounded like a military demonstration. It was game time. They exited the ship via the cargo hold's airlock. The chamber was purged of air before lurching, then the floor proceeded to descend, carrying them down to the asteroid's pockmarked surface.

As soon as their boots hit the ground, Jones waved an arm and his team fanned out to the left. Joxy could feel the surface dust and gravel sliding underneath her feet, and imagined the crunching sound that was supposed to go along with it. She led her team into the dome settlement, maintaining cover as they anticipated an ambush. She couldn't help but think how those VOrg lab buildings could help a place like this.

Joxy spoke into her suit's comm. "How we looking up there, Tano?"

"Heat signatures indicate that most of them have retreated inside that big dome up ahead. You have three sigs, fifty meters, positioned out front."

"That must be our welcoming party."

"Their weaponry is antique. Not sure if it would even scuff your suit."

That weird feeling in her gut was aching. *Who the hell are these people?*

"Jones."

"Go ahead, Cap."

"What are you seeing?"

"Ghost town."

"We got three. My side, big dome. Go around and flank both sides. If provoked, then we'll catch them in a crossfire."

"Aye-aye."

Joxy and her team used their suit's thrusters to swiftly dodge between the smaller domes, closing the distance to targets. They took cover behind a piece of broken mining equipment. She snuck a look; their position offered a clear line of sight. The three figures still stood there, just watching them.

Jones came over the channel. "We've got eyes."

Looking again, she saw her men behind the targets, hugging the dome, edging closer. They clearly had the drop.

"I'm coming out. Everyone look sharp."

She inched her way out from behind the rig, rifle at the ready. If they were going to attack, now would be the opportune time.

"Stop right there," ordered an amplified voice.

Joxy stopped, mere meters away. She took a deep breath, then cued her own suit's mic.

"I just want to talk," she responded, trying for a nonthreatening tone.

Two of them looked to the one in the middle. No doubt they were conferring on their own private channel.

"Who sent you?"

"The owners of this rock. An organization operating out of the Sega System, VOrg." She was hoping they had heard of it. And when the three men brought up their old guns to bear, she knew that they had.

Joxy stepped to the side, aiming through her own sights. "Whoa, whoa, whoa! Calm down, you're surrounded. Don't fire," she pleaded, not for herself, but for their own sake.

Jones's team swept in behind the hostiles, looking for any reason to dust these guys, Joxy knew full well.

"Guns down," Jones barked. "Put 'em down now!"

They hesitated, clearly surprised by the sudden rush of force. Their survival instincts finally kicked in, and they dropped their weapons. Joxy breathed a sigh of relief. These people weren't bandits; they were amateurs. She bet that if she checked their rifle cartridges, she'd find not a single one of them fully loaded.

Joxy stepped in. Brigs and Rooney came jogging up from behind. "All right, let's calm down," she said. "Is there somewhere we can comfortably chat?"

The one in charge motioned toward the dome behind him. His body language indicated his fear, but his voice remained sturdy. "We can go inside here, if you'd like."

No one could see it, but Joxy was sure they could hear the smile on her face.

"Perfect."

* * *

"We were sent to take out a dangerous group of bandits. When you didn't attack or even attempt to defend yourselves, a red flag went up for me," Joxy explained.

"We are nothing of the kind," said Keith, the old man in charge. "We've held a righteous claim of squatter rights to this asteroid for generations. Back before it was ever registered."

The cushions that they sat on were vibrant and comfortable, if not well worn, their colors and condition matching the thin, patterned carpet and plastic furniture that gave this communal dome its warm, homey vibe. She was able to take her suit off inside. The air was kind of stale, which meant the air purifiers were probably struggling to recycle all the breaths being taken by what appeared to be the asteroid's entire population inside.

Feeble-looking men, women, and children crowded around in order to watch this meeting unfold. Joxy recognized the wide-eyed looks of fear and desperation on their faces. The Devils opted to keep their suits on. They'd positioned themselves around their captain to create an armored wall between her and the masses.

"You didn't respond too kindly when I mentioned VOrg," she said.

Keith scoffed. "Did you not see our destroyed domes when you flew in?"

Joxy nodded. She'd seen them and was pretty sure she knew who had left them in that state of disrepair, too.

"That was VOrg," he continued. "A few months ago, they attacked. It was a warning. They could have easily wiped us out if they wanted to, but we think they assumed we would pick up and leave afterward. They didn't expect us to go public. We reached out to this quadrant's local Galactic News affiliate. It was a little bit of bad press for them and of course they denied it." Keith wiped at the corner of an eye. "My wife and son were in one of those domes."

"I'm so sorry to hear that," Joxy said, scooting closer to the old man. "What does VOrg want with this asteroid?"

"That's just it. We don't know why the sudden interest. These families have been mining this rock for centuries. There're very few precious metals left, no large deposits that we're aware of." Keith gazed at the floor, shaking his head. Then, as an afterthought, he said, "There were some analysts here a while back, maybe a little over a year ago. I overheard them talking about some substance or another. NH-something . . . sorry, my memory is a little fuzzy. I didn't think much of it at the time."

"Was it NH2I?" Joxy asked, a cold rage building inside of her.

"Yes, I believe was it. Is it rare or something? I had never heard of it until then."

"It's rare enough that VOrg would send death squads to take you out." She pointed both thumbs back at herself.

The crowd around them murmured anxiously. Joxy scolded herself for using such alarming language.

Keith held up a hand, gesturing for his people to remain calm. "I see. What do you suggest we do? We have but a single, shabby shuttle for transport and no place to go. This is our home, Captain. I know it doesn't look like much, but it's ours."

"If we leave," Joxy said, "then VOrg will just send someone else behind us. Someone that will follow orders and unknowingly end the lives of a few hundred innocent people." Joxy paused a moment for this to sink in. If it wasn't them, then it would be someone else. VOrg wouldn't stop until they had what they wanted.

Everyone went quiet. It felt as though the dome itself was holding its breath.

The corner of Joxy's mouth twitched. "I think I've got a plan."

CHAPTER 7
NOSTIC AND THE FLOWER

Joxy sat cross-legged on her perfectly broken-in captain's chair, making minor course corrections while twirling the small cube in her hands. The anomaly wasn't moving, but they somehow kept going off course. *The Legacy* would veer off ever so slightly even though its AI was supposed to prevent that.

Half of Joxy's adolescent years were spent growing up alone aboard the ship after her father's death. The emergency destination Bran had sent her to was a tiny moon of some insignificant exoplanet, where a cache of food and water had been stashed. The years dragged by, and it didn't take her long to start discovering some of the ship's secrets.

The Legacy's systems were advanced beyond that of standard military grade. One day, while roaming through archived audio files, Joxy made a startling discovery: the ship's AI was programmed to speak using her mother's voice. The mysterious mother who had supposedly died while giving birth to her. The woman whom her father claimed to have deeply loved, but rarely discussed. Joxy felt little connection to the voice, and it pained her every time she heard it because it reminded her of the parent she actually knew. She tried several times to remove it; unfortunately, it ended up being embedded in the ship's hardware and could not be deleted or changed. For this reason, she was hesitant to engage the AI unless absolutely necessary, relying mostly on Tano. It was Tano who had reassured her (at least half a dozen times) that the disruptions to their trajectory were nothing more than a little void interference.

"What's your plan once we get there?" Raygo asked.

He was sitting on a nearby couch. The past few weeks had dragged by. There was no more tinkering to do on the cube, only the crew's antics seemed to pass the time. This wasn't even the first time he'd brought up the question, and the answer was always the same.

"I'm not sure. A part of me hopes we don't find anything." She placed the cube down on the floor and sighed. "Don't get me wrong, I'm not in any hurry to get back to the universe proper. But I am hoping this is as exciting as it gets. The Nocturians pay us the same either way. Plus, we've already had enough excitement on this mission with that Commander Vaughn A-hole and his astros."

Raygo understood. He was trying to limit his expectations as well. Except, he was hoping that they did encounter something, anything. Having all the answers became monotonous sometimes. There had to be more to existence. He longed for there to be. Surely, he wasn't the culmination of humanity, that possibility had plagued him for years.

He was getting anxious. Thus, the recurring questions.

"And if it's one of our long-lost neighbors?"

"Then we'll invite them over for a nice round of skid and ask why the hell they couldn't have met us somewhere closer," Joxy said with false bravado. "Besides, if things get too dicey, then we'll see what our little cube here can do."

"Assuming the damn thing doesn't take us out, too." Raygo held up his recovered hand as the two of them laughed uneasily.

* * *

An escape pod sat in one of the warship's hangars, it's hatch shut. Rope-like robotic tendrils rose from the floor, torching their way around the small, egg-shaped bubble of life. More tendrils extended down from the ceiling, pulling the top half off and setting it aside. Inside, Commander Vaughn was still strapped in, gasping desperately at the sudden flood of air. His wobbly, bloodshot eyes tried to focus on the image of a comically large man approaching, but his consciousness faltered as his chin lolled to his chest.

Kurd fanned the air in front of his nose. "Whew! Someone get this man cleaned up, then dump this trash back out." He hurriedly walked away, gagging.

Vaughn woke up in an infirmary. He thought he was dead. He was the only body in a long row of cots. The room was blindingly white and reeked of cleaner. It didn't take him long to realize that he was on board a ship, a big one. He breathed a sigh of relief. What confused him, though, was that this vessel was not a Segan design.

The absurd thought of being on board *The Legacy* flashed through his mind. He sprung up, but a wave of nausea forced him back down. The last thing he could remember was spiraling uncontrollably. He had barely reached the escape pod in time. Some of his astros could have fit in with him, but he didn't have time to spare as he shut them out, mashing the red eject button.

His starduster was destroyed shortly after. The explosion sent flames and debris at his pod, damaging it. He watched his atmosphere gauge as its needle neared zero, his only chance for survival leaking out and causing him to spin. His last words before blacking out had been some curse or another meant for Captain Joxy.

A cup of water sat on a wall-mounted table beside him. He greedily gulped it down.

"Ah, you're awake," someone off to the side of him said.

Vaughn didn't want to risk anymore nausea. He tilted his head ever so slightly, only enough to make out the portly man he'd seen earlier, standing in the entrance to the infirmary, his body angled so that it would fit.

"Who are you?" Vaughn murmured. Half of his face buried in the pillow.

"I was going to ask you the same thing. Imagine my surprise when I found you all the way out here in the Void. But first, why don't you take those pills that were beside your cup. They'll help you with the sickness."

Vaughn dreaded the effort it would take to look for the pills. Without lifting his head, he reached out an arm, blindly feeling around the table. The stranger entered the room, managing the narrow path to his cot. Then he reached over Vaughn, their bellies touching. Pulling back, the man handed him the two white capsules. It could be a trick, Vaughn thought as he popped them, but he was too woozy to care. His guest sat on a cot beside him, testing the limits of its durability.

"I'll go first. My name is Kurd, emissary to the Nocturian Lord Emperor. You are currently onboard one of our warships." He paused briefly, letting the weight of his words sink in. "Based on your uniform we were able to determine you're a high-ranking officer from the Sega System. Now, you need to listen carefully. Tell me exactly who you are, and what you're doing out here. Exactly."

Vaughn hesitated. He wasn't sure what all he should tell this Nocturian. Answering questions was not something he was accustomed to, nor was being in such a vulnerable position. They could space him at any time. How long would these Nocturians tolerate a suspicious foreign officer if he didn't cooperate? He doubted anyone outside of this ship knew he was still alive.

Kurd's meaty fingers tapped against the cot's frame, and Vaughn knew he was growing tired of his silence. "Before you answer, let me just say this: we are currently in the midst of a very important, very secret mission. Your immediate future depends on your cooperation." Kurd shifted his bulk, the cot straining under the load, as he flung his arms wildly about, indicating the large expanse of the Void that surrounded them. I am very eager to hear your explanation as to why someone such as yourself would be way out here."

Vaughn's nausea mercifully drifted away, relief creeping in. He attempted to sit up, this time without becoming sick. A paper gown crinkled. They'd put him in a paper gown? An eyebrow arched at Kurd.

"You were—" Kurd cleared his throat. "You were quite the mess when we found you. Not hurt or anything, just . . . sick." The Segan sighed. "My name is Commander Vaughn. Commander of the Segan Armada. I was leading three stardusters in pursuit of a bounty, when we were savagely attacked."

"And who was it that attacked you, Commander?"

"The ship we were pursuing," Vaughn grumbled.

Kurd feigned astonishment. "Are you telling me that a single ship took out three of yours? That must either be some vessel or a hell of a captain. Tell me, who were you pursuing?"

"Just a bandit popular among the inner galaxies. I doubt you'd have heard of her in Nocturne."

"Try me."

* * *

"That can't be right," Joxy thought out loud.

Sitting up, she pulled the holo closer. The data was acting funnier than it normally did out here, and the AI, or Tano, wasn't doing any better at making sense of it. She thought there must be a glitch with the system, until she looked out the window and saw flashes of light.

Scans indicated that they were now mere minutes away from the anomaly. Klaxons erupted, warning that *The Legacy* was on a collision course. Joxy strapped herself in and advised through the ship's comm for everyone else to do likewise. Fingering her cracked display, she reversed drives in an emergency braking procedure.

The ship's design and propulsion system were meant to absorb and redistribute forces so that high g's wouldn't kill a human or mech. No matter how well a ship is designed, sometimes shit is just going to get thrown around. *The Legacy* reached the edge of its limits. Joxy's eyes felt as though they were about to pop out and roll around on the bridge. Her harness was cutting into her Eskin, threatening to slice through.

Given the immense pressure, she couldn't see and only hoped that her heart wouldn't quit pumping. They made drugs to counteract these effects that were supposed to help keep you alive. Unfortunately, she had no time to prepare.

It lasted only seconds, but it felt like hours. Her ship had successfully decelerated and now approached the anomaly at a manageable speed. The feeds said they were only a couple hundred miles away from whatever was out there. Joxy looked up from the holos and out the window. She inhaled sharply. Floating out in the darkness, shining in its own luminescence, was an elaborate geometric pattern of some sort.

"What the hell is that?" Tano whispered in awe.

Raygo and Tano stood behind Joxy's chair, the three of them baffled by what they were seeing. She hesitated to get any closer. They may have been hundreds of miles away, but in terms of being in space, it was too close for comfort. *Way too close.* Sliding her finger, she pulled back on the throttle, bringing the ship to a relative stop.

"That, my friend, is what we were sent here for. Tano, go make sure the crew is all right," she said without looking away.

Joxy unbuckled her harness, then stood up to stretch, rubbing at her sore shoulders.

"I'll be feeling that for a while," she said with a groan.

Raygo still had his hands resting on the back of her chair. He hadn't taken his eyes off the anomaly.

"It's mesmerizing," he said.

"That pattern definitely isn't natural, someone created it. I sent out a comms beam, but it's responding like nothing's there."

She stepped up to the window, putting her nose to the polymer. From their current position it looked to be about the size of a small moon, about the same size, in fact, to the one she grew up on. A faint iridescent glimmer flashed across its surface.

"It's a Flower of Life," Raygo declared. Shocking himself at his own revelation.

"A what?" Joxy was confused. What did a flower have to do with anything?

"Flower of Life. It's one of the oldest known symbols. Considered a divine design; it symbolizes the unity of everything." In a few quick strides, Raygo made his way from behind Joxy's chair to join her at the window. "Someone had to have placed this giant, ancient symbol all the way out here. But what is the purpose?" He talked faster now. "I couldn't imagine anyone with hostile intentions provoking such an image, Joxy. This," he pointed toward the object, "pattern represents togetherness. So, can we not interpret that to mean we are in some way connected to who-ever put it here?"

"It's cute, but what do you think it's supposed to mean to us?" she asked.

Tano made his way back onto the bridge. "Everyone's all right, Captain. Just a little banged up is all, nothing major."

"Thank you," Joxy gestured outside. "What do you think about that?"

He walked past Raygo and took a place between the two of them at the window. Mech faces weren't known for conveying as much as a human's, but Joxy could tell that he was in the midst of some serious pondering.

"Well, for one, it's beautiful." He cocked his head to the side, then shrugged. "Maybe it's a portal? It doesn't appear to be any kind of ship or planet that we're familiar with. Surely, it's not some piece of Void art deco.

Joxy slid him a skeptical look. "A portal. To where?"

"That's why we're here," Raygo said slyly. "To find out."

She tapped her thigh, an anxious habit. Her head twisted back and forth between the two of them. She shrugged noncommittally. "Okay. So, let's agree for one second that this is a portal. Do we go in . . . or does something come out?"

Raygo was looking past her. He pointed out the window. "I think we're about to have an answer."

A bright, iridescent wave washed through the anomaly, lighting up individual sections of the shapes as it passed. Tano darted for his station. Indicators were flashing all over his holos.

"Captain, we're picking something up. It's making its way from the anomaly."

Joxy rushed to her own controls. "I'm bringing up . . . "

"Wait!" Tano shouted. "Scanners are showing that it's—it's human."

Her jaw dropped.

"Human?" she asked, incredulous. Is someone floating out there in a fucking space suit? I need more information, Tano, or I'm about to dust this thing."

Tano's hands flew about his station's holos, no doubt while simultaneously controlling the ones pulled up through his holo vision. Raygo stepped around Joxy and crept toward the window.

"It's human all right," Tano confirmed, but he sounded confused. "There's no ship, suit, weapons; no nothing. I'm not even sure if they're clothed, but they're heading straight for us."

Joxy was scrolling through the same data he was looking at. Although it sounded impossible, he was right. She calmed herself, knowing the pivotal moment was on its way. Soon she'd know if things would be friendly or violent. She was prepared for either.

"Fucking Void," she said with a snort. "Things just keep getting more interesting. Get everyone locked and loaded. I'm going to flash the lights for the starboard air-lock; hopefully this thing takes the hint." She hopped up and threw on her jacket. "Have the crew meet us there." Out of habit, her hand swung to her lower back. A pang of sadness shot through her chest.

Joxy looked to Raygo with a mischievous grin.

"What?" he asked innocently.

"You're the smartest . . . so, I'm going to let you take the lead on this one. You're our best hope of communicating with whatever's headed our way."

"I believe this may be out of my league as well." He chuckled. "I'll give it the ole college try. Just don't let me die, please."

It wasn't that long ago she would have laughed off such a preposterous request, having believed him to be invincible. But the encounter with the cube had changed this misconception. Anything was possible, especially when something completely unexplainable was floating towards her ship.

Joxy shot him a tense smile.

Stopping at an intersection on the midlevel of the ship, they stared at the starboard air-lock hatch. The lights on their side were flashing, which meant the lights on the other side of the small chamber would be, too. A majority of the crew filed in from the other three directions, piling up at the intersection where Joxy and Raygo stood. The Devils were the closest.

"Tano filled us in," Jones said. "Orders, Captain?"

The low whine of charging lasers mingled with the click-clack staccato of mechs checking mags. Joxy's adrenal glands were pumping full throttle. Before she could respond, Tano chirped over the comms, causing her to almost jump out of her skin.

"Target took the hint and is approaching the air-lock. On your command, Captain."

She took a deep breath. "Secure this level. Nothing makes it past this junction without my say so," she ordered Jones.

Jones fanned everyone out, placing them along the halls at strategic intervals. He ran back and forth, ensuring that everyone was in their proper position with their safeties off. Raygo stood with his back to the wall on the opposite side of the hall. Joxy and he were the two closest ones to the air-lock.

"Okay Tano, we're ready down here."

"Opening exterior hatch . . . now."

The only indication that the hatch had opened was the lights went from flashing yellow to flashing red. Red meant the chamber was in vacuum. A human couldn't survive that. The scans had also said that whatever was coming at them didn't have weapons. *But that doesn't mean it doesn't have any,* Joxy thought. The surrealness was sinking in, and she couldn't believe she was allowing this thing on her ship. Was it too late to run? This was happening too fast.

She shook the uncertainties from her head. "Look sharp, guys," she said, more to herself.

The flashing lights stopped. Some of the crew could be heard readjusting their weapons. A tiny ding, ding, ding surprised everyone as it reverberated through the passages. They all exchanged questioning looks.

"Did it just knock?" Lily asked in disbelief.

Such an obvious question, yet so strange. The mood lightened a little.

"Tano, please open the interior hatch for our guest," Joxy said with a small smile.

The clamps surrounding the hatch disengaged. A slight hiss escaped the popping seals and the door swung open. A dozen heads peeked around corners as a pale being stepped over the threshold of the ship. It smiled at the sight of weapons whose operators stood with mouths agape.

The humanoid's head was a perfect circle equipped with eyes, ears, mouth, and nose, but it had no obvious sex. Joxy considered it a male even though its features were round and soft, only the lack of any discernable breast allowed her to leap to such a conclusion. Completely hairless, he stood there naked and smiling. He raised his hands in greeting. Everyone quickly shuffled back behind the walls for cover. Joxy contemplated ordering her men to open fire but resisted the urge. Instead, she peeped her head back around the corner.

Joxy frowned. "What the hell do you want?" she asked in a strained voice.

The humanoid didn't respond.

Joxy went back behind the wall. Raygo was staring at her. "Talk to it," she mouthed. He shrugged, then stepped into the hall. As he opened his mouth to speak, their guest spoke first.

"I can understand you, Captain Joxy." He spoke loudly and she easily heard him. He then addressed Raygo. "How are you all?"

Raygo flinched. He wasn't sure if the being was asking about all of the crew, or just asking him. For some reason he believed it was the latter.

"I'm fine?" Raygo stuttered.

The being lowered his hands to his sides.

"In your language, my name is Nostic. I am the gatekeeper of what you refer to as the Void. The doorway between your dimension and mine. As for what the hell I want, well, you may want to sit down when I tell you."

Raygo turned to Joxy. His eyes said, "What the fuck?"

The crew stood by in shock, no doubt figuring it best that their captain and resident BAI handle the situation. Starting to feel silly for hiding herself away, Joxy stepped out from behind the wall.

"We'll skip over the fact that you already know who we are," she said. "Let's get right down to this other dimension and what exactly you and the rest of your species are."

"The Others."

"Yes, you and the others. What are you?

"The Others. In your language, that is what we are known as."

Joxy's hand tapped at her thigh as she cleared her throat. "I see. Why don't we take this conversation up to the bridge where we can be seated comfortably and help ourselves to a much-needed drink."

* * *

Back on the bridge, Raygo stood at the captain's bar fixing drinks for Joxy, Tano, and himself. No doubt the rest of *The Legacy's* crew was doing the same. Typically, protocol required keeping a clear and sober mind; however, protocol never addressed what to do when encountering an alien species. Therefore, protocol be damned. He yelled over his shoulder, "Nostic, you're sure you don't want a beverage?"

"Unnecessary, thank you."

"Suit yourself," Raygo mumbled.

Joxy sat leaning forward with her elbows on her knees on a couch directly in front of where Nostic was sitting. "I changed my mind," she declared. "Let's start with how you know Raygo and myself."

"We've been monitoring your species for a long time. The universe, and its many wonders, has allowed only a few handfuls of sentient beings. Out of those, humanity has reaped the most destruction. Humans are actually among some of the least advanced, yet that did not stop your kind from venturing further than any before you. Unfortunately, it was with the sole intent of exploitation."

Nostic fondled the cuff of a sleeve. Tano had dug up some clothes that were a close fit. Joxy thought he looked uncomfortable in his attire. She figured it was his first time in clothes, and only just realized the mistake in assuming that he needed to put some on. Never mind that now, more important matters were at hand.

Raygo walked over to Tano's station, handing him his drink. The mech kept one eye on the portal and the other on the drama unfolding before him. He propped his feet up as Raygo joined Joxy on the couch, drinks in hand.

"The Others inevitably lost faith in humanity," Nostic continued. "A dead end in the ever-ongoing experiments of the universe. But I have observed your species for too long to give up. I believe I know the heart of man: how you destroy, but you also create. There is natural good in all of your kind, it's just getting harder to find. That's when I began my search for those who would be worthy. The proper representation of humankind to move forward. Thus, my interference in your lives. This meeting is no accident, I've had this planned for a time now."

Joxy sat back and downed her skid in one gulp, her face puckering up. This was a lot to take in. While Raygo sat quietly beside her, she could tell something was going on in that complex head of his. His cup sat full in his hands.

"Wow, um, okay," she said, her eyes roaming around the room before landing back on Nostic. "So, you're saying you've chosen us," she gestured to herself, then Raygo, "to join you and *The Others*? Well, where did you want us to join you, and why?"

"Yes, why us?" Raygo echoed distantly.

"And why not me?" Tano grumbled over his station, fairly positive that no one was paying him any attention.

"Humanity is the last grand experiment. No one else is coming along." Nostic paused a moment, tugging at his other cuff now. "Of the species before you, few have managed to advance outside this dimension. Those who didn't eventually succumbed to their own destruction. You are on the cusp of this advancement, but you are quickly running out of time.

"The discovery of what you term NH21 was by design. VOrg's concept of Biological Artificial Intelligence was by design. I've had to pull some extra strings to expedite the process. Otherwise, humanity will cease to exist, and I will lose what I consider to be my interdimensional siblings."

The bridge was quiet other than the soft gurgle of a pot of stim. Joxy was wondering how stout that cup of skid had been. Surely, she'd heard incorrectly. Was Nostic really insinuating that he possesses the capability to affect their lives so drastically?

She looked over and noticed Raygo's eyes boring into the being, saw the pain and anger flashing through them. She was aware of the losses that it took to create him, to create his siblings, and knew, without a doubt, that the same awareness raged through him at this very moment. Perhaps some of the blame that they both placed on Veruna should instead be placed on this character?

Nostic read him. Seeing Raygo's anger building for what it was. He looked through the BAI's eyes and into those of the many within.

"I have put a lot of faith in you. Without those sacrifices, all of your species would become extinct. My actions of intervention have had great consequences for you, as well as myself. Please try to understand."

Raygo noticeably battled with logic. Many have died so that they might be saved. The fact that they would have died anyway, and their death was for a greater cause, was a hard concept to get on board with. Joxy filled the awkward silence, asking the question that was probably in her best interest to leave unasked.

"So, out of the trillions of people scattered all throughout the universe, how did a few savvy bandits such as ourselves win this lottery?"

Nostic smiled without showing his teeth, but the humor did not reach his eyes. He tilted his head forward giving the captain a knowing look.

"You are not the crew of outlaw bandits that you have been labeled as. I've watched you, Jim, and the rest of your crew time and again fight for what is right," he gestured to Tano. "You've repeatedly helped the helpless. And now, in my own way, I am doing the same for you."

Tano's expression didn't change. Joxy was caught off guard at the mention of Jim. It meant Nostic had watched them for a while.

"Could you have saved Jim then?" Joxy's throat tightened.

"Jim becoming sick was not part of my plan. The universe, and all its possibilities, had implemented one of its own. In order to save a rare example of what you humans call love, I had to improvise. The plan was always to have Jim emulate, just not so soon. I wanted you both to have the choice."

Joxy was suddenly horrified. "Are you saying that I'll have to emulate, too?"

"But why even emulate?" Raygo blurted out. "Can we not as humans continue on into the next dimension? Even as a BAI, we're just a collection of individuals, just . . . a lot less individual."

She saw the gleam in his eye. Jim was at the forefront. She scooted a little closer to him while she nodded her head in agreement. The idea was not appealing in the least.

Nostic was patient. He'd known this would all require some explaining. "Your brains have evolved to process the stimuli of this dimension. You would overload your neural network if you were to experience a higher dimension. The Freedom Element, NH2I, is extremely ironic being that it is essentially the key to all of this. It's how my species, and those before us, were able to progress. It's how you will transcend as well."

Raygo sat his cup down without taking a single sip. He stared at both of his hands, turning them around. "You stated the universe is ending. How long do we have, does this decision need to be made today?"

"It's hard to say exactly. The universe grows weary of being plundered, its parts destroyed in days what took billions of years to create. I placed a wormhole in front of your ship to get you here sooner. We do not have weeks to waste, I . . . "

"So, you get to decide who lives and who dies," Raygo interjected. "Who gets to carry the torch for the human race. What gives you the right?"

Nostic focused the full weight of his stare on him. "Nothing gives me that right, my friend. Absolutely nothing. I am in a position to help a worthy species from becoming extinct. Roles reversed, I'm confident you'd do the same. My plan is not perfect, and neither am I."

Joxy watched as Raygo's shoulders noticeably slackened. She could feel his intensity come down a few notches. She understood what he was asking and why. It was a valuable insight into the reality ahead and those who inhabited it. Reaching over, she grabbed his hand. They locked eyes and smiled at each other. Joxy had always played around with the idea of emulating into Raygo if for no other reason than to be closer to Jim. But those had only been daydreams. She wasn't sure if she could actually bring herself to do something so extreme. Even if her life did depend on it. She didn't think she could make the same decision that she made for Jim, for herself.

"Well then, Nostic," she started in an apprehensive manner, "where do we go from here? Do you have a means to emulate, because, and I'm sure you are aware of this already, *The Legacy* doesn't. On top of that, surely you don't expect me to just leave my crew behind." She leaned back against the couch with her arms crossed over her chest, holding Nostic's stare. "If you know me as well as you claim, then you know that will never happen."

Nostic beamed, which was still more of an awkward smile than anything.

"I admire the love and loyalty you hold for your crew. I cannot even imagine you moving on without them. Of course, they're welcome—if they'll follow you, that is."

Tano shot up from his seat like a rocket, snapping to attention.

"Captain, if I may, I believe I speak for the entire crew when I say that we've followed you to the ends of this universe and will follow you to the end of the next."

Joxy's chest swelled. "Thank you, Tano." She cocked her head and arched a brow in Nostic's direction.

He forced a strained laugh, although genuine, he hadn't yet mastered the human emotion. "That settles it then. Now, for the tricky part of the plan."

Joxy quit smirking. Before Nostic could continue, Raygo chimed in. "You don't have a way to emulate, do you?"

Nostic slowly shook his head. "Unfortunately, no." He looked to Joxy. "The good news with that, though, is you all won't have to emulate into Raygo. The bad news, you'll have to return to Sega City and get into the VOrg labs."

Her mouth dropped. "But I have a bounty on my head out of Sega. We just destroyed three of their ships on the way out here."

"That would be suicide," added Tano.

"I did say this part of the plan was tricky, didn't I?" Nostic said.

Raygo sat up. "What are you suggesting?"

"VOrg has created more BAIs in recent years. They learned from the first batch and made the new ones exceptionally more malleable. You still have three siblings that they keep isolated. I'm sure they'll be happy to join in our little adventure. I will set a wormhole that will take you back to the edges of the Void. There you will find two warships that you should be well aware of."

The shock of discovering that his two brothers and sister were still alive was evident in Raygo's wide eyes. With what little Joxy remembered of them, she knew that they shared a unique bond with one another. Raygo had shared his fears with her, that he hoped Veruna had not taken her anger out on them when he left, and how he regretted not taking them with him. Even though he knew how much they meant to Veruna, the woman was completely unpredictable at best.

Joxy tilted her chin up. "I knew those damn Nocturians were try-ing to shadow us."

"Commandeer one of those ships. You'll need it in order to get into Segan territory. Make your way to Sega City and VOrg headquar-ters. I leave the rest in your capable hands, Captain Joxy."

She stood up and started pacing between the two couches.

"You make it sound so simple. But there's a lot of room for some-thing to go wrong. You've put a lot of faith in this rag tag team of ours. What if we don't succeed?"

"The fate of humanity depends upon your success," Nostic replied somberly.

Joxy stopped pacing and looked out the window toward the Flower of Life portal. It winked back at her as she tried to fathom the wonders beyond. She let out a breath that she hadn't realized she'd been holding.

"Let's get this show on the road then."

* * *

"Emissary, we've located *The Legacy*, but . . . "

Kurd gestured for the soldier to spit it out.

"She's popped up behind us, sir."

"Well don't just blabber about it to me," Kurd shouted. "Tell Captain Long to intercept."

The two NGS-14s sped toward *The Legacy* on a path to intercept. Captain Long, of vessel one, noticed that a small anomaly was registering on his feeds not far from where scanners had discovered the ship. Scans showed that the ship materialized out of nowhere and was steadily mov-ing away from the sudden anomaly.

A soldier spoke up from his station. "Ten minutes until intercept."

The veteran captain acknowledged with a nod. "I don't want to lose them again. Something strange is going on here. Keep an eye on that anomaly," he ordered.

Down in the cooler, Captain Vaughn lay strapped inside a capsule. It wasn't that long ago he'd threatened Joxy with the same fate. Tubes connected to his veins intertwined around him. The chemicals being pumped throughout his body would ensure the normal performance of his internal organs all the while keeping him in a state of paralysis, but completely awake. The worst part about the cooler was experiencing every second of it. He swayed in his harness when the ship made a sudden acceleration, and wondered where they were headed in such a hurry.

Vaughn was completely blindsided when Kurd informed him that Joxy was currently under the employ of the Nocturian Empire. At first, he thought it a joke, until two soldiers had marched into the infirmary and restrained him. He thrashed about haphazardly in a weak attempt— to do what? He didn't know but was in no condition to put up much of a fight. At least he had tried, he told himself now.

Walking through the bridge, Kurd stepped up beside Captain Long. Long's eyes drifted, hardly concealing his contempt.

"What do we have, Captain?"

The Captain wished that this annoying man would just let him do his job. If anyone else had bugged him as much as Kurd had on this trip, he would have spaced them long ago. But the Emissary was too close to the emperor, and he didn't dare cross him.

He sighed. "We're moments away from *The Legacy*. By now they definitely know we're coming but have yet to stop. On the other hand, they haven't sped up either. It appears they're wanting to put some distance between themselves and an anomaly we believe they appeared from."

"Anomaly?" Kurd asked. He rushed over to the nearest holo.

"Correct. Scans are picking up some unusual data. We believe it's how they were able to maneuver behind us."

Kurd anxiously scrolled through the feeds. He started to sweat.

"Two minutes to intercept," a soldier announced.

"Make a course correction," Kurd blurted out. "Change of plans. We're headed for that anomaly."

"But sir, what about *The Legacy?*" Long's patience seemed to be wearing thin.

"Have Captain Richards continue with intercept. No one is to speak with Captain Joxy or her crew. Make sure that is understood perfectly. Then have them reconvene at our location."

Long gave the order for the course correction. Pulling up his own holo, he attempted to hale Captain Richards of vessel two.

"Captain, we are changing course. You are to continue with rendezvous. Kurd has ordered that you are not to converse with *The Legacy* crew. Will send you coordinates of our new location afterwards."

Richards rolled his eyes, and Long responded with a smirk. Neither of them knew what was going on with all the secrecy. Both captains assumed Kurd was just enjoying his position of power.

"I'll inform you once we have *The Legacy* aboard, then we'll head your way."

"Thank you, Captain. We'll see you soon." Long closed the holo.

"We're approaching the anomaly, Captain," another soldier announced.

Kurd and Captain Long both stepped up to the main observation window. In the midst of the pitch blackness sat a swirling gray mass. Sporadic flashes of lightning could be seen inside of it.

"Scanners are going crazy!" someone shouted.

Captain Long hesitated, never in all of his years in space had he seen such a sight.

"All right, let's pull back," he ordered.

"We have no thrust," came the response. "Thrusters are not responding. Captain, we're being pulled toward it!"

Kurd spun on his heels as the drama unfolded.

"Captain, do something!" Kurd screamed.

Long pushed a soldier aside and took up his position at the station. He scrolled and tapped vigorously, but he couldn't get any part of the ship to respond. He shouted across the bridge.

"Are comms with Nocturne still up?"

"Affirmative, Captain."

"Send them our coordinates." Long looked at Kurd. The large man was frighteningly pale. "Inform them of our situation."

Kurd spoke in a weak voice. "Get word to the emperor. Tell him I said to send our entire armada."

CHAPTER 8
MONGREL

Five years earlier . . .

Joxy strode into Veruna's office where she noticed at least a dozen holos floating throughout, showing multiple feeds featuring a new discovery that had been made the day before. Several galactic news stations competed for exclusives regarding the new element found on Golton, racing to capture as much media content as possible before the bigger universal stations trickled in and took over. Joxy stopped and took it all in, fighting hard to hold back a pleased smile. Apparently, this little-known rock had become an overnight media sensation.

"As you know, it's not often that a completely unknown substance is discovered in this day and age. We're being told by initial data reports that this discovery could drastically change the industries of medicine, construction, genetics, and military as we know it. It's quite . . . "

"I'm standing here with Keith Becker, Golton's community leader. Keith, how does it feel to be a part of history, of discovering what you all are already calling the Freedom Element . . . "

" . . . whose wealth has just skyrocketed . . . "

Joxy continued into the room and found Veruna sitting in an isolated section of the office stationed behind a large Earth wood desk. The desk was easily the most expensive thing in a room full of expensive things.

"I don't give a damn about what concerns our shareholders have. Remind them who's in charge and buy up everything—yes, everything those balloon heads put on the market. No, I don't care how much it costs. Just do it!"

With a violent thrust of her hand, Veruna swiped away the holo connection, her gaze landing on Joxy. The captain stood stiffly, staring at a spot on the wall just above Veruna's head. She feared that if she were to make eye contact the old woman would read her betrayal.

"Have a seat," Veruna hissed.

Joxy chose the closest seat to the desk. If nothing else she didn't want to appear frightened. Veruna clasped her hands atop the polished wood and gritted her teeth. "Please, Captain, brief me on how such a disaster came to be. I gave you such a simple objective. One I had no doubt you would be able to handle."

Joxy wanted to point the finger at Veruna, at VOrg, for sending her to kill a bunch of innocent people for the sake of obtaining a resource. For treating the situation as if the community of miners was less valuable than the minerals they mined. This only proved that Veruna didn't know what she and her crew were all about. But she said nothing. Instead, she stuck to the plan. In order to successfully pull this off, she had to.

Joxy met the woman's gaze. "The asteroid was already surrounded by media ships when we arrived. Upon reconnaissance of the target location, I decided the mission was too risky. It appears that something valuable was discovered. Half the universe is keeping up with it."

Veruna thrummed her fingers along the desktop. Her mouth a slanted thin line.

"I see." She leaned back and assessed the Captain. "I just want to make something perfectly clear." Her voice was now frighteningly calm.

"If you ever give me reason to doubt your loyalty to our agreement, I will remove Jim from Raygo and upload his consciousness to the most derelict vessel in the universe. I will make him a pet for my pets. Do you understand the threat, Captain?"

Joxy's throat constricted. She had found the perfect holster for Jim's gift, and the kager rested on her back. Grotesque images of using the knife on this psychopath flashed across her mind.

She cleared her throat, not wanting her voice to falter. "I understand completely, but let me assure you that I have every intention of honoring our deal. I feel as though I owe you everything for what you have done for me and Jim. What occurred was merely bad timing. Failure will not happen again."

Joxy felt disgusted with herself. Even more so when she saw the genuine contentment wash over Veruna's face.

"See that it doesn't," Veruna said.

Joxy looked down at the floor, really trying to sell it. "Yes ma'am."

Veruna smiled at that, and it seemed as though all was forgiven, at least for now. "Would you like to visit with Raygo? I can arrange for you two to have some alone time." She gave Joxy a conspiring look. "Whatever you have in mind, dear, just let me know and I'll make it happen."

Joxy did her best to keep the thrill of that idea below the surface. She had so many questions she needed to ask Raygo, but after the perceived failure of this first mission, she'd been afraid Veruna would withhold access to him. "Some time alone would be nice."

"He has an apartment a couple of floors down. I'll have someone come up to escort you. Relax, and take all the time you two need."

Veruna called for an escort. A simple bot arrived on the lift dressed in an unfashionable tuxedo. It was from an ancient era; back when Earth society was at its peak. Veruna must like the nostalgia. *Typical for someone like her*, Joxy thought.

The butler bot took her down to another lobby, not unlike the one at the lab level. The exception was that this one actually had people loitering about. Extremely beautiful people whose presence seemed to radiate throughout the room. Their heads turned toward her.

Joxy's face blushed uncontrollably at their gaze. A part of her felt inferior in the presence of such remarkable beings, until the logical part of her brain reminded her that their thoughts were human in nature as well. Two men and a woman parted for them as they made their way to the hallway beyond. The beautiful people were silent, acknowledging her with nods and smiles. She blushed even more as she scooted by them wearing something like a smile of her own. When she'd finally passed them all, she laughed at herself, embarrassed by her reactions. Freaking BAIs, they must be Raygo's siblings, she surmised.

She and the robot hadn't quite reached the end of the hall when they stopped in front of a pine wood door. They had already passed three others: birch, maple, and oak. She thought pine was the prettiest and was surprised to see normal doors in a place like this. The bot rapped soundly on the door three times before swiveling around and making its way back to the lift.

"Thanks," Joxy mumbled as she watched it go.

The pine door creaked open on its metal hinges.

"Joxy!"

Before she had a chance to respond, Raygo swept her from her feet into a firm embrace. She looked up into his eyes, where she noticed the gleam and that his head was cocked in a familiar angle as he took in her face. All she could do was smile back at him, feeling both happy and sad, as she longed for Jim's actual lips.

"When did you get back?" He set her down gently, then motioned for her to come inside.

"Only a few hours ago," she said as she entered the lavishly decorated apartment. It appeared Raygo had a wide range of taste, which made sense considering how many people resided within him. Screens, acting as artificial windows, lined the walls. Beautiful scenes of canyons and gardens, each one creating the sense that you were no longer in the private sector on Sega City.

Joxy spun back toward him, disappointed to see that the gleam was already gone, and wondered at how the politics inside a BAI must work. She added it to her ever-growing list of questions.

"I just spoke with Veruna. She's furious about the mission. Have you heard?"

He pointed to a holo. "How could anyone miss it? It's being broadcasted on every station. Even ones that don't usually show the news."

Joxy threw off her jacket and slumped on the couch. She didn't regret helping Keith and his people, but Veruna's threat weighed heavily.

"What do you think of the discovery? Someone else will get their hands on that stuff now. VOrg might have some competition."

"Undoubtedly others will manage to obtain some NH2I, but I know Veruna will secure most of it. These people don't know what they're doing. They'll be lucky if some rogue system, desperate for power, doesn't come and invade their little rock."

Joxy was appalled. He spoke as though he were completely disconnected.

"Everyone's watching them right now," she fired back. "Who would risk such an attack?" She didn't tell him it had been her idea to go public.

"As I said, someone desperate. There are plenty of them out there."

Yeah, and VOrg is one of them, she almost said aloud. She decided to switch topics instead. "Are the other rooms I passed where your siblings live? I think I ran into them in the lobby."

Before he could answer, she stood, deciding to give herself the grand tour. Without meaning to, she found herself walking into the bedroom. The bed was enormous and looked comfortable. She flung her body on top, creating waves of wrinkles in the covers and causing some of the decorative pillows to fall to the floor. Her body melted into the cushion.

Raygo followed her into the room, smiling at her antics. "I guess they would be considered my brothers and sister. At least that's how Veruna sees it. Bobby, Marlow, and April are their names. Marlow's the one with the pointy nose."

Joxy lifted her head slightly from the mound of pillows. "But you're Veruna's favorite, aren't you?" she asked.

"I'm not too sure sometimes," he said with a laugh. "We tend to disagree on certain important matters."

She considered that for a moment.

"Have none of you ever thought about leaving? I know—"

A voice in her head came through loud and clear. It was Raygo. *"Careful what you say. This apartment, hell the entire planet, is monitored. I can assure you, Veruna is watching and listening."*

Her eyes widened. She stared at Raygo as though she was seeing him for the first time for what he was, which was something far from human. It hit her that the strong possibility of being surveilled by Veruna must account for his disconnectedness.

He followed up with spoken words.

"No, we owe everyone here at VOrg a lot. In most instances, like Jim's emulation into this body, they saved a life, or consciousness, however you choose to look at it."

Joxy remained unmoving on the bed, speechless.

"Act normal," the voice said again. *"Veruna is not aware of this ability, yet. This is how my siblings and I communicate without VOrg listening in."*

She thought back to the quiet BAIs in the lobby and was willing to bet they were having a private conversation as she passed through.

Sitting up, she managed to spit something out. "VOrg seems to help a lot of people. I'm happy to be a part of it now, and hopefully I can make a real difference."

Joxy was obviously shocked to discover Raygo had telepathic abilities, but she still had room for disappointment in herself for not expecting Veruna to be surveilling her. Especially here. *Why else would the old bat be so willing to let me meet with him?*

"Focus your thoughts," Raygo said, startling her. *"We can communicate like this. You just have to focus. I'll pick up on the radiation from your brain waves."*

"I'm excited to hear that," he said, sitting on the bed beside her. "Together, we can all move forward as a species. Conquer the stars, as Veruna would say."

Joxy lay back down. She was skeptical, knowing she didn't have telepathy, or whatever mental skill Raygo utilized. "I'm exhausted," she said as she rolled onto her side. She looked into his eyes. "Will you stay with me?"

Raygo lay down beside her. He threw an arm over her side and pulled her toward him. "Of course."

Joxy tried to focus her thoughts on what she wanted to say. She kept repeating the same sentence in her head and was beginning to worry whether she was doing it right. *"We'll lie here and pretend that we're asleep, so it doesn't look strange if we talk like this."*

His laughter came into her head. *"I heard you the first time. You've got it figured out. Simple right? We'll lie here and pretend that we're asleep, so it doesn't look strange if we talk like this."*

She was lost in the moment. Her heart thump-thumping against her ribs. His touch was gentle, caring. His warm breath tickled the small hairs on the back of her neck. Just for a second, she imagined that it was only Jim embracing her, then she eased back to reality.

"It's kind of creepy, you reading my thoughts." She smiled, nestling her face deeper into his tunic. *"So, tell me, why have you never left? You're the plaything of an egomaniac."*

"What I said earlier is true. In a sense we do owe Veruna our lives. And yes, we could leave, but where would we go? VOrg is a universal organization with branches everywhere. I think you underestimate their range of influence. We'd be on the run. That's no better than what we have here, now."

"I'd rather be hunted than enslaved." She sent the thought with some anger.

"Perhaps you're right."

Joxy could feel him hesitate as though he deliberated something important. *"We are tired of Veruna parading us around like some sideshow. Life has become more tolerable since you and Jim entered into it. Your love has given us something more to live for."* He squeezed her a little tighter. *"If you want to run off into the stars, we're with you."*

Joxy curled a handful of his tunic in her fist as she tried to keep her body from shaking. She knew Jim was in there, convincing them.

"What about your siblings? Would they come with us?"

"I'm not sure. Besides, it's too risky. I know they feel the same way I do about Veruna, but that doesn't mean they'd flee from her. If we mention something, then one of them could . . ." He didn't want to finish the thought.

She tried to imagine one of the three BAIs she crossed in the lobby betraying them. Maybe they were content with existing here. He was right, too risky.

"Any idea on how we might pull it off?"

Raygo was quiet for a few minutes. She listened to the rhythm of his breathing, a trance that almost put her to sleep. She jerked when his voice finally reappeared.

"We'll wait until Veruna has another mission for you. That will allow you to get off planet without appearing suspicious. She's not going to let you out of her sight until then. She wants to make sure you're going to hold up your end of the bargain. It's possible she is already anticipating your attempt to do something like this."

Joxy gave that some thought. *"And what about you?"*

"I'll suggest that I tag along to ensure the mission is a success. It's reasonable enough given your last task. Maybe she'll go for it."

"If she doesn't?" Joxy played the skeptic. Veruna was unpredictable.

"I've got a few tricks up my sleeve." She could hear his smile.

Joxy had to get out from beneath Veruna's clutches. She knew she would have to act as though everything were normal until the woman needed her again. *"Let's just hope it doesn't take long,"* she thought.

Something was bugging her, and she needed to clear the air.

"Did you know that Veruna sent me to kill a bunch of innocent people? That my mission was to remove bandits, except they weren't bandits. They were just a small mining community that happened to be squatting on an asteroid that VOrg wants." She tipped her head back in order to judge his reaction.

"When Veruna snatched you away from the lab after the emulation, I didn't know. I wasn't even expecting her to send you out so soon. After I

realized you were gone, I did a little digging. I was so relieved when I saw the first news feed. You're too clever. I knew you figured something out."

Joxy gave a throaty, disgusted snort. *"She's absolute evil. Does she answer to no one? Is she not held accountable for her actions?"*

Raygo sighed, familiar with this type of frustration. *"Veruna is the leader of VOrg. VOrg is the leader of innovation. Humanity has always sacrificed for innovation."*

To Joxy that sounded like a corporate script, and she would never accept it. She knew people weren't perfect, but she believed they should all be working together, not tearing each other apart. Have we not learned anything from the ruins of our predecessors? Overwhelming evidence shows that multiple civilizations were the cause of their own extinction. Would humanity follow that path, leaving crumbs behind for another species to perhaps one day find?

Joxy pondered all of this while she snuggled up to humanity's latest innovation. She now knew firsthand the sacrifices some were willing to make for it.

Joxy didn't remember falling asleep, but when she woke, the room was dark other than a thin line of light seeping through the cracked bedroom door. She lay alone in the massive bed; a blanket had been pulled over her. While her eyes adjusted, she wiped the drool from her cheek. Noises came from the other side of the door and so did the intoxicating aroma of freshly brewed stim. Her stomach growled. She couldn't remember the last time she'd eaten.

Sliding out of bed she had a sudden flashback of being back at their vacation suite. The smell of stim, a box with a bow, and Jim . . . sprawled out on the floor. She tripped over her own feet but managed to catch herself at the end of the bed. Tears threatened her eyes, but no, she was done with crying.

Joxy gained her composure, then opened the door the rest of the way. The light made her squint. Raygo stood in the open kitchen scrolling through *The Sega City Times* on a holo. Golton was front page.

"Says here that a private company, Bubonics, is buying up a good chunk of the NH2I. I'd be willing to wager they're just a shell for VOrg. I can't find much information on them."

She hopped up on a stool at the counter. Raygo slid her a steaming cup.

"Well, I hope they're able to get it all," she said tossing him a wink. "If it helps VOrg move us all forward, then so be it." She did an exaggerated shrug.

Joxy got a kick out of the charade, ever mindful now of Veruna's surveillance. Picking up the mug she gently blew across the inky black surface before attempting a tiny sip. Of course, the potent brew still scorched her tongue, but the effects were worth it. Instantly perking up, she set the cup back down.

"I'm not sure if Veruna is planning to give you your own apartment or not," he said with his eyes glued to the holo. "But you're more than welcome to stay here if you'd like. It wouldn't be any trouble." His eyes quickly darted to hers, then back to the screen.

She decided to mess with him a little. "Uh, I don't know . . . "

"I mean of course you probably need your own space. I understand, I—"

Joxy got her chuckle.

"Yes, I'll crash here, silly. I don't want to be alone in this place, besides, I want to get my money's worth, too. Jim's not getting rid of me that easily." She thought she caught the gleam flashing across his eyes.

Raygo's body relaxed. They laughed together, and Joxy was beginning to think that everything might just turn out okay.

"If I'm going to live here, though, I need to know, why pine?"

"Why what?" His face scrunched.

"Pine," she repeated. "Why is your door made of pine wood? I've been wondering ever since I noticed that each of your doors were different."

"Oh, well, in addition to its obvious beauty, there's something about its smell. It puts me at ease." His crooked smile expressed some sheepishness. "I know it sounds corny, but it's true."

It did sound corny, she agreed. She was expecting some symbolic meaning behind it. The simplicity of his answer put Raygo in a more human light.

"No, that's a good reason," she said softly. "I like the smell, too."

In the past, Joxy had only smelled pine-scented perfumes and aerosols. Nothing came close to the real thing. From then on, that's how she would imagine Earth smelled.

The holo in front of Raygo pinged. He shot Joxy a warning look before accepting the call. A holograph form of Veruna sitting at her desk materialized on the counter between them.

"Good morning, you two. I hope everyone had a restful night." Her voice sounded weary. "There's been a development, and I'd like to speak with you Raygo. Joxy, why don't you freshen up, then meet us in my office? This involves you as well."

After a clipped nod, she disappeared before either of them could respond. *The Sega City Times* rematerialized in her wake. Joxy thought Veruna was probably tired from watching them last night. She celebrated that small victory.

Raygo stared at her. *"Our opportunity may have come sooner than we were anticipating,"* he said telepathically.

"I'm not a fan of sudden developments," Joxy said aloud. "It has me a little worried. Why do you think she wants to speak with you first?"

Raygo frowned. "I'm not sure." He gulped down his stim; Joxy's was still too hot. "The bathroom is down the hall on the left. The laundry is the closet beside it. *Don't appear too eager up there, or she'll know something is up. Play it smart, and we'll pull this off,*" he assured her.

"I would love to see the look on her face." Joxy grinned.

"I don't want to be anywhere near that look," said Raygo. *"Matter of fact, I plan to be on the other side of the universe when she has that realization."*

"I'm going to head on up," he said aloud. "Wish me luck. I'll see you in a few." He gave her a wink before leaving.

She heard the front door creak open, then close. Sitting there alone, she contemplated the situation. Her hands were still wrapped around the mug, the *Times* still open and floating in front of her. *Veruna hadn't wasted a single day,* she thought. Another mission was already in the works, no doubt, and this one might even be more fucked up than the last.

The summons coming so soon normally would have pissed Joxy off, but because she and Raygo had a plan, she was glad for it. Now they wouldn't have to wait around, driving themselves mad, wondering when it would come. It bothered her, though, that Veruna wanted to speak with Raygo alone. She wondered what it could be about, then found herself questioning if she could truly trust Raygo. She berated herself for even having such a thought. Jim was in there, so of course she could, right?

After taking another sip of stim, she made her way for the bathroom. Walking around the counter she noticed the holo and how its front page displayed the Golton community posing in the big dome, all smiles. She turned off the holo, pleased with herself. It'd been weeks since her last real shower, and she eagerly disrobed as she padded down the hall. *The Legacy* had a lot of nice features, however, a decent-sized shower with good water pressure wasn't one of them. With no water allowance for the residents of these apartments, she stood under the hot water for as long as she could stand it.

When she got out, her skin was pulsing red and clean. She dried off, then picked up the kager from the sink and secured it to her back. The blade was never out of quick reach. Looking up she caught the stare of her own reflection. She wondered what her father would think of her now that she'd blossomed into a strong young woman.

I became fierce for you, Daddy.

Joxy knew her father would have liked Jim. She wasn't sure if he would have approved of their adventures, not to mention being in cahoots with an organization like VOrg, but she'd be back to roaming the universe before she knew it, she assured herself. *Just have to put on one last show for the woman who thinks she has all of the answers.*

She nodded to her reflection, then went into the bedroom and dressed. Knife, jacket, and now hygiene. She felt and looked like a captain. Showtime. As she walked out of the apartment, she took it all in one last time. This lavish life could easily be hers. All she had to do was submit. She laughed at the ridiculous thought. Other than the shower, she much preferred her cabin—and life—aboard *The Legacy*.

No one sat in the lobby as she passed through this time. The entire floor was eerily quiet. On the lift ride up, Joxy fingered the hilt of her kager.

As she approached the top floor, she detected a muffled voice. Joxy cocked her head to the side, trying to make out the words. None emerged clearly enough to decipher until the lift stopped and its doors opened.

" . . . do whatever I tell you. You're a fucking weapon, not a human, a fucking weapon. You hear me?"

Veruna was screaming.

Joxy considered getting back into the elevator and waiting for Raygo to return to his apartment, but she knew she was being watched. Instead she knocked on the wall beside the open door and crept with a bowed head into the office. Raygo stared at a spot on a wall, seemingly unfazed by the ass chewing. The old woman reared back her hand, then whipped it forward. Her hand stopped centimeters from his face. Raygo had reacted with terrifying speed, grabbing her wrist.

Veruna's head snapped up in surprise, then became fearful. But the moment of fear dissolved under a new wave of rage. Joxy realized just how unstable the woman was as she jerked her arm free, releasing another string of obscenities. Veruna made her way back to her desk, her lower lip still quivering in rage. Using both hands, she attempted to fix her hair before plopping down into her chair. Her gaze soon found Joxy approaching.

Sitting up, she smoothed out her dress. Her eyes softened as Joxy moved closer, the unpredictable woman's mask slipping back into place.

"Don't be alarmed, dear. I was just reminding Raygo how important he is. I admit, sometimes I can be hard on him." She glanced in his direction. "But he understands, don't you Raygo?"

"Yes, Veruna. I understand." His voice slipped into the detached tone Joxy had heard before.

Veruna smiled at Joxy. Joxy didn't like it, but she had to play along.

"He's humanity's future." Joxy declared in mock astonishment. "Hell, if he doesn't understand that, then no one will." She spun in her seat and shot Raygo a disapproving look. Veruna laughed aloud, eating it up.

"My, my, this one may be tougher on you than I am. You might want to watch out Raygo."

Raygo exhaled loudly, then took a seat beside Joxy.

"I'm not sure how you expect me to save humanity when I can't even save myself from the two of you," he said.

Veruna pointed a hand at Joxy. "Maybe the captain here can finally toughen you up. Work on him for me, will you?"

"I'll do what I can." Joxy saluted. "For the sake of us all."

Veruna let loose another guffaw.

"You're enjoying this way too much," Raygo said telepathically.

The corners of Joxy's mouth twitched. *"Just having a little fun."*

Veruna slapped the top of her desk, the joy present mere seconds ago, vanished. "All right, now that we've gotten that out of the way, let's get down to business." She leaned back in her chair and continued. "We've been buying up most of the NH2I coming off that little rock. No one knows it's us, of course, but we are encountering a little competition. There is a shadow entity buying up what we can't. Our systems have tracked the transactions to a far-flung system known as Subway."

Joxy's breath caught, and her eyes involuntarily darted to Raygo. A sick feeling rose from her gut.

Veruna leaned forward. "Is something wrong, Joxy?"

"No, it's, well, that's where we think Jim got sick," she said, speaking truthfully. "There was a freighter with stolen supplies and—" Joxy swallowed, unable to continue.

"Ahh, I see" Veruna seemed to ponder that for a moment. "Will this be a problem?"

"No, no," Joxy stammered. "I can handle it."

Veruna leaned back again. "Very well, however, I feel as though I must be blunt about this. Whatever you find there, I want it destroyed. Eliminate our competition." She pulled up her desk's holo. "I'm sending you the coordinates. I want you to make a strong statement out of whoever this is. Are we clear?"

"Crystal."

"Don't disappoint me again."

Joxy didn't like the idea of venturing back into the Subway system. It was risky. Whatever affected Jim in that system might affect her or another member of her crew, and may even be able to do the same to a BAI. She couldn't go through that again; then again, if everything went accordingly, she wouldn't have to.

Joxy hitched her thumb at Raygo. "You could have told me all that without him here."

"He's a reminder of what's at stake. Also, he'll be joining you on your trip." Veruna looked like someone who had just pulled back the curtain for a big reveal. Only more smug. "I want Raygo to get his feet wet. A little action may just give him the spark he needs."

He started to object. "But I—"

Veruna cut him off. "But you will go and help Captain Joxy on this mission," she said in clipped words. "It'll be a good bonding experience for you two. Try not to embarrass yourself, Raygo." She glared at him with contempt.

"I'll get something out of him. Jim's in there, and he's a fighter. You'll be pleased when we return," Joxy said with a nod.

"That's exactly what I want to hear." She waved her hand in a dismissive way. "Don't waste any more time. Those fuckers out there keep driving up the price."

Joxy and Raygo stood as Veruna seemed finished. But then, an afterthought: "Raygo, why don't you take Mongrel with you," she said. "He hasn't been out in a while."

Raygo nodded before walking away. Joxy trailed behind, unhappy with this last-minute addition. *Who the hell is Mongrel?*

"Not who, but what. Things just got a little more complicated."

* * *

"Where are we headed?" Joxy asked as she chased Raygo out the front of the building. "Slow down and talk to me."

Raygo stopped in the middle of the sidewalk. Joxy almost ran into him. No one else was around.

"This isn't good, Joxy." He shook his head. "Not good at all. We're going to one of VOrg's storage facilities. One of their most secure. It's practically a bunker built to house Veruna's worst atrocities."

He started back down the sidewalk. Joxy grabbed his arm and spun him around.

"Stop walking away from me, damn it, and tell me what this Mongrel is. Why are you so worried, what does it change?"

"Everything. It changes everything."

She stood there, staring back at him expectantly, one hand on her hip.

"Okay," he said with resign. "Mongrel was part of a program that VOrg was working on before they created BAIs. They were genetically designed to be the supreme killing machine. One was so good at it that he killed the others in the program. His name is Mongrel. He's Veruna's lap dog and doesn't come out of his cage often. I don't know why she's making us bring him along."

"Well, if he's that dangerous, then I'm not letting him on my ship. Let's go back and tell Veruna how insane her suggestion was."

Raygo laughed. "It wasn't a suggestion. It was an order. And if we don't take her pet, then I can assure you that she will not allow us off planet together."

Joxy snatched the front of his tunic. "How the heck does she expect us to keep this thing from killing us? Can we not just throw it out an airlock, toss it a bone, and continue on our merry way?" She released his tunic, then paced around him in a circle.

"It's not that simple," Raygo said. "We won't be doing anything to him that he doesn't let us. He's our babysitter, fiercely loyal to Veruna. She can monitor what he sees, and he will do as she commands. We now know for sure that Veruna doesn't trust us."

They finally reached the lightrail station. Raygo entered a destination into one of the station's terminals, then glanced back before stepping into the light. Joxy followed shortly after. They arrived at an area that could be best described as the middle of nowhere. Except for a few squat buildings, there was nothing to see. It was that rare time of day where both of the planet's two blue suns could be seen in the sky at the same time.

Joxy surveyed the desolate landscape. "This is a very remote location for a storage facility. I'm guessing VOrg atrocities don't include toy goods."

"'This is where they keep the toys they can't afford to play with."

The two of them made their way up to a boxy, gray building. The building's only features were that of a fairly noticeable automated-weapons system. Wall-mounted lasers panned back and forth while larger cannons on the roof idled silently. Raygo informed her that typically they wouldn't have been able to get anywhere close to here. Normally the system would have started shooting as soon as they stepped from the station. Veruna had granted them access. A well-hidden recessed door slid open. As they entered the dark interior, a bank of lights switched on and illuminated the grated platform on which they were standing. A wide, steel ramp descended further into the darkness before them.

"No lift?" Joxy asked.

"Afraid not."

The lights in front of them came on as the ones behind faded out. The feeling was a little disorienting. At one point Joxy stopped, both directions were in complete darkness, her only comfort being the small bubble of light that enveloped them.

"How far does this go?" she asked.

In answer, the next string of lights came on and lit a massive metal door. Joxy's mouth went slack. Six-inch-diameter bolts lined its perimeter. She figured the door was more for keeping things in than keeping them out.

To the left of the door, a panel flickered to life. Raygo entered a code, then stepped back as each bolt clanged as it pulled back. A seal broke and cold fog seeped through its cracks. Joxy was thankful she brought her coat as a shiver ran through her body. Grabbing a handle, Raygo effortlessly swung open the door.

"I would have tried to prepare you for what you're about to see," Raygo said, "but I doubt it would have helped. Some things just have to be experienced to understand."

Inside was a vast cooler. Separated polymer cells stacked floor to ceiling. They contained creatures of the sort contrived from nightmares. Joxy knew the beasts were all awake, the drugs preserving and paralyzing them, not allowing for sleep.

Her heart pounded in her ears, and she gulped. "Th-this is insane."

Some of the bodies of these creatures, obviously mutated, indicated that at some point they had been human. Others were completely unrecognizable. It was a horrifying sight, one that took every ounce of her courage to stay in place even though she desperately wanted to take off screaming.

Raygo put a hand on her shoulder to help calm her nerves. "Believe it or not these are some of the more successful experiments. Come on, Mongrel is kept in the back."

Joxy's neck hurt from craning it all about, wanting to be a witness to every horror. Her fear transformed into something hot and angry, and soon she burned with rage. Maybe some of these things had once been volunteers, but she knew that VOrg probably forced most of these people into it. No amount of knowledge was worth this price. These were once normal people with normal lives. Her hatred for Veruna soared. A vision of the people of Golton trapped in these cells flashed across her mind's eye. Her jaw flexed.

"Who all knows about this place?" Joxy was no longer cold.

"Very few. Even the puppet politicians don't have a clue."

"Somehow, someday, I'll make her pay," she growled.

Raygo looked over at her, and she realized her fists were clenched and that her shoulders shook.

"And I'll be there with you," he said.

They arrived at the end of the chamber and encountered another giant vault. Entering a code, the bolts pulled back from this door before it swung open. No fog appeared this time, but a soft rumble could be heard as much as it was felt.

"Holy shit," Joxy exhaled. "No. There is no fucking way that *thing* is getting on my ship."

"Let's just calm down. It's been ordered not to hurt us. It should obey."

"*Should?* What the hell do you mean, should?"

Tubes connecting to the monster's leathery skin popped off, startling them both. A puss-like fluid dripped from their ends as they sprang to the floor, coiling around long, sharp claws. Mongrel's eyes blazed feral red. Joxy felt paralyzed by his gaze. Slowly the beast raised itself on all fours, arching and stretching its back like a panther.

Huge fangs clacked as they chomped at nothing. Muscles rippled throughout its body, vibrating like someone had struck a chord.

Mongrel furiously shook his head back and forth, slobber flinging against the thick polymer, then oozing down. Standing upright on its hind legs, he scratched at his chest with a single claw. He walked upright with surprising stability to the barrier, then stopped in front of Joxy and Raygo. The polymer pane didn't seem thick enough. Not nearly.

He paused to appraise them both as saliva dripped from the corners of his mouth. To Joxy, it appeared as though the monster was weighing the pros and cons of eating them.

Raygo started to speak. "Mon—"

The thing erupted in a deafening roar. His breath fogged the pane in what resembled a Rorschach ink blot.

"Nope." Joxy turned back. "Nope, nope, nope. No F-ing way. Not my ship. Nope."

She stormed out of Mongrel's chamber, strode through the first room of horrors, and crossed the hall of darkness. This time she didn't even bother to see all that she could.

Joxy had seen enough.

CHAPTER 9
TRICKERY

"Captain Richards, comms are up. I'm transferring them over to you now," a station's operator announced.

"I would not have ordered something so strategically inappropriate. To go chasing after some anomaly, alone," Richards grumbled to himself. The fact that Kurd required such a thing made him detest the obnoxious man even more. What was all this running around really about? Perhaps it would be prudent of him to slip in a few words with this Captain Joxy, even though he'd been ordered not to.

His holo pinged and the image of a stunning young woman materialized in front of him. The bandit captain's reputation had reached even his small circle of acquaintances, though this was his first time he'd seen her image. All of the stories he'd heard implied that the woman was more dangerous than she appeared. He had to remind himself of this, because other than the sly grin in her holo likeness, she looked ready to host a ball for some star system's high court. He made a mental note not to underestimate her, but he couldn't get over how beautiful she was. Richards was uncomfortably reminded of his age.

"Captain Joxy." He was all smiles. "I am Captain Richards of the SS NGV 2 warship. My orders are to give you a lift. Do you copy?"

"Yes, Captain. We are ready to dock."

"We're opening hangar doors. Pull around to starboard. I'll be coming down personally to greet you."

"That will be nice. I'm looking forward to meeting you." Joxy winked.

The wink threw him off. *Is she flirting with me?* Surely not, but maybe. No, can't be. She had something in her eye. She's not interested in an old space head. He entertained the thought with a goofy smile. One of his hands fidgeted with a gold button on his uniform.

"Captain ... Captain? Is everything all right, sir?" an officer asked, concerned. Richards found himself blushing. What in the universe was wrong with him? *Get yourself together old man*, he chided himself.

He cleared his throat. "Yes, excuse me. Yes, I'm fine, Lieutenant. Get an escort team together and do it quickly. We have a guest to greet."

The officer hesitated. "Do you think that's a good idea, Captain?" I mean, these are bandits we're harboring. They're running scans of our ship as we speak, sir."

Richards's face burned crimson. "That was an order, soldier! Do not question me again, or I will bring you up on charges. *The Legacy* and crew are under the employ of your Lord Emperor and will be treated as such." He paused to wipe the spittle from his lips. "Have I made myself clear, Lieutenant?" he said with a snarl.

The subordinate's jaw moved, but words failed him. Instead, he snapped to attention before briskly walking off the bridge to gather an escort.

Captain Richards dabbed at his forehead with a hanky before plucking his cap from beside the holo screen. Switching the screen to mirror, he adjusted his cap and ironed his uniform with his hands. Refolding the hanky, he placed it smartly in a front pocket. He popped a mint as he made his way off the bridge.

* * *

"Did you just wink at him?" Tano asked, incredulous. "What's that all about?"

"I don't know. I panicked. I'm not used to flirting, and I wanted to disarm him a little. To give us the element of surprise, you know?"

"Oh, I think you surprised him, all right," Raygo said. "I bet he's weighing his chances right now."

"Well, screw you guys." She brushed them off with a laugh. "Maybe he'll have flowers and chocolates waiting for me as I commandeer his ship."

Raygo and Tano both shook their heads in amusement. Tano piloted *The Legacy* to the warship's starboard side. The vessel eclipsed the billions of stars behind it, completely filling Joxy's view from the bridge. The hangar was already open, leaving a gaping hole in the side of the warship, sealed off by only a thin shield membrane. Tano guided into its berth.

Nocturian fighter vessels lined the hangar in racks. Their profile resembled a baseball bat, giving them their nickname, Bats. Soldiers in heavily armored power suits scurried about like ants. Not for the first time, Joxy questioned Nostic and this plan of his. A small army inhabited this warship.

It took them a few minutes to find an empty dock; the hangar was practically full. Tano slid the ship into the bay; clamps clanged and lights flashed, then everything went still and silent. No one appeared to pay any mind to the new cargo.

"Tano, is everyone in place?" Joxy asked.

"Yes, Captain, they're all ready."

"Good, Raygo you're up."

Raygo pulled her to his body and wrapped his arms around her. He looked into her eyes. "I'll see you on the bridge, be safe."

His body drifted away as he de-atomized in her arms. Joxy stared at the emptiness.

"You, too," she conveyed to him telepathically.

Tano tossed her a recoilless automatic pistol that she snatched from the air. She tucked it into her waistband in the place her kager usually occupied. He slung a belt of gravity grenades over one shoulder and a plasma rifle across the other. His mech tech did not include weaponry, but that did not mean he wasn't a proficient fighter.

"I've left a skeleton crew behind to watch the ship and in case we need to make a fast break. Otherwise, all hands on deck," Tano said. "We'll need all the help we can afford to pull this off."

Joxy clasped a hand on his arm. Her grip was tight, eyes deadly serious. "If something goes wrong, promise me that you'll take *The Legacy* and run. Head to Sega and make a break for the emulation lab. Complete this mission, Tano, with or without me."

He clasped her arm in return. "Don't talk like that. We're all going to make it."

"Promise me." Joxy shook his arm. "Promise me, no matter what, you'll do whatever needs to be done." She looked the other way for a second, then back. "And take care of Raygo, too."

Tano loved how selfless his captain could be. Of course, he couldn't leave her behind, no matter what transpired. He knew she was worried, and for what it was worth, so was he. But he would never leave this warship without her.

"Yes, Captain, I promise. Whatever it takes." Tano could not look her in the eye.

Joxy stared at him a moment longer before releasing his arm. The two of them made their way down to the air-lock. The same one Nostic had used, the one that currently linked them to the NGV2.

Most of the crew packed the halls. About thirty of them lined the walls leading up to where The Devils stood at the front of the pack. They were positioned at the intersection before the air-lock hatch.

"Jones, how we lookin'?" Joxy asked.

The squad leader snapped to. "Weapons hot, arms are cocked. Hoo-ah!"

Joxy turned slowly, making eye contact with as many of her men as possible.

"Listen up! You all know the stakes by now. We must win this ship. It's our ticket into Segan territory. As you know, *The Legacy* here has a little bit of a bounty on her head." The halls filled with anxious laughter. "But that's never stopped us before, has it? Everyone stick to the plan and execute your roles. Let's show these Nocturians why they've heard of us in the first place!" She threw a clenched fist into the air.

Her crew jeered and an excited energy filled the cramped space.

"Wait for the signal," she told Jones.

He gave a curt nod, then patted the air to quiet everyone down.

The lights above the air-lock quit flashing, and its clamps disengaged. Joxy swung the door open, letting it rest against the wall. She stepped inside and in a few strides was at the exterior hatch. A small light changed from red to green. Taking a deep breath, she opened the hatch just a crack, not any further than she had to.

Joxy slid out, leaving the door slightly ajar behind her.

* * *

Captain Richards stopped by one of his ship's many lounges and retrieved a beautiful bouquet of artificial flowers from the center of a table. Embarrassingly, it took nine lounges before he finally found a vibrant enough imitation that he liked. He was old school, and as luck would have it, one of the vendings actually offered a small tray of chocolates. Richards recognized it all for what it was, his stars were aligning.

There were not many prospects aboard a military vessel, even in this day and age, with women flooding the ranks, very few were visually worth a second glance, in his old-school opinion. The tours were long and boring. Being stationed on the outskirts of the known universe didn't elicit much action, and he'd been ashamed more often than not at who, or what, he awoke to in his cabin, snoring beside him. Richards could feel it in his old bones, this Captain Joxy had hit on him. Boy, it had been a while since a female had taken the initiative. He tried, but failed, to think back to when that may have been.

With pep in his step, the captain sauntered toward the hangar. He led the way with a cocky, tooth-filled grin plastered on his wrinkled face. A small convoy of four high-ranking officers joined as his entourage, playing background to his ego. For this initial courtship, his first impression, he wanted to appear important. His plan was to have Joxy bagged before they ever reached vessel one, to hell with Kurd's orders.

The four officers followed closely behind, their strides matching pace with that of their Captain's. They rounded the corner together, arriving at the air-lock to *The Legacy's* bay. No lights flashed, and the ship lay secure in her berth. Richards stood there shifting his weight from foot to foot, palms sweaty. He felt like a young man waiting on a date. His officers flanked him, two to either side. He knew that this beautiful woman would be impressed and appreciative of his small gifts.

The air-lock seal broke, and the hatch eased open. A radiant, soft-featured woman slid through the narrow opening, popping out into the hall. *She's even prettier in person*, Richards thought. Joxy stood to her full height, looking every bit the captain that she was.

Richard's heart hammered inside his chest. He spoke hurriedly, tripping on the first few words before taking a deep breath and gaining his composure. "Captain Joxy, welcome aboard the SS NGV2, finest vessel among the Nocturian Armada."

He watched in awe as Joxy stepped up to him, stopping but an arm's length away. He took in the way her soft, full lips were slightly parted, how her easy eyes were half lidded, and how she stood with both of her legs firmly planted.

"Thanks for your hospitality, Captain Richards." Her tongue brushed her lips. "It's quite fortunate that you found us way out here."

"Th-These are for you," Richards stammered as he remembered his gifts.

Joxy received them graciously, although he noticed some sweat on them as he handed them over.

"Awe, thank you. You shouldn't have, really." She brought the flowers up to her nose. "They arc wonderful."

Blushing, he held out his arm. "Allow me to escort you to the bridge. Have you ever been on a warship before?"

"This is my first. I'm so excited." Joxy grabbed his arm, and they started off.

His teeth flashed a dirty smile. "Then I have much to show you."

"Shall we start at your cabin?" Joxy asked.

The officers raised their brows at one another. Maybe their captain did have some game.

Richards was momentarily speechless as he couldn't believe that these gestures were actually working.

Back on *The Legacy*, Jones heard the signal. The air-lock door crashed open as a wave of mechs swarmed forth. Richards and his small entourage spun around at the sound, eyes wide as they were caught completely unawares.

Joxy slammed Richards to the floor. His face landed beside a tray of scattered chocolates and broken flowers. He lay there stunned and bruised as the ship's air system blew colorful petals down the halls.

"Women," he moaned in pain.

* * *

Joxy's crew made quick work of the officers. Subduing them with restraints and gags, they dragged them into a nearby mechanical closet. She had already handled the captain and was standing him back up. His hands were secured behind his back, a bluish-purple bruise blossomed across the left side of his face.

The Devils split up, leading their own teams on detailed assignments. Jones's team, along with Joxy and Tano, would escort Captain Richards back to the bridge. Brig's team would hit the engine room. Lily, armory. Rooney, whose men had stripped the officers of their uniforms, would keep the halls clear. They couldn't afford Nocturians roaming around. Rome stayed back to guard the ship. Everyone knew their role; now it was time to execute.

"You won't get away with this," Richards snarled.

He attempted to launch a bloody loogie at Jones, but Joxy jerked his restraints up, causing him to yelp in pain instead.

"Please be quiet, Mr. Richards, and above all else, be cooperative. We will be taking over your lovely vessel, and if you play nice, then I may let you have it back when I'm done. Although, I cannot promise that it will be in one piece."

Richards started to protest but was only rewarded with another bolt of pain. From the scans Tano ran, he was able to concoct detailed blueprints of the warship. They led the old captain through the labyrinth of passageways as though it was *The Legacy* herself.

Joxy's heads-up display indicated which twists and turns to take, avoiding heavily trafficked routes. Jones held point alongside her, both arms weaponized. Behind three crew members, Tano brought up the rear. Rounding a corner, not far from the bridge, they encountered a small group. Between Jones having the drop, and the crewmen seeing their captain restrained, they didn't resist, as they, too, were bound and gagged before being deposited into a closet.

Joxy halted at the last bend before the bridge. Whispering, she said, "All right, fan out and cover as many stations as you can. We don't need any alarms before we can secure the ship." She tugged Richards closer, speaking into his ear. "You will order your crew to stand down, and hand control over to my men." She dug her pistol into his back. "Do you understand?"

"I'll do my best," he said, nodding anxiously.

"For their sakes, you'd better." She pushed him forward.

They quickly covered the distance to the bridge. Joxy froze as she took it in; she couldn't believe how big it was. This was going to be hard to cover. Disposable cups littered most of the stations. A stiff odor of sweat and stim permeated the room. Jones took off for the farthest station, followed by Tano and the rest of the team.

None of the station workers seemed to be aware of what was transpiring. Naively they believed that their warship, especially the control room, was impervious to being besieged. It wasn't until their captain made a strained announcement to obey the mechs by their stations—as well as a weak declaration that they would not be harmed—that they realized something was happening.

Holos reflected in their startled and confused eyes as they snapped into the reality that mechs leveled guns at them. They soon noticed that their captain, flanked by some striking woman, was pale and bruised.

"Listen to your captain," she told them. "This vessel is now under my command. Obey the orders of my men and you will not be harmed."

"Some of these men would rather die than follow your orders," Richards mumbled.

"For those of you who would rather die than be under my command, do something stupid and we will be happy to oblige," Joxy announced.

She nudged Richards to the closest station, one that Tano was covering. Placing her pistol to the operators nape, she ordered him to pull up the ship-wide comms. The operator gulped as the pistol dug into his skin. His fingers flashed across the holo screen.

Joxy told Richards to "order everyone aboard to their barracks and that they have ten minutes to get there. Anyone roaming the halls after that will be disobeying a direct order and shot on sight."

"I don't ..."

Joxy moved the pistol back to Richards, twisting it into his uniform. He cleared his throat and leaned in to the comm.

"Men of the SS NGV2, this is your captain speaking. I am ordering you all to return to your barracks, immediately. This is not a drill. Everyone has ten minutes to comply, or under Galactic law will be subject to extreme punishment. Return now. Thank you."

Joxy reached over and shut off the comms.

"You did good." She turned to Tano. "Monitor their movements. Once everyone is in the barracks, secure the doors. Alert Rooney and his team of any stragglers. Let the others know we have the bridge and to proceed as planned."

Tano kicked the operator off the station and took his place. Joxy scanned the bridge. The Nocturians and her own men glanced at her expectantly. Out of the corner of her eye, she caught movement, a station operator was inching his hand toward a discreet little red button. He was too far away for her to stop him from pressing it.

The air on the bridge swirled to life, sending cyclones of debris all over the place. Everyone's hair stood up, and ozone replaced the smell of stim and sweat. Joxy stood there grinning, her hair wild like Medusa's, minus the snakes. She spotted Raygo materializing behind the station. A hand shot forward, and there was a cry of pain. The station's operator was plucked from his seat and handed off to the nearby mech who was at first confused, then embarrassed when he realized he'd missed something important.

"Way to have our backs," Joxy said, grinning.

"What would you do without me?"

"Be stuck here alone in Armageddon."

Jones yelled from across the bridge. "Captain, the other warship just vanished!"

Murmurs spread throughout the room. Joxy ran to where Jones stood pointing at a scanner screen.

"Did he just say our sister ship vanished?" Richards braced himself against the closest station's console. "What in the hell is going on?"

Joxy looked to Raygo and jerked her head toward the overwhelmed captain. The man's pallor had somehow grown worse, and his lips produced incoherent mutterings that neared the edge of madness.

"Handle that please," she said.

Raygo briskly, but gently, escorted the old captain from the bridge before he had a complete meltdown. In a way, Joxy felt sorry for him; his entire life had just been upended, his power and ship stripped from him.

Jones scrolled through the data feeds. Joxy passed him a knowing look. The other ship had gone into their wormhole.

She shrugged. "I guess Nostic will handle that one?"

CHAPTER 10
RUN FOR IT

Five years earlier . . .

Joxy emerged from the bunker of horrors and into the suns' bright light; she raised an arm to shield her adjusting eyes. Over her own heavy breathing, she could still make out the screams and death throes coming from deep inside the bunker. Mongrel was in there feasting on the other abominations. She knew that Veruna was allowing this to happen, and Joxy hoped that the creatures' cocktail of drugs prevented them from feeling the pain.

Halfway back to the lightrail, she heard Raygo hollering for her to stop, or to at least slow down. She ignored him. When he finally did catch up to her, she was weeping. Before he could say anything, she buried her face in his chest, her body heaving with sobs.

"It's going to be all right," he said, his hands brushing across her back.

"No, it's not. Veruna has us trapped." She stopped crying and stood on her own as she dried her face. "Did you see that thing? What are we going to do once it's on my ship? Its claws could shred right through the hull. He might be able to survive the vacuum, but we cannot."

"He's our only ticket off this planet. I don't like the idea any more than you do. We'll figure it out. In the meantime, we'll set a course and play along. Maybe we'll find some information on what happened to Jim while we're out there."

Joxy considered that last possibility and her heart wrenched. Was it possible to find who was responsible for his illness, and how much was she willing to risk doing so? Maybe this shadow entity would have some answers. Her pain and fear transitioned into hope and anger.

Raygo scanned her suddenly calm face with a worried look of his own.

"Uh, did I say something wrong?" he asked.

Joxy laughed to herself at the irony of her revelation. It brought clarity.

"Actually, you said something right. We're going to go check things out, do a little poking around, but not for Veruna, for Jim. Mongrel may even turn out to be of some use." Raygo raised his brows. "We'll set him loose on whoever we find is responsible."

Joxy's smile was manic. She was falling in love with the idea more and more. Why didn't she connect the dots back in Veruna's office? With VOrg's resources, she could conduct her own covert mission while seemingly carrying out her assigned task.

Raygo shrugged. "Sounds good to me. I'm just relieved you had a change of heart. Besides, a part of me is curious what we might discover out there as well." He flashed her a smile.

"Yeah? And I bet I know which part," she said, punching him playfully in the shoulder.

They turned around and made their way back to the bunker. Lasers swiveled, tracking their movements. Veruna, no doubt, was monitoring the feeds. The door was still open. An ear-splitting sound from inside staggered them both. An enormous hand curled around the door's frame, its claws easily digging into the exterior of the bunker. Almost too big to fit, both sides of Mongrel's body scraped along the entrance as he lugged himself out.

Outside, unrestrained, his presence became even more terrifying. Joxy became overwhelmed as she tried to piece together which animal's genes provided each body part: its skull, a mix of lion and elephant; its legs, horse and cheetah; the arms and hands, ape- and human-like; the torso clearly a guerrilla's. The long claws were anyone's guess. A boney, spiked tail wagged behind him. She thought she'd seen a similar feature on a creature from an old Earth children's book. They were dino-somethings.

Everything about Mongrel was exaggerated, his features larger than the ones based on their ancient ancestors. He stood on hind legs again, stretching to his full height and resting his gaze of contempt upon the two standing before him. He bared his fangs and snarled, his long snout wrinkling. A mysterious limb of some sort still clung to his teeth, swaying gently out of the corner of his mouth.

Joxy fought back a lemony buildup of saliva. The sight was repulsive, and her distaste obvious. In response to her expression, the monster opened its maw even wider, revealing another row of serrated teeth. Surprisingly, the creature spoke. Its voice, deep and throaty yet disturbingly human.

"So, where are we headed?"

Joxy fumbled for words. Mongrel's voice matched his appearance. It was rough, to say the least, but she did not expect such a normal question from such a creature. As her brain raced for a response, he used a single claw to pluck the limb from his teeth. Tossing back his head, he sent the morsel down the hatch and followed it up with a satisfying burp.

Raygo looked to Joxy and cleared his throat. She blinked back at him a few times. "A system known as Subway," Raygo answered.

"Yes, um, the Subway system," Joxy followed up. "Veruna wants us to take you with us just in case we need help with whatever we encounter out there."

Mongrel exploded into a guttural laugh.

"Veruna's already uploaded to me what she is expecting, and it sounds a lot like babysitting. I'm probably not supposed to be telling you this, but I'm going to in the hope that you actually try. First, I'm supposed to make sure that you two lovebirds don't run away. Secondly, I'm tasked with turning Raygo here into a lean, mean killing machine. The second one will be pretty damn hard, if you ask me."

"She knows we're going to run." Joxy couldn't keep her hands from shaking. *"How could she know?"*

"If she knew for sure, then we wouldn't be leaving at all."

Raygo took a step forward. "You'd be surprised," he quipped.

Mongrel released a low growl. Joxy ran up between the two of them. She knew Mongrel could shred her to pieces in one swipe. She wasn't too sure of what Raygo was capable of, which was just as frightening.

"You two stop now," she demanded.

They could not afford to fight, not yet, but Mongrel was already advancing. With Joxy almost in reach, the beast unexpectedly fell to his knees. Grabbing at his massive head with both hands, he bellowed in what could only be described as excruciating pain.

"Stop. Please, stop." Mongrel whimpered, "I won't hurt them. I promise."

Joxy furrowed her brows at Raygo. He tapped a finger on his head.

"Veruna," he said matter-of-factly.

✳ ✳ ✳

Tano sat at his station, clearly uncomfortable as he stole glances over at their new guest every now and again. Mongrel had boarded *The Legacy* and headed straight for the bridge, apparently familiar with the ship's layout. Finding an empty corner, he curled up on the floor. From his breathing, along with the steady rise and fall of his massive chest, one might assume that he was sleeping.

Tano didn't think so.

Joxy had asked him to keep an eye on this beast while she gave Raygo—the name didn't feel right when he knew Jim was supposed to be in there—a tour of the ship and a chance to meet the crew. Joxy had told him that Jim's consciousness was a part of Raygo's character, as were quite a few other minds. As a mech, Tano found it hard to imagine. In the back of his own mind, he believed VOrg might be playing them. He'd have a chat with this so-called BAI.

Mongrel let loose a snoring sort of hacking sound that almost caused Tano to fall from his seat. He reached under his station's terminal, feeling for the pistol he kept hidden, relaxing a little as his fingers brushed the grip. The temptation to snatch it and dump the clip was enticing. He jerked his hand away before he did something foolish.

Joxy and Raygo arrived on the bridge. Raygo flashed Tano a friendly smile. He returned one that was skeptical. *Yeah, we'll see who's really in there,* he said to himself. Joxy eyed Mongrel, his tail wrapped around him all nice and snug. She imagined him lying, like he was now, in Veruna's office. The perfect pet for such an evil little woman.

She fell into her captain's chair. Raygo took a seat over on the couches not far from Mongrel. Tano kept a wary eye on both of the VOrg creations.

"Tano, set course for the coordinates VOrg provided," Joxy ordered. "Tano . . . "

The mech punched away at a holo, mapping the quickest route, avoiding asteroid farms and the most hostile galaxies. Being on an official mission for VOrg would merit its own safeties of travel, but there were some who'd attack for that very same reason. After all, they were not the only bandits in the universe.

"ETA is forty-seven hours, Captain."

"I'm putting the crew on alert. We take no chances on this one. I want everyone to be ready, no surprises. Let The Devils know we'll be running recon once we've reached destination."

"What would you like me to do?" Raygo said.

"What can you do?" she asked, sounding genuinely curious.

Tano was curious as well. He expected Raygo to elaborate on some super-awesome ability, one that might be helpful when it came time to dispose of Mongrel.

"Jim's memories are my memories. I can manage the drives, control weapons system, run the stim pot." He placed a finger on his bottom lip. "Even fly *The Legacy* if you'd like."

Joxy and Tano both erupted into laughter, but for different reasons. In order to pilot *The Legacy* someone with authority, typically the captain, had to permit it. Joxy had granted Jim access years ago. Would the ship's AI recognize him in Raygo?

"I have to get used to that," she said, still laughing. "Although I wonder which memories got lost." She chucked a holo across the room to him. It slid to a stop right in front of where he was sitting. "How about for now you keep tabs on weapons." She leaned back, playfully twirling a lock of her hair. "And make sure our stim pot keeps a fresh brew."

Tano didn't like the idea of handing over their weapons to this VOrg tech. He wasn't in the habit of questioning his captain, but for the sake of her safety and that of the crew, he had to find out if his old buddy was indeed part of this BAI.

Tano decided on a question that only the three of them would have the answer to. "Jim."

Raygo slid the holo to the side and looked across the bridge. "Yes, Tano?"

"Before I became a mech I had a lovely wife and two precious daughters. They were the entirety of my world. My reason for living."

Raygo nodded, "I remember, my friend, and as you know, I am deeply sorry that you lost them."

Tano swallowed hard. "What were their names?" He watched Raygo intently. There was a gleam to the BAI's eyes.

Joxy observed the exchange in silence. Tano appreciated her allowing him this opportunity for assurances. He desperately needed them. And if Jim was in fact now a part of this being, then he, too, would understand.

"Your wife's name was Tanya," Raygo answered. "Your two daughters, twins, Mila and Styla. Before emulating, your name was Jacob, and you worked at a shipyard. Many people died that day during the cataclysm. You barely escaped with your own life, your body all but destroyed. I know that it may be hard for you to understand, and even harder, maybe, to accept, but Jim is a part of me. I share the sorrow he feels for your loss as well as the joy of your friendship."

Tano sat back and gaped, his mind racing through countless scenarios. How much of his previous life was on public record? Who all knew he had once been a man named Jacob? Did VOrg have the means to trace his cryptic past? Most daunting of all, was Jim's consciousness really inside this guy?

He found it hard to accept. There was just too much at stake. He questioned his own judgment. There was only one thing left that would put him at ease. He pointed to where Joxy was sitting. Her eyes grew big as she threw her hands up.

"What, Tano? What more do you want?" Frustration had made its way into her voice.

"See if *The Legacy* recognizes him. Let's find out if he can still fly."

"Were his answers—"

"It's fine," Raygo insisted. "I was actually curious myself."

He hopped up and covered the distance to Joxy in just a few strides. Taking her by the hand, he helped her up from the worn-out seat. She backed away, allowing him space.

Raygo sat. He swiveled his head between the two observers. They stared back curious, expectant, but disappointed as nothing seemed to happen. Tano was about to say something when a soft musical tone was emitted onto the bridge. Mongrel stirred but remained curled in place.

The Legacy's AI spoke in its default voice: "Welcome back, Captain Jim."

Raygo nodded with a big smile. "Glad to be back."

Tano shot forward and extended his hand. Raygo grasped it firmly as it wildly shook.

"My God, it really is you. I'm so sorry . . . "

Raygo placed a hand on his friend's shoulder. "It's okay, you were just being cautious. I would've done the same. Trust me, I'm as relieved as you are."

Joxy joined them, and they all embraced. They were family. They loved one another and would always be there for each other. Tano acknowledged that this ship, and the beings on it, were all that any of them had. It's why they needed to be free from VOrg, from Veruna, to live their lives together how they deemed fit—not at the whims of a psychopathic overlord.

Over in the corner, Mongrel lay silent, one eye open, watching their reunion.

* * *

For the most part their voyage was uneventful. Other than a small, terribly equipped party of bandits that futilely tried to ambush them, not much happened. Joxy didn't even return fire, the would-be bandit's munitions never came close to penetrating the ship's shields. She simply sped up the drives and watched as tiny red icons vanished from the scanner screen.

Mongrel didn't budge, laying claim to that corner of the bridge. Tano assumed he had had his fill back at the bunker and was just sleeping it off. His synthetic body cringed as he recalled Joxy and Raygo's account of retrieving the creature. He was thankful he wasn't having to deal with the beast. The less drama the better, until he could figure out what can be done with him. A sense of dread lingered as he was not looking forward to that moment.

Raygo ran diagnostics on the weapons system, and their efficiency jumped up 31 percent. Tano was impressed. It was Jim and himself who had originally set up the system. Over the short span of this journey, the two of them had reconnected. They both held a strong affinity for Joxy, and their own relationship was just as important. The longer they were around one another, the more Tano understood the concept of BAIs and how advanced they really were. Raygo was continuously developing, learning, and grasping at knowledge and capabilities that teetered on the edge of impossible.

Joxy had informed Tano of VOrg's agenda to use these beings to lead and control humanity, to create a godlike ruling class that would usher in the next step in human evolution. Veruna would be pulling the strings, and by default, she would be the most powerful person in the universe.

"How does it feel?" Tano asked Raygo. "When I became a mech I went through an adjustment period where I felt invincible, no longer fragile in my natural body."

Raygo took a moment before answering.

"It was not until rather recently that my own thoughts seemed to emerge." He glanced at Joxy. "Thoughts that contrasted greatly with those of VOrg. A moral compass, if you will, seemed to materialize. The shroud covering my eyes, lifted." He paused briefly again before continuing. "Perhaps Jim's emulation created the spark. His love, his courage, the catalyst for what I, we, are now.

"It's . . . humbling. The knowledge and power. What are they but useless tools without the awareness to properly wield them. Jim awakened such awareness, and through our opened eyes, discovered that VOrg's— that humanity's—constant desire to be in control is not the way of the universe. There is too much chaos, and to think that one might be in control is to be ignorant of that fact. For true knowledge, one must submit to chaos."

Tano attempted to wrap his mind around that answer, but it only left him with more questions.

"And how do we submit?" he asked eagerly. He, too, wanted such knowledge. A part of him yearned for it.

"By being part of the solution, my friend. Look at the ruins that litter our universe. All the comings and goings of past sentience. One day humanity will have to atone for its exploits or be held accountable for their sins."

What Tano was hearing sounded ominous. He didn't know how to be a part of the solution. Hell, anything not pertaining to *The Legacy* was pretty much irrelevant to him. He decided to change the direction of the conversation.

"You have become wise," Tano said. "But you still can't brew a decent pot of stim."

Their conversation drifted into less serious talk, as they discussed which animals might have went into making Mongrel.

The UPS indicated that there are thirteen planets inside the Subway System. None of which registered as naturally habitable. Tano didn't like what he was seeing on the feeds, and apparently neither did Joxy.

"Tano, have The Devils meet me at the armory. We're suiting up," she said.

Mongrel roused himself. "You aren't going anywhere without me."

Joxy shrugged. "I don't have an environmental suit that will fit you."

Mongrel laughed as he stood, his head scraping the ceiling. "Well, it's a good thing I won't be needing one." He shouldered past her and Raygo. "I'll see you in the cargo hold."

Joxy watched as Mongrel made his way down the hall. His back muscles rippled while his tail swung casually, brushing the wall, leaving faint scratch marks. Tano watched as his captain's eyes widened with rage. By the time they managed to expel the monster from their ship, it might be scraped to pieces. With Raygo in tow, she stormed toward the armory.

Tano came over Joxy's comm. "The coordinates have us landing on the second planet from their sun, or at least what's left of it. This whole system is saturated with radiation. Probably why they're here in the first place."

"Copy that."

* * *

Joxy didn't want to waste any more time than necessary in the armory, not with Mongrel being unattended aboard her vessel. His orders may have been to keep an eye on her, but she liked having an eye on him as well.

"Tano, keep tabs on Mongrel. Make sure he doesn't stray from the cargo hold."

"Already on it, Cap."

Joxy and Raygo rounded the corner into the armory where The Devils were already getting prepared. She stopped short of running into Jones, then addressed her team.

"Everyone should add a layer of bio before suiting up." Her Eskin offered some protection, but not enough. "The scanners have picked up extreme levels of radiation out there. Enough to fry organs and eat away at your synthetics."

She rifled through the thick, rubbery undergarments until she found one her size. She noticed the way Raygo eyeballed them.

"Mongrel claims he can survive out there without atmo, even with the high levels of radiation. How would you hold up?" she asked him.

Raygo shook his head. "Don't know. Never been off Sega City before."

Joxy snorted and tossed him a bio. "Better safe than sorry. Suits are over there." She pointed.

After sliding into the thick garment, Raygo began adding the environmental-control layer that was the armored suit. Jones came up and handed him a recoilless slug chucker, each bullet self-propelled by their own mini rockets. In theory, Raygo was now ready to kick some ass.

"You know how to use one of these things, don't you?" Jones said with a smirk.

Joxy remembered the countless hours Jim spent with Jones at the range before he'd become sick.

Raygo turned the gun over in his hands. "I may remember a thing or two about a thing or two."

Jones clapped him on the shoulder. "Good to have you back," he said, looking him in the eye. "It's good for the captain, which means it's good for us all."

She wasn't meant to hear it, but she had.

They both turned to look at her. She continued to buckle on an armored plate.

Jones clapped Raygo on the back once more for good measure. "Don't worry, I'll watch her six." This time he'd nearly whispered, but again, she'd heard him. Then he walked off and joined the rest of The Devils.

Joxy stepped up, front and center.

"Listen up! Everyone knows why we're here, but that doesn't mean I want you to go out and get yourselves killed. Not so VOrg can make more money by eliminating their competition at our expense. We are going to have ourselves a little look-see, and if it doesn't feel right, then we're going to tuck tail and run. No shame in living, huh?"

"Hoo-ah."

"Good. Glad we're on the same page. If target location looks accessible, then we'll penetrate. Mongrel will be running with us, and of course he stands out more than a pimple on a prick. So I want everyone to mind their distance from him and spread out. Not sure how tactical he is, but I do know he can eat things that are our size."

The Devils did not so much as flinch. She wondered what was running through their heads. Their discipline made her proud as she struggled not to let slip her own fears. What if this turned out to be ground zero for what happened to Jim? She wasn't even sure what she should be looking for.

"Stay close to me," she urged Raygo. *"I couldn't handle something happening to you again."*

Raygo spread out his arms while looking down at his suit.

"I think I'm buttoned up pretty tight."

Joxy snapped her kager into a hip holster, shouldered a tri-directional laser rifle, then proceeded to lead her men to the cargo hold, where Mongrel waited by the giant cargo door, lounging atop some crates.

"It's about time," he growled. When he hopped up, the cargo he'd pulverized simply by sitting on it littered the area. He sized up the mechs, then scoffed. The Devils spread out around him.

"Something you wish to say?" Jones asked, stepping forward. Both arms had weaponized into gravity grenade launchers.

Joxy wanted everyone out of the hold and off her ship before this escalated further. "Talk to me, Tano. How are we looking?"

"Coordinates lead to a natural formation inside of a deep valley. Nothing stands out on the scanners. Whatever we're looking for must be buried deep in the bedrock. I'm setting us down at the top of the valley. It's too narrow for us to enter. You're going to have to propel down."

She didn't like the idea of scaling cliffs, but at least they had the high ground.

"Once you touch down, depressurize the hold and open the bay door. We're taking the ramp. Mongrel won't fit on the lift."

The hatches leading into and out of the hold began to close, signaling it was time. "Helmets up," she announced. She tapped a button with her chin and her helmet's visor slid into place. The rest of her crew did likewise.

Alarms blared and warning lights flashed. As the air was pumped out, the noise faded. All Joxy could hear was the sound of her own breathing inside the suit. She opened a teamwide channel. Communicating with Mongrel would be its own challenge.

"Everyone look sharp," she said.

To Mongrel, she pointed two fingers at her visor, then one finger toward the door, using the universal sign to pay fucking attention. He responded by extending his middle claw, another universal sign.

Vibrations traveled up through Joxy's suit as the massive door slid open. A ramp extended from the exterior threshold, a plume of reddish-green dust sprouting from where the metal landed on the planet's surface. Joxy glanced at Mongrel, hoping to find him on his knees, dying. She wasn't that lucky.

Jones took point and led them into the unknown. They made their way to the cliff's edge, staring down into the steep valley below. There were zero signs of habitation. Scans picked up a hollowed-out formation on the valley's floor. It ran for about thirty feet before abruptly ending. It was difficult to determine if the area was a natural cave or an engineered tunnel. Either way it was a promising place to start. If anyone was here, they'd be buried deep to protect themselves against the radiation. There wasn't much in the universe that could survive topside here.

"Tano, you're our eyes up top. Have the crew on standby in case we need rescuing. And Tano?"

"Yes, Captain?"

"Remind me to decontaminate the hold after this."

"Aye, aye."

Joxy pointed her arm at the ground and shot a spike. Tethered at its end was a carbon Teflon cable that was light and strong as hell. Raygo held up his suit's forearm curiously before aiming down and firing. The cable ran through the suit to a spool hidden between the shoulder blades. By opening and closing their gauntlets, they could engage and disengage the cable's braking system.

Leaning over the precipice, their backs faced the valley floor and their eyes pointed skyward. Joxy chinned her comm.

"Take it nice and easy," she said. "Remember, no one dies here."

As one, they pushed off the ledge. They grasped for purchase along the cliff's face as they descended. The valley was in essence a giant wind tunnel that caused them to sway, making their descent even more dangerous.

Mongrel leapt over the edge, his extended claws digging deeply into the rock; sliding down, he leapt again. Repeating this pattern, he managed to scale the wall quickly. Joxy saw him pause below and look up at them, his contempt evident as he shouted something no one could hear because of the vacuum. Whatever it was still pissed her off.

Their boots finally hit the flat surface of the valley floor. Small particles tinkled against their visors. Joxy fired another spike, and the cable detached from her suit, securing itself to the bottom of the cliff. The suit's heads-up display lit a path for them that led to the formation. It would have been almost impossible to orient themselves otherwise.

Following the green path on their visors, Joxy hung back while Jones took the team through a maze of boulders and ancient riverbeds. Mongrel paced impatiently at the entrance to the destination. As soon as he spotted them, he turned and entered the cave's darkness. Everyone remained silent as they followed behind at a distance.

Lights from their suits illuminated the walls. It became apparent that this feature was in fact man-made. The walls and ceiling were too smooth, indicating that cutting lasers had carved this tunnel. On their way inside, Joxy thought she had seen a faded letter *V*. Any other letters that may have been there before had been windswept long ago; that is, if it wasn't just her mind playing tricks on her.

The cavern was enormous. Joxy figured that *The Legacy* could fit comfortably inside of it. Suit scanners mapped its layout, relaying to the team's heads-up displays where deep holes and large boulders determined their winding path forward.

"There's a door up ahead," someone pointed out.

Just then, a door came into view on their displays.

Mongrel reached it first, but he stepped to the side as the others came up behind. It was smaller than the cavern's entrance, and Veruna's pet would have to slide through on his belly if he was to make it. The smooth metal door seamlessly meshed with the cavern's walls. Jones ran his hands along the surfaces looking for a way to open it.

Lily helped him search. "This is old," she said. "There's got to be a hidden terminal somewhere. I can probably hack it."

They continued to run their hands over the walls, when Jones finally found a small, unnatural feature the same color as the rock. He twisted, pulled, and pushed it, and a section of the wall slid away, revealing an older-style keypad.

Jones stepped back. "There you go," he said. Lily slapped him a high five.

She stooped over the keypad. "Everyone might want to back up. There's no telling what's on the other side."

They all did except Mongrel.

"You think this is the place?" Joxy telepathically asked Raygo.

"I don't know. Someone went through a lot of trouble to keep this place hidden, but where's the security? It doesn't feel right."

Lily removed a gauntlet, then morphed one of her slim fingers into a prong that she slid into a port on the side of the pad. After a few breaths, a seal popped and the door slid open, vanishing into the rock. The desolate, radioactive surface was in complete contrast to what they had just discovered underground. It took a bit to register what exactly they were seeing.

"This must have been an old access tunnel, clearly forgotten," Lily whispered.

None of the people strolling past could have expected the wall to pop open, and by the looks on their faces, they were as surprised to see a group of beings in armored suits as Joxy and her team were to see them. The people gaped as the team entered their facility, and when some of them spotted Mongrel sliding through the doorway, screams of terror erupted. Pedestrians dropped shopping bags, spilled drinks, and stopped pushing strollers and carts, to shove and trample one another in a desperate effort to put as much distance between themselves and the unforeseen, terrifying intruders.

The screams weren't as loud as they should have been, some of the atmosphere was leaking out the door behind them, just not as much as it should have been. Joxy noticed huge vents above their entry that prevented that from happening. Lily was already accessing another keypad, and as soon as Mongrel's tail cleared the threshold, she closed the door behind him. The effect was like someone turning up the volume.

They had stepped into what was essentially an underground city. One consisting of mostly pristine offices and labs, dotted here and there with cafés and restaurants. The area was colossal and supported by a domed structure stretching high up into the air.

Joxy was amazed at the vast and populated discovery hidden from the universe. She tried reaching Tano but only detected static. She slid her helmet's visor up, as did the rest of her team.

"Comms can't penetrate the rock," she said, but everyone's attention was on the pandemonium unfolding in front of them. People were desperately crawling over one another to escape this sudden intrusion. "We'll split into two . . . "

Mongrel launched himself at a ten-person security force marching into the plaza. The first row of officers knelt, took aim, then fired at the intruders while the second row open fired at the airborne beast descending upon them.

Joxy, Raygo, and The Devils leapt for cover behind a low, decorative wall. Apparently, security around here shot first and asked questions later. Considering the appearance of Mongrel, she didn't blame them. Joxy risked a peek above the partition to see how the abomination was holding up.

Gore sprayed across the plaza, coating office windows, people, and security alike. Mongrel's razor-sharp claws tore through the armored security as though they were nothing. All firepower was now trained on this immediate threat, though their munitions showed no obvious effects.

"Advance," Joxy ordered, taking advantage of the distraction.

Staying low they proceeded forward, taking cover behind a fountain. They each took aim, with Joxy pulling her trigger first. Three enemy combatants went down. Raygo dumped slugs that screamed into a mass of armored bodies. The Devils were slinging plasma and chucking grenades. Friendly fire didn't appear to be an issue as Mongrel continued with his melee.

The slaughter lasted only a few minutes. The body parts of scientists, businessmen, and techs had entangled with parts of deceased security officers. There was no one left alive in the plaza. Joxy's team was at the very center of a ring of death. The only screams to be heard came from a distance, further into the subterranean city.

The team crept out from behind the fountain, its once-clear water now crimson. Mongrel came back to them, drenched in blood, cleaning himself like a cat.

"You did good," Mongrel said in between licks. "Veruna is pleased."

Raygo didn't respond. His jaw flexed instead as he observed the carnage.

"The main labs and offices will be at the center of the city. That's where we must go. I'll clear a path." Mongrel bounded off, stifling the closest wails as he went.

Stepping over splayed limbs and dodging puddles of blood, Joxy made her way to Raygo, who stood there in a trance. She placed a hand on his shoulder. "Are you okay?"

He rested a hand on top of hers.

"For years Veruna has tried to manipulate me into killing, to become a weapon like Mongrel. And now she's finally done it."

Joxy spun him around. "You're nothing like that monster," she shouted. "You hear me? You can love and have compassion. You're unique. Anyone can kill, so don't you dare feel sorry for yourself. You did what you had to do, and no one is going to hold that against you."

She reached for his chin, tilting it toward her.

"Don't let Veruna make you into something you're not."

Raygo cast his eyes down as if ashamed of his own pity. His eyes locked on something on the ground, his body stiffening. Slowly he knelt beside a corpse outfitted in a black armored uniform, a security officer. Raygo twisted the man's uniform for a better look. Mouthing the word stitched into the fabric.

Bu-bon-ics.

Pulling Joxy down, he pointed. Her mouth dropped.

"Do you remember that name?" he whispered, but her reaction had said it all.

Joxy shot back up to her feet, waving Lily and the rest of the Devils over from their perimeter positions.

"There's no time for questions. I'll explain later, but we're getting the hell out of here, now." Her team nodded, ready for further orders. "Lily, get that door opened back up. As soon as we're through, shut it and destroy the panel. Everyone, break for *The Legacy*. We're leaving Mongrel behind. Let's move!"

Led by Joxy, the team sprinted, but Raygo didn't budge. He remained behind, kneeling beside the body, fire burning in his eyes. She ran back to him, dropped to her knees and said, "Come on. This is our chance. We can run and not look back."

Raygo took a deep breath and nodded at her. The two of them rose to their feet. He reached over and entwined his fingers with Joxy's.

"Let's never, ever look back," he said.

Hand in hand they ran toward their future together.

Lily had just managed to pop the door when they caught up. Everyone ran through as a bone-rattling roar chased them into the cavern. Joxy chinned her mic.

"Close it!" she screamed.

The door slammed shut, and Lily fired a few plasma rounds into the terminal. They weren't just running for their freedom now, they were running for their lives. They had almost made it back to their cables when corpses and debris shot past them, bumping and scraping along the valley floor and cliff faces. An image of Mongrel destroying the atmospheric control vents on his way out flashed through Joxy's mind's eye. Leaving the unhindered vacuum of space to viciously siphon out the contents of the underground domed city. Their mission had been nothing more than a coverup to terminate the liability of one of VOrg's shell corps.

Hooking to their cables they took off up the valley wall. Joxy glanced down between her feet and her heart dropped. Mongrel, leaping dozens of feet at a time, gave chase beneath them.

"Tano, we're coming up," Joxy shouted in the comms. "We've got some company. Target cannons at Mongrel. We're about to breach the precipice, and make a run for it. Be ready!"

"Damned beast," Tano muttered.

"What was that Tano?" Joxy was still yelling into her mic.

"Crew is at the ready," Tano said. "Cannons are primed. Soon as he comes into view, we'll light him up like a supernova."

No one bothered to brake as they approached the top of the cliff and were flung up and over its edge. As soon as their boots hit dirt, they pumped their legs and propelled their suits at full speed. The suits, designed for microgravity, allowed them to move swiftly; unfortunately, Mongrel could move even faster.

The ground shook beneath their feet as *The Legacy's* cannons opened fire, targeting an area that was close behind them. Joxy stumbled a step when she turned to get bearings on the beast. He was nowhere to be seen among the destruction. The ship was already in motion when they reached it. They had to jump just a few feet to clear the ramp. Several of them spun as they surveyed the ground they had just crossed. It looked like a war zone. Craters littered the surface, giant plumes reached for the subtle atmosphere. There was no sign of Mongrel. He had to have been obliterated.

They'd done it. They had escaped him, deceived VOrg. The last laugh was theirs.

Joxy followed Raygo and the Devils back into the hold. Just as she was about to enter, the ramp lurched slightly. She drew her kager blade as she spun around.

Mongrel stood panting at the ramp's end. His unnaturally long tongue hung limp from the side of his mouth, long strands of saliva dripped from it. His hide was charred and, in some places, flaking off. Joxy began to wonder if he could be killed at all. What would it take?

She gripped her kager tighter and stepped forward.

Tano came over her comms. "Captain, I can't retract the ramp with you still out there."

"We have a bit of a problem," she breathed.

She nervously crept further onto the ramp. Mongrel's mouth was moving, but of course she couldn't hear what he was saying out here.

Putting the kager between her middle fingers, she raised the fisted gauntlet. He smiled wickedly, then lunged for her.

Joxy instinctively extended the knife, bracing for impact. She tossed up a prayer that it would find the beast's heart. But the impact never came. Opening her eyes, she realized that the ramp was now empty. She ran to the edge. Leaning over she spotted two bodies clinging together, free falling through the air. A tall plume reached out and consumed them.

"Raygo!" Joxy screamed into her helmet. Chinning her mic, "Tano swing back around. Raygo just tackled Mongrel off the ramp!"

Joxy dashed for the bridge, still outfitted in her armored suit. She hopped into her chair, madly pulling up holos.

"Where is he, Tano? Please tell me you've found him."

"Not yet, but I'm still scanning. There's a lot of interference from the dust clouds. We'll find him." Tano couldn't look in her direction. "That was a long fall, Captain."

Joxy pretended she didn't hear him. She wouldn't entertain that possibility. Swiping and scrolling, she manipulated the ship's scanners to target specific areas, calculating the trajectory of *The Legacy* with the area and velocity of the fall. She tried to grid the best search locations.

After over an hour of scouring the planet's surface, her hope dwindled. Thanks to the scattered remains of Bubonics's employees, there were plenty of false alarms. She'd tried countless times to reach out to Raygo telepathically, her heart breaking a little more each time there was no response.

Joxy held back the tears, which wasn't too hard as numb as she felt. She was done with crying. She had lost Jim twice, barely making it through the first time. Waking her screen with a gentle punch, she set course back to Sega City, hell bent on a suicide mission of epic proportions. Since VOrg had been operating out of here, then it was probably something they were working on that had gotten Jim sick. All very ironic at the end of the day. A breeze blew through the bridge. The unusualness of it didn't hold her attention for long until it continued to happen.

The air around her tasted and smelled like something was burning. She looked to Tano, both of their eyes wide, wondering what in the universe was going on. She wasn't sure if they were being attacked, or . . .

Something was starting to materialize at the center of the bridge. Joxy's fingers dug into the leather armrest as she watched, mesmerized by the bright flickers of light in the air, before random fragments of body parts began to ooze together to form their solid molds. It was like watching ice melt in reverse. In the span of a few breaths, Raygo had somehow managed to conjure himself back aboard *The Legacy*.

Joxy's face paled, while Tano rubbed his eyes as if his optical sensors might be malfunctioning. Raygo's armor displayed metallic grooves that eerily resembled claw marks. He spun around, taking in his own body. Astonishment flooded his voice.

"I can't believe that worked. Pretty cool, huh?"

Joxy sat there, speechless, staring in disbelief.

"Pretty cool indeed," Tano said. Something on his controls drew his attention. He selected it. "Uh, Captain?"

She didn't respond.

"Captain, we have another problem," Tano said more forcefully.

Joxy snapped from her daze and groaned inwardly. *What now?*

"What is it?" she asked.

Tano uploaded an image to all of Joxy's holos. It was a picture of them, the entire crew of *The Legacy*. All except for Raygo. Above their pictures, in giant pulsing letters, a headline read: "Galactic Bounty: Dead or Alive."

"Fuck," Joxy huffed.

CHAPTER 11
VERUNA AND THE SIBLINGS

Joxy steered the NGV2 warship on a course set for Sega City. Most of the Nocturian crew had ended up making their way back to their barracks without incident—minus the lingering handful Rooney's team had to mercifully escort themselves. Brigs succeeded in taking control of the engine room, a key element to Joxy's plan. If the engineers would have managed to secure themselves inside, or heaven forbid, decided to self-destruct, then the siege would have been over. Fortunately, no one had felt like dying, and it all transpired without a hitch. She was very pleased with how efficient her own crew had been.

Lily arrived back at the bridge, almost unrecognizable, while sporting next-gen Nocturian mech tech. She stood several inches taller, with more guns and shield regulators broadening her shoulders and back. Twirling around, she showed off her new pearl and garnet glossed upgrades.

"I found this sweet tech down in the armory," she said. "There wasn't even anyone guarding this stuff."

Joxy whistled. "You're packing some serious heat there, girl. What else they got?"

"Come on. There's plenty." Lily waved for The Devils and some of the other mechs to follow.

Joxy smiled at her crew's eagerness. "I'll catch up later," she yelled after them. She didn't feel comfortable leaving the bridge. Not when there was so much for her to keep an eye on, trying to maintain control of a warship.

Joxy ordered all the station operators to be taken back to their quarters along with Captain Richards. Tano overrode every single hermetic door from his station on the bridge, effectively trapping all the Nocturians and securing them inside. At first, the old captain tried to protest, but when Joxy mentioned she would toss him in the cooler, he quickly got with the program. If all went according to plan, they would need him soon enough.

Joxy kept tabs on the warship's crew through the vessel's security system. For a while they had paced around, confused. It wasn't long until they started to grasp the seriousness of the situation, and things began to turn ugly. In shifts, and for days, the sailors lashed out at the hatches confining them. Unequipped with power suits or any formidable weapons, their efforts were futile. Eventually they tired, probably realizing it was fortunate that they were still alive. Joxy felt for them, knowing most were probably good men, loyal to their galaxy. But if given a chance, they would kill her crew without a second thought. She knew this because she would do the same.

Joxy and Raygo were the only ones on board who knew the layout of the VOrg complex. They created a diagram and put it up on a holo so that Jones and the rest of The Devils could examine it, too. It was crude, but it served its purpose as they discussed how best to proceed to the emulation lab from their landing site.

Jones stood up and made his way to the holo map. Pointing, he said, "We should land here. Blow the lightrails to prevent a ground force flank, then make our way up to the HQ block by block."

It'd been five years since they'd visited Sega City. If the layout was the same, or even differed slightly, then Jones's plan was the best approach. There wasn't enough time to contemplate all of the what-ifs. They just had to go in and execute the best they could.

Joxy picked up where Jones left off. "There we'll split into two teams. We need to capture Veruna, if we can. That would make everything run a lot smoother." Joxy didn't say so, but she wanted to make Veruna pay.

"What if she's not there?" Lily threw out.

"She'll be there," Raygo responded.

"Raygo's siblings are vital to pulling this off," Joxy continued. "There may be other BAIs as well, and you should consider them hostile."

Raygo positioned himself in front of the holo map. All eyes were on him.

"I'm confident my brothers and sister will understand what we're trying to accomplish, but there's a good chance Veruna has brainwashed them." He took a deep breath. "Worst-case scenario is that you will all emulate into my body."

The room went silent.

Joxy really hoped that alternative never became a reality. Yes, it was better than dying, but she wasn't digging the idea of them all being crammed into one vessel. No offense to Raygo. Besides, humanity needed more than just one ambassador; some diversity in the next dimension. Although it went unsaid, she knew everyone hoped for the same thing: that Raygo's siblings would cooperate and want to join them.

At their current speed, they would arrive at the Cemetery, the galaxy in which Sega City was located, in about twenty-four hours. The name of this war-torn galaxy was fitting, as unrest between the systems was an ongoing problem. Over the years it became apparent that the Sega

System would reign supreme as VOrg developed their corporate empire. Because Sega no longer needed to partake in these petty rivalries, the other systems learned to leave well enough alone.

Joxy watched Raygo idly toy with the small cube they had taken from Commander Vaughn.

"You think there will be any more of those things waiting for us?" she asked, nodding to the cube.

"It's complex, finicky. I doubt VOrg even knows a whole lot about what it is they've created."

Raygo had the forearm holo controls pulled up. Kicking off with his legs, he rolled across the bridge in his chair to where Joxy sat and held the cube in front of her eyes. "The casing is comprised of many different layers of NH2I," he said. "Inside is a good-sized black hole–worth of energy, as in, a massive amount."

Joxy found it hard to believe that such a small device could harness such power. She nodded in a vague way, indicating he should go on.

"The science behind it is spontaneous at best, and even I don't quite understand it all. They've somehow managed to control the absorption of such density. It's way beyond what our G-drives can do. Whoever has this controller," he held up the forearm piece, "can decide what molecules, or even trace atoms, that this thing targets."

"And what if no one added a filter?"

"Unchecked, it would consume everything within its gravitational influence."

Joxy leaned back in her chair and eyed the little cube.

"Maybe we should chuck this thing out an air-lock," she said.

Raygo jerked his hand away. "We may need it if we find ourselves in a jam. I'll keep an eye on it and make sure that it doesn't suck up your ship." He laughed.

She punched him playfully in the shoulder. "You better. What do you think happened to the other warship?" she asked. "Think they tried going through the portal, or are they floating around, wondering what to do?"

He shrugged. "Guess it depends on whether or not Nostic has graced them with his presence."

"Better for us if they've attempted to enter the portal. One less obstacle in our journey, for now." Joxy sighed. So much rested on their shoulders. Her shoulders, in particular.

"Is humanity truly damned if we fail? If so, then is it not wrong of us to keep the rest of the universe in the dark? We finally have our answer to The Great Expansion, yet the rest of humanity will never learn of it." She shivered at the thought. "It just seems harsh, like our species' existence was trivial."

She was aware that Raygo didn't always share her views, and she had a hunch that he believed keeping humanity in the dark was for the best, a mercy, even.

"I believe in Nostic's belief in us. Though *The Others* are not eager for us to join them, and they even deem us unworthy, he is still taking a risk to save a piece of humanity. He sees the good in a sea of evil. For all we know, he has chosen other humans as well. We may not be the only hope, but it's an honor to have been chosen."

Reaching, he grabbed her hands. His touch still so foreign and cool even after years of knowing him, but the gesture was warming. She noticed the gleam in his eye and thought of Jim.

"Pandemonium would ensue across the universe if we shared what we know. Our chances of success would drastically decline as chaos erupted." He squeezed lightly for emphasis. "We will be doing them a kindness by keeping them ignorant. No one wants to know they are about to die, that their dreams would not be coming true, their destiny cut short."

It pained her, but Joxy agreed.

Barreling toward Sega City, she knew that her entire life had prepared her for this moment. Their cause was righteous, and she pitied whoever got in the way.

"Veruna," she whispered. "I'm coming for you."

* * *

"I repeat: you are an unauthorized military vessel about to enter Segan space territory. If you do not correct course immediately, you will be fired upon!"

Tano chuckled to himself. He could hear the anxiety in this greenie's voice and was willing to wager that the astro wasn't more than a month or two out of camp. Stuck with the monotonously dull job of watching scanners all day, every day, the kid probably spilled his stim all over his station when a Nocturian warship popped up on the screen. By now no doubt his superior was elbowing him out of the way.

"This is Captain Roschek, Commander of the Segan Armada," a new voice chimed in on cue. "Correct course, or we will slag your vessel."

Tano couldn't help himself. "I thought Captain Vaughn was the Commander of your armada."

There was a brief lull. Tano imagined the commander's lips sputtering to form a retort.

"Captain Vaughn is considered MIA at this time. Do you have information as to his whereabouts? Is the Nocturian Empire responsible for his disappearance?" Roschek's voice grew impatient. "Is this an act of war?" he shouted.

Tano heard something slam and was barely able to contain his amusement as he disconnected the comm's link. *That'll really piss him off,* he thought.

Everyone was back aboard *The Legacy,* still sitting in the warship's hangar. From his own cozy station, Tano had full control over the warship. The Nocturian crew, along with their captain, were still tucked away. At the appropriate time, Tano would release them and give them control of their ship, although by that time they'd probably be in a fight for their lives.

Tano's holos indicated that they were now being targeted by multiple Segan ships and a network of planetary defense cannons. This was about to be quite the dance.

The mech spoke calmly into his comms. "This is our stop."

"Copy that. Touch us down safely," Joxy responded. She and the rest of the crew stood by in the cargo hold, ready to infiltrate VOrg.

Engaging the NGV2's auto defense system, Tano then set a flight path that would leave the Segans chasing the warship all over their system. The goal was to create a distraction, but if it wasn't enough, then his next action should help. Opening the warship's hangar doors, Tano dropped all the BATs out on autopilot to swarm the gap between the Segans and themselves.

The Legacy dropped with them.

Blending in with the mass of ships, they drifted toward Sega City. BATs dropped like flies all around them. Tano had maneuvered so that the swarm acted as a shield and kept them well hidden.

Most of the Segan firepower concentrated on the Nocturian warship as hoped; however, huge clusters of stardusters poured forth from hangars and engaged with the BATs. Tano disengaged from the swarm, dropping into the artificial atmosphere of Sega City. He switched over from the G-drives to fission thrusters. Warships and fighters were not typically space-to-land vessels, so he didn't worry himself much about anyone tailing them, for now. This didn't stop the planet's defense cannons from recognizing them as small tertiary guns opened up against *The Legacy's* shields. Tano pointed the nose of the ship down, diving through atmosphere as fast as possible to avoid sustaining any major damage.

He checked the holos to see how the Nocturian warship was holding up and noticed their shields had fallen to 30 percent. He unlocked Captain Richards and his crew from their prisons, putting their lives in their own disadvantaged hands. If they immediately fled the Cemetery, then they had a good chance of escaping with the ship, and their lives, intact.

The flight path lit up a line on Tano's holo. He was excited to be the one flying, as this could be his last time. *The Legacy* had fairly efficient space-to-land capabilities. As a Starborn-class vessel, which was not small by any means, the ship could easily travel where most others couldn't.

Sweeping over VOrg's complex, he fired a few shots from their own cannons, successfully sabotaging the nearby lightrails. The mech whooped in delight. After landing *The Legacy* at the predetermined location, Tano unstrapped his harness, grabbed his pistol, and took off running to join the rest of the crew. All hands were needed on deck for this one.

* * *

"Ah, damn it, Tano," Joxy cursed as her body jerked first one way, then the other. She and her crew waited in the hold, ready to descend the ramp and storm VOrg headquarters. Their suits' magnetic boots held them to the floor, locking their feet in place. Due to Tano's maniacal maneuvering, their bodies still swayed dangerously, forcing them all to cling desperately to any buttoned-down cargo within arm's reach.

Joxy began to regret not piloting herself. If it wasn't for the strong desire to lead her men out, then she would have. In a brief moment of weightlessness, the crew floated in their suits as *The Legacy* nosedived toward the planet's surface.

She breathed a sigh of relief when her ship leveled back out, her hot breath inside of her helmet sticking to her sweaty face. The hold still seemed to be spinning around. Disoriented, she placed a hand on her armored knee, then pushed off to help herself back to her feet. Joxy held on to a cargo strap for balance. The cargo door lights flashed as it screeched its way open, serving as an impromptu rallying call for the crew. Out of the corner of her eye, Joxy spotted Tano racing to join them.

She took point, flanked by Raygo and The Devils as she sprinted down her ship's ramp, pressing up a road with her entire crew in tow. She had briefed her men about how little activity seemed to take place outside of the labs, and that during her last visit the streets were practically devoid of pedestrians. Still, much as last time, the emptiness felt creepy.

Posting up behind one of the odd-looking lab buildings, she scanned the area ahead. Seeing that the path was clear, she ran to the next building and repeated this process. Every time they advanced, Joxy would station one of her men behind to help cover their rear. These buildings had no obvious doors; based on prior experience, she knew they could pop up anywhere.

In the back of her mind, she wondered how long it would take the Segans to look into the single ship that had entered their atmosphere. She hoped the Nocturians would keep them distracted for a little while longer. Repressing these thoughts, she went back to focusing on the task at hand. Sweeping the streets, Joxy had the gnawing feeling that there were less labs than the last time she passed through.

"Weren't there more labs than this?"

"Five are missing," Raygo responded instantly. *"They must have needed the material, which means they've been very busy."*

Busy making what? she wondered. Surely all that NH2I didn't go toward making more BAIs. One of the men shouted in alarm behind her. As she spun to see what was going on, Jones called out beside her.

"We've got movement up ahead."

Gaping doorways sprung open on every building, spawning the familiar Med Hub bots known as ROBs, who rolled out and positioned themselves along sidewalks and in the roads. Joxy peered skeptically at them. What were these medical robots doing out here?

She chinned her comm. "I don't like the look of this."

No sooner had her voice cut out did the usually harmless robots begin shooting. VOrg must have kept this alternate militia on standby, a smart move seeing as no one would have suspected ROBs of being a standing army on Sega City.

Sufficiently weaponized, ROB after ROB flooded the streets from the labs, crowding Joxy and her crew from every direction. Some of her men were already down, with waves of bots washing over them.

The Legacy's crew returned fire, littering the ground with silicone and carbon parts as they desperately tried to push back the tide. Joxy and her men were bunched so close together that using the comms was pointless.

Joxy slid her helmet's visor up and shouted, "Tano use the ship's guns to lay down some fire. We need a lane cleared!"

Tano accessed *The Legacy's* weapons systems as he dodged laser rounds and returned fire with his pistol.

"There must be some **underground** tunnel network linking the labs with the Med Hub. No way they were all hiding inside, there's too many of them." Raygo paused to fire. "Might explain why we hardly ever see anyone around here."

Small and heavy cannons roared to life nearby, flashing exaggerated shadows across the faces of the buildings. At such close range their resonance was deafening. *The Legacy's* line of fire was such that it could only cover one of the main roads and a handful of side streets. This still left quite a few routes by which the ROBs could attack and swarm them.

Lily huddled next to Jones. Their position was being overrun, and they wouldn't last much longer. Without either one of them letting up from shooting, she informed him of her simple plan.

"It's time we see what this tech can do," she shouted over the cacophony. "Cover me!"

The Devils barely had time to react before Lily sprinted for the middle of the road. Her two hand-cannons cleared a path as concentrated fire from the rest of her team provided some protection. Slapping one of her armored breastplates, the new weapons tech kicked in. Small sections of armor and skeletal structure whirred and buzzed as it shifted around. Then eight pivoting barrels sprouted from her hardware, munitions unknown.

Lily shouted for everyone to get down.

"Here goes nothin'," she growled.

Her systems didn't seem to have any problem syncing with the upgraded tech as her new gun barrels ignited with light. A pulsating ribbon of energy sprang forth from each barrel as they pivoted to account for every direction the bots attacked from. ROBs, debris, and chunks of road and sidewalk all vanished, disintegrated by the spiraling beams of bright light. Even the sides of some of the NH2I labs brandished deep gouges, though they remained intact, and in some places looked to be healing themselves.

Jones and the other mechs who had dabbled in the Nocturian armory made their way over to adjacent roads. The VOrg labs acted as barriers and funnels, and the upgraded mechs were able to bottleneck the flow of attackers. Piles of ash littered the streets as ROBs relentlessly threw their bodies against the energy beams' onslaught.

Joxy advanced with the remaining half of her crew, moving up a street that ran parallel to the main drag up to headquarters. *The Legacy's* cannons still boomed away behind them.

"Ship scanners are picking up several Segan airborne coming in fast," Tano's voice came through her helmet, loud and clear.

Joxy nodded once and set her jaw.

"Make sure shields are at full power," she said. "As soon as they come into range, start targeting. She's our ride out of here so keep her safe. If she gets swamped, use the net array. I like that thing."

Time was running out. There was a short pause in cannon fire before they opened back up, this time at the sky above. ROBs had cut through a lab, exiting the rear and flanking Joxy's crew. Darting down a nearby alley, she found herself running onto the main drag. VOrg headquarters lay directly in front of them.

Jones caught up to her. He looked her square in the eyes. "We'll make a stand here. Hold them off to buy you some time, then we'll catch up."

Joxy swallowed. "Don't take too long. Get in, and let's get out." She made to walk off but then stopped and flung her arms around the tough, old mech. "You better be in that lab when I get there."

He didn't answer. Just gently squeezed her before turning to whistle Lily and some of the other recently modified mechs on over. The small group stepped into the center of an intersection, placing their backs to one another, effectively cordoning off the last stretch of road leading up to VOrg's headquarters. It took heavy casualties to make it this far, and there was no telling what Veruna had waiting for them ahead.

Joxy did a quick head count. Raygo, Tano, the rest of The Devils, and only four remaining crew would accompany her inside after leaving Jones and his team behind to buy them time and guard their rear. It would have to be enough.

Raygo addressed everyone remaining in his depleted force. "Veruna has most likely been watching our every move since entering this system. She's toying with us. The med bots were just a test."

At that, most everyone gripped their weapons tighter.

They made their way through the Roman-style courtyard with the sound of munitions and explosions at their backs. Joxy didn't need to glance behind her; she was confident Jones and his team would hold. Her body tensed for battle when the entrance to the headquarters opened without warning. She instinctively raised her rifle, fully expecting something to come charging out at them. It worried her when nothing did.

Raygo took point. "We are going to make a run for the lift. Everyone knows their roles. Get in and get out."

They'd been over the plan countless times. Tano and his team were to secure the labs while Raygo and Joxy's team rounded up the siblings. Everyone was to meet back at the lab for emulation. Raygo looked around at the nodding heads, everyone except Joxy.

"I'm going to the top floor," she said. There was no room for negotiation in her voice.

"We should stay together," Raygo said. "As long as we can make it back to the lab, we won't need Veruna. Joxy, please".

Joxy's eyes became steel. "Veruna has taken everything from us and countless others. Her day of atonement has come, Jim."

Raygo conceded with a grin. "The thirst for vengeance runs through my veins as well," he said. "At least take Rome and Rooney with you."

The two mechs stepped forward, flanking their captain.

"What about little ole you?" Joxy asked sarcastically.

"I think I can handle my siblings," he said with a laugh.

They made their way into the building. Aside from the clomping boots, trickling water from the fountains, and low hum of the air system, the place was eerily quiet. Crossing the foyer, they entered the lift without incident. Joxy thought it would have been better to have already engaged hostiles by now. At least the anxiety of anticipation that was driving her mad would be over.

They all crowded into the lift together, leaving very little in the way of personal space. Even with having a full load, the lift took off without struggle. There was no screeching or groaning as it shot upward through VOrg's headquarters.

Joxy stared back at her reflection in the lavish, gold-paneled walls and doors. *What a sight we make,* she thought. *My rag-tag crew of bandits.* She smiled with pride.

The lift stopped at what Joxy hoped was still the floor that the emulation lab was on. Tano's stop. He stepped off, followed by Brigs and four crewmen who quickly fanned out and secured the lobby. Their attention focused on a long stretch of hallway leading to the lab. Tano spun back around to face them, his face grave.

"Don't drag your feet. I'll try to have everything up and running by the time you get back." He wanted to say more, a lot more. Instead he snapped to attention and threw them a salute.

The last thing Joxy saw as the lift doors slid closed were her men bravely rounding the corner into the hall. All she could think about was how long that hall had been. How dangerous it may be now.

Joxy locked eyes with Raygo's golden reflection. There was nothing left to say. It was time to get the job done. She caught the two Devils smirking behind them. She knew her men got a kick out of her and Raygo's unusual relationship. It was just one more thing that she had to adjust to. Unsurprisingly, it had made the couple the target of many jokes and jibes, some so vulgar that she made sure to commit them to memory for later use.

Joxy casually took a step back. Throwing her elbow, she managed to hit Rooney right in the solar plexus. He vomited a whoosh of air. The mech staggered into the wall behind him, coughing as everyone laughed.

His hands were on his knees. Shaking his head, he managed to let out a grunt. "I've had that one coming for a while."

The mood had lightened, the stress of the situation receding a little. They were family, and as long as they had any say in the matter, they would continue to live in the next dimension as well. Humanity's next step. Their next journey.

The lift stopped once again, and Rome and Rooney moved to the doors as they opened. The lobby looked the same as it had when Joxy first saw it, when she passed Raygo's siblings on her first and only visit to his apartment. There had been a brief moment, years ago, when she imagined that apartment might become the setting of her and Jim's new life.

Raygo wrapped Joxy in his arms, embracing her so tightly she could feel the pressure even through her armored suit. The next thing she knew he was stepping off and headed down the hall. The doors closed, and he was gone all too quickly. The lift began its ascent to the top floor.

"Be careful," Raygo said.

* * *

It'd been over five years since he last walked this stretch of carpeted hall. Its design modeled after a once-famous Earth hotel. He had expected there to be more doors, knowing Veruna had created more BAIs, but everything remained the same. Even his pine door could be spotted; he supposed Veruna had expected his return all along.

Well, he was back now.

With hands in pockets, he stood there staring at April's door, debating on whether or not to knock. Did a warm welcome await him? Had he even been missed? Their situation had only allowed them to be so close. Conversation had been strained; paranoia prevalent in all of them, especially in the beginning. A strong bond prevailed, however. One that VOrg would be hard pressed to destroy, or so he hoped.

His hand was a few centimeters from the door when it opened. His sister, April, stood on the other side and stared back at him. He didn't know what he expected her reaction to be. Shock maybe. Instead her eyes imparted a soft scolding, and to his relief, forgiveness.

"I knew you would come back for us," she said with a smile she couldn't contain. "Bobby and Marlow were skeptical. But once we heard the fighting going on outside, I knew it was you."

Two figures came out from behind the door. Bobby and Marlow stared at their brother in disbelief. Grins crossed their faces before they all embraced one another. Raygo squeezed his eyes tightly together as long-suppressed emotions welled up inside of him.

"I feared Veruna had broken all of you. That you had become her weapons, her fake gods." He pulled them in even closer. "Then I feared that she would kill you if you didn't."

"No, brother," April said. "When you left, Veruna was so concerned that we would attempt to escape that she locked us away up here, isolated. She threatened to torture all of us if even one of us tried anything. She made more of our kind, Raygo. Although we're not allowed any contact with them, we can sometimes pick up on their thoughts. I don't think they're aware of this ability yet, but they're an evil breed. Veruna must have altered their genome or corrupted their consciousnesses in some way before emulation because they are nothing like us." She bit her lower lip.

Bobby shrugged. "After you took off, everything changed. We were no longer her prized possessions. Like we were a bad batch, or something." He flashed a smile. "Maybe you should have thought to take us with you."

Raygo took a step back, hurt. "I did have that thought," he whispered. "But it was too much of a risk." A risk for their safety, but an even greater risk for Joxy and himself. He knew that they were aware of what he was implying. If anyone should have understood his paranoia, it would be them.

Marlow grabbed Raygo by the shoulders, garnering his full attention.

"Tell me, tell me about your adventures," he said.

Raygo firmly grasped his brother's arms. Time was running out. People were fighting to buy them every second.

"I promise we'll have time to catch up later. Right now, I need your help." He was already pulling the lot of them toward the lift. "We have to get down to the emulation lab."

They stopped in the lobby. He looked to them gravely. "This is going to sound crazy, but the future of humanity depends on us getting to that lab."

Bobby's face was unsure, but none of his siblings questioned him. Raygo chinned his mic.

"Joxy, Tano, I have them. We're headed to the lab, copy?"

"All clear down here," Tano responded. "Place looks hurriedly abandoned. I am familiarizing myself with the equipment. Shouldn't take long."

"Joxy, what's your status?" Tano asked.

Static.

"Joxy, come in," he said.

"Are you all right?" Raygo asked her telepathically.

His heart began to beat a little faster. April frowned at him, concern washing over her face.

"Is there anything we can do to help?" she asked.

Raygo closed his eyes and took a deep breath.

"Take the lift down to the emulation lab. There you'll find a mech by the name of Tano. He'll tell you what to do. I'll catch up."

"But how—" Bobby started, but Raygo was already de-atomizing. The three of them stood in shock as the lift doors dinged open.

"He has to show me how to do that," Marlow said in awe.

* * *

Joxy reached Veruna's office. Rome and Rooney gawked at the wastefulness of such luxury. The two of them seemed to be having a hard time focusing as their captain led them through a maze of cushions, tables, holos, and plants. The sections had been moved around, she noted. The path to the old woman's desk more meandering than before.

And there she was, sitting with her feet propped up on her desk, watching them. The three of them approached with caution. The smug look Veruna wore worried Joxy. This was too easy.

"I must thank you," Veruna said, her voice like a purr.

The two Devils had Veruna covered. Uneasy, Joxy pressed the rifle harder into her shoulder, her eyes scanning the room, checking for any indication that they had just walked into a trap.

"Don't thank me yet," Joxy spat. She inched her way closer to the desk. "You've gotten away with ruining countless lives for far too long. How do you live with yourself?"

Veruna raised her hands over her head, the universal sign of surrender, although her smile only widened.

"Everything I have done I have done for the sake of humankind. Great civilizations are built on the backs of the many, and I have been building the greatest civilization of them all." Arms still in the air, she spread them wide. "Look at what VOrg has created—"

"What VOrg has destroyed, you mean," Joxy shouted.

Veruna waved it away.

"A matter of perspective, my dear. BAIs are the future, and my name will forever be synonymous with them. Now, I must thank you for returning Raygo. I knew it would only be a matter of time. He is still my greatest creation."

Joxy's finger trembled above the trigger as she took aim.

"History is written by those who win," Joxy said softly.

Veruna snapped her fingers.

Simultaneous grunts rose from either side of her. Looking to her right, she watched Rooney collapse to his knees, weakly clawing at a gaping hole in his chest. She spun around just in time to see Rome's face hit the floor.

Rage boiled up from Joxy's chest. As she screamed and intended to fire at the woman behind the desk, strong hands ripped away her gun and helmet, and covered her mouth. Joxy fought with all she had to get loose while being dragged to a nearby chair. By the end of this scuffle, one of her eyes was swollen, and she found her hands and feet bound. She tried to topple the chair by swaying her body, but it would not budge.

Veruna continued to speak with an air of supremacy, but Joxy wasn't listening. Instead, with her good eye, she was trying to see who her attackers had been. Craning her neck, she found ten good-looking people standing at attention behind her, eyes forward as though they were oblivious to her spewed curses.

Just by looking at them she knew these were VOrg's latest BAIs. They must've gone with a larger sample size this time, which would account for the missing labs. She spit a glob of snot and blood to the floor and took a moment to collect herself, purposely avoiding the sight of the bodies of her fallen comrades. How did this bunch manage to sneak up on them, she wondered. Then she noticed a faint aroma of charged particles and understanding dawned.

Joxy thought she heard Veruna say her father's name. Her head snapped to attention.

". . . used to work for VOrg. He was one of our most brilliant minds. We had feelings at one point, Bran and I. Your father was such a good lover."

Joxy's face paled. Veruna was trying to manipulate her, to play mind games. Her father never would have worked for VOrg. It went against his character, against everything she knew the man to be. Veruna had to be lying.

"My father would never work for an organization like yours," Joxy said with a snort. "He despised people like you."

"There's a lot your father never told you. For instance, did you know he was the one who designed the Starborn-class ships?" Veruna paused a moment while Joxy shook her head in disbelief. "Bran built *The Legacy* for *me*."

"No," Joxy breathed. She knew her father had his secrets, but this? This was just too unbelievable. Had he ever told her how he even came by *The Legacy*? No! She wouldn't allow herself to get trapped in Veruna's tangled web. "You're lying!"

"Am I?" Veruna mocked. "Why do you think you were always on the run? Who do you think put that bounty on him, the same bounty that was put on you and your crew? Poetic, is it not?"

"If my father built *The Legacy* for you, then why would he have stolen it?" Joxy spoke with confidence, feeling as though she had caught the deranged woman in her web of lies.

Veruna peered down her nose at Joxy from behind the desk, an air of amusement tugging at the corners of her lips.

"Bran was blind to what it was we were accomplishing here. But he was blind by choice. Your father was allotted unimaginable resources that kept him content for a time. It wasn't until later in life, about the time you came along, that his self-righteousness seemed to awaken."

Veruna eased back in her chair. The supple leather groaned against her body. Her smug façade expressed how much she enjoyed destroying the image of Bran in his daughter's mind.

"When your mother passed away while giving birth, you were all he had left. He didn't want you raised here on Sega City. He thought I might one day corrupt his precious little girl. I was offended by this, of course. I had to remind the ungrateful man of all I had given him, but still, he insisted on leaving. And I could not allow it."

Joxy ran through memory after memory of her father, searching for any kind of sign in his character or actions that might suggest even a shred of what Veruna said held truth. To observe memories of her father in this new light saddened and confused her.

"Your father stole *The Legacy* one night and took you with him. He fled into the depths of the universe. As much as I hated to, I put the bounty out, and you know the rest. You have lived the rest."

Sitting there, stunned, Joxy struggled to wrap her head around it all. Her father had never told her of her birthplace, but had he hinted at it? Veruna had known her mother, but were they ever friends? She tried to imagine her kind and caring father working for such evil. Could he have really been that ignorant? No, she wouldn't think of him like that. The man who raised her spent every second keeping her safe; that's who her father really was.

She inhaled deeply, then exhaled slowly.

"I would not be the woman I am today if not for my father and the decisions he made to protect me. I am proud of him, and I love him. Tell me, does anyone love you Veruna?"

Veruna's face darkened, her body shaking. "How dare you," she muttered.

She gave a curt nod to the BAIs posted behind Joxy. Joxy heard them shifting around. She thrashed in her chair, desperate to see what they were doing.

She noticed that the BAIs had a hint of fear in their own eyes. When she finally saw the reason why, her heart leaped into her throat. She choked back the screams that were fighting to be released, not fully believing what she was seeing.

Mongrel came up behind her. His stench of rotting gore almost caused her to pass out. His hot, gag-inducing breath spilled over her and filled her lungs. The fumes caused her eyes to fill with tears, which leaked down her cheeks. She took shallow breaths, careful not to inhale too deeply.

Joxy didn't dare speak, afraid of what tasting his odor might do to her. She wasn't in the mood to vomit on herself. Body trembling in the chair, she locked her eyes on Veruna. If Joxy was going to die, and if Veruna had a sliver of soul left, then she was going to try her best to haunt the woman.

A tendril of saliva oozed onto her suit's shoulder plate. The viscous goo continued to flow, dripping off of her chair, and puddling on the floor. Silently she thanked the heavens that it hadn't landed in her hair. A foolish thing, she knew, considering she was about to be eaten.

"I've missed you, Captain," Mongrel said in his raspy, gurgling voice.

His sharp, cruel eyes radiated hunger. A long claw scratched idly at his belly while awaiting his master's command.

Joxy wanted to prolong the inevitable.

"How did you survive that fall?" she asked, genuinely curious.

The beast let out a throaty roar of a laugh. Beating a fist against his chest he shouted, "I am Mongrel! Nothing can kill—"

Veruna slammed a hand down on top of her desk. "Enough! Shut up and eat her already, you vile creature."

At this, Mongrel looked hurt. His eyes darted down at Joxy, their eyes met, and he smiled with all his horrible teeth.

A gentle breeze stirred around them. Joxy's hair began to move, a lock caught in the corner of her lips. The smell of ozone mingled with Mongrel's stench. Joxy cocked a relieved smile at the realization that she might actually make it out of this alive. Veruna's expression remained none the wiser as she sniffed curiously at the air around her.

The light breeze turned into a gale. Joxy burst out in manic laughter, though it was drowned out by the confused commotion of Veruna's BAIs.

"Oh, no," Mongrel growled.

Joxy blinked. Raygo had entered the room.

Heads turned, staring past Veruna. The evil woman blinked back at them, and for the first time that Joxy could recall, she appeared frightened. Veruna tried to maintain some sense of composure while she started to spin around. But two strong hands latched to the sides of her head, and her eyes grew wide.

In a single, fluid motion, Raygo jerked his arms.

There was a wet pop when Veruna's neck broke.

Cartilaginous disks ripped apart as nerves and connective tissues tore away from the spine. Her head hung loose over her slack body. It looked as though she might be taking a nap. Raygo stared down at her, frowning, then reached over and brushed closed her eyes.

Mongrel roared, swiping Joxy out of the way with the back of his hand, sending her tumbling hard to the floor. Her shoulders screamed at the impact, her bonds somehow tightening against her wrists and ankles. The beast lunged over Veruna's desk, his claws out, teeth bared, as he frantically tried to reach his creator's murderer.

Obviously expecting this type of reaction, Raygo de-atomized at the last moment, sending Mongrel crashing into the wall. Joxy flinched when Raygo materialized right beside her. Reaching behind his back, he pulled out the cube and winked at Joxy. Spinning on his heels, Raygo lobbed the device into the middle of where the other dumbfounded BAIs stood gaping. He tapped quickly at the controls on his forearm.

The sides of the small contraption sprang open, and a consuming brightness flashed. The BAIs threw their arms up in an attempt to cover their eyes. Small pieces of them were already disappearing. Soon came their helpless screams.

Even with the filter Raygo and Tano had worked out, Joxy felt a steady tug at the core of her body. Not enough to draw her in, but enough to want to get far away as quickly as possible. Kneeling, Raygo quickly unbound her, the blood flowing back to her limbs in a tingling sensation. He helped her to her feet, but she almost collapsed to the floor when Mongrel released an eardrum-piercing bellow. He pounced at them. The cube pulled harshly at his airborne body as he flew through its bubble of influence, causing the spitting and clawing abomination to crash down to the floor, feet away from his intended targets.

Mongrel's long claws were embedded in the floor up to their cuticles. What remained of his hind legs floated behind him, the stumps shortening as the cube devoured them. His deafening screams overrode those made by the BAIs.

Then, all at once, they ceased.

Joxy trembled uncontrollably. Raygo turned and hugged her tightly as the last traces of Mongrel's snout vanished. Still embracing, he brought his forearm up behind her back and turned off the cube, its sides clamping shut with a click. He buried his face in her neck.

That had been a close one. Joxy knew that if Raygo had been only seconds later that she wouldn't be standing there. Words weren't needed. They both were all too aware of this fact. Raygo gripped the side of her arms, looking her dead in the eyes, he raised a brow. Taking a deep breath, she steadied her nerves and nodded that she was ready to continue with the mission.

He walked over to Veruna's desk. The woman's hair had shortened a couple of inches indicating where the cube's area of influence had ended. He swept the tangled mess of hair from her face, noticing that even in death she seemed to wear that trademark smirk of hers. There was only one thing left to do. He got on the comms.

"Tano?"

Joxy went to retrieve her helmet and found it lodged under a sofa. She placed it back on.

"Have my siblings arrived yet?"

"Just a few minutes ago," Tano said, his voice sounding distracted. Joxy figured he was busy getting the emulation machine going. She could hear other voices in the background, too.

Raygo's shoulders appeared to relax at the news that his siblings had made it to the lab okay.

"Will it work?" His anxious eyes darted to Joxy.

"I believe it will." Tano paused, but Joxy could still hear him tapping away on a holo. "Jones and his team haven't made it here yet. They're not responding."

Joxy kept the worst thoughts from invading her mind. *Maybe they're still busy fighting to buy us time.*

"Okay," Raygo said. "Then we'll have to get started without them." He locked eyes with Joxy. "I'm sure they'll catch up."

Raygo grabbed Joxy's hand, and they ran together through the office and on to the lift. Stepping inside, Raygo removed his helmet. Joxy did the same.

"This is the moment of truth," he said, turning to face her. He picked up her braid and tossed it back over her shoulder, then pushed loose strands of her dark hair out of her eyes. "Are you ready?"

CHAPTER 12
A NEW LOOK

When the Nocturian fighters flew from their warship in a swarm, Segan AI detected a Starborn-class vessel in the midst of the cluster. After it became obvious that the Nocturians were attempting a rapid retreat, Commander Roschek felt it important to personally pursue the lone vessel that had branched off and managed to breach Sega City's atmosphere. Besides, he'd never seen such a ship in person; that's how rare they were.

He eventually found the ship parked on the outskirts of VOrg's massive complex, over by what was now a cratered lightrail station. His own ship's AI placed the image of a year's-old bounty upon his holo. Apparently he'd stumbled upon an infamous bandit vessel. Pictures of the ship's captain and its crew swept across the bottom of the bounty poster. Taking caution, he ordered his small fleet of accompanying vessels to land on the far side of the complex, where there was exceptionally less damage, and so that his forces were spread out as to better track down the bandits.

His men successfully swept through and cleared the streets, only having to eliminate a few dozen of the bloodthirsty ROBs themselves. Roschek hoped to encounter a VOrg official as they followed the trail of destruction up to the courtyard of the organization's main building. At the very last intersection of the road leading into the courtyard, he came across what looked to be five heavily armed mechs, frozen in their final moments, partially covered in a thick layer of soot. He figured they belonged to the bandit captain's attacking party. The tall pile of ROBs stacked all around them suggested that they had not gone down without a fight.

Something troubled the commander that made the back of his mind itch. What were the Nocturians using these bandits for? He wasn't sure why, but he felt that somehow Vaughn played a role in this; he just couldn't connect the dots as to how. A single warship sent to assault a planet, or more specifically, one of the universe's most dangerous corporations just didn't sit right.

He was missing something vital.

Roschek didn't like the situation at all. VOrg had never even called for assistance. He and his men arrived just shy of the massacre, with soot raining down on the buildings and bodies, creating a blackened graveyard. He could taste the ash with every breath. The sight of so many ROBs had at first confused him, until one of his officers pointed out that the med bots had been weaponized. But why?

VOrg was an entity unto its own, with Segan military keeping out of their affairs. The commander wasn't blind to their political influence, nor was he a fool. Sega City was threatened and it was his job to defend it. He just had to proceed with caution.

He stood inside of VOrg's courtyard with an entire company of Segan Marines at his back, leaking out into the roads and alleys beyond. He should have felt more than confident with any decision that he made. He didn't.

"Commander," a marine said, snapping a salute. "No one is responding from inside."

Roschek's next move was a forced one, and he dreaded the potential repercussions of it.

"Spread out," he ordered the platoon leaders around him. "Start clearing these labs." He spoke the next words with even greater resolve: "I want these bandits captured *alive* for questioning. Go!"

Groups of marines broke off to span the entire complex. Roschek took a deep breath. He was fully committed; now he had to save the day, or it would be his ass.

Two platoons remained with the commander. He would personally lead his marines to confront these Nocturians, bandits, or whoever they were. With tactical efficiency they charged from the disaster outside to the quiet tranquility of the entrance lobby. The abrupt contrast staggered them. Roschek had been expecting the carnage to continue.

The place looked untouched, and it unsettled his nerves. He started to question his decision. Had VOrg already handled the invaders? If so, he should turn around right now. They moved further into the lobby. Posted near the lift was a directory.

Roschek decided he would take some of the men up to the "Main Office," where he hoped to get clarity on the situation, plus a nice pat on the back. Starting from the top down, the rest of his marines would break into small teams and clear the building floor by floor, flushing out any stragglers.

Each marine was well outfitted in powered armor suits equipped with standard-issue battle rifles. Because they were bulky, several elevator trips were necessary to transport the teams to their assigned floors. Roschek and his team went first. In the lift's golden reflection, he fantasized that he and his men were knights in shining armor, here to save the damsel at the top of the tower.

The lift pinged, snapping him from his fantasy. The doors opened. Segan Marines fanned out, covering the entirety of the enormous office in seconds.

"All clear," a marine shouted.

The wealth on display in this single office could buy planets. The thin wood molding alone was worth more than he'd make in five life-times, not to mention the vibrant aquatic life that most likely lived fuller lives than he did inside of their clear, sealed portions of the office walls. Roschek never felt so strongly that he did not belong somewhere. Such a place did not exist in his world. His palms began to sweat. Someone shouted his name.

"Commander, sir, you need to see this." A marine called to him from the far side of the room.

Slouching behind a giant wooden desk was the body of a withered old lady, the damsel they were there to save. Her neck unnaturally twisted, the flesh rolling over itself. The woman's eyes were closed, mouth slack, but with the corners of her lips slightly upturned, as though she were relieved that the fight, which was life, was finally over. Roschek knew exactly who she was and that the situation had just become a million times more complicated for him.

He would be responsible for capturing the people who murdered the most powerful woman in the universe. Even in her current condition, the sight of Veruna emanated power. He had only seen her once before, at a dinner party, where she was the center of attention in the midst of presidents, ministers, and monarchs. Her grandeur was not lost in death.

She was an icon to many, though undoubtedly the dread of many more. Most on Sega City knew who she was, honored that their planet played host to her organization. And yet, this was looking more and more like an assassination. The lone vessel and diversion tactics helped to sup-port that theory. But the Nocturians were all the way on the other side of the universe. Roschek doubted that VOrg's reach went that far. First Captain Vaughn and now Veruna; he couldn't conceive Nocturne's angle.

Roschek's comm roared to life, tearing him from his conspiracy theories.

"There's activity going on down here at one of the main labs. You'd better come quick."

The commander's head snapped up. His marines stood around the desk, awaiting orders. Without a word he stormed off toward the lift. As his men rushed in to flank him, one of the marines tripped over a strange-looking cube.

"Ah," the marine shouted, grabbing at his ankle before kicking the cube across the floor.

"Careful," another marine said. "There's no telling how much that thing might be worth."

"You men better not break anything in here," Roschek warned. "Now come on, follow me."

Roschek's team piled back into the lift. He yelled into his mic with annoyance. "What floor, you idiot?"

"Three levels down from you," one of the team leaders stammered.

"Hold tight," he growled.

With Veruna gone, some of the pressure lifted from his shoulders. As far as he was concerned, her demise left no question as to who was actively in charge. There was no longer any reason to tread lightly; this was his show now. His newfound confidence bolstered his bravado, turning him back into the strong, coldhearted leader he'd always been.

Roschek's foot tapped impatiently against the lift's marble floor, willing it to descend faster. The man wanted answers. He couldn't wait to drag these scum back to a Segan interrogation chamber. After all was said and done, a promotion would be warranted. Even if Captain Vaughn did by chance return, perhaps he'd maintain his post as acting commander. Roschek was giddy at the thought.

Ping. The elevator doors slid open. There was a staccato of clacks as nervous-looking marines swiveled their rifles around. He could tell his men were on edge, unnerved by being in VOrg headquarters. He was sure that they, too, had heard rumors about some of the nightmares that took place here.

Roschek's face burned crimson. "Damn it, don't point your guns at me you fools!"

The marines stepped back and lowered their weapons with a sheepish hunch of their shoulders. Looking beyond this trigger-happy bunch of dummies, the commander noticed his team leaders bunched around four painfully beautiful people. They brought to mind angels from the Bible stories his mother used to read to him.

He parted the crowd in the lobby, eventually making his way up to these strangers. They didn't strike him as assassins, and they were actually unarmed. Something about them was familiar, though.

"Who are you?" Roschek demanded.

One of the strangers stepped forward, extending a hand in greeting. Roschek shook it, its coolness unsettling.

"My name is Raygo." He smiled as though his name alone explained everything. "Behind me are Bobby, Marlow, and April." They smiled as well. April even gave a small wave. "We're VOrg property," Raygo continued. "BAIs, to be exact."

The term was vaguely familiar but eluded Roschek. Unconsciously, he cleared his throat.

"I am Captain Roschek, acting commander of the Segan Armada." He hesitated for a moment, thinking how best to continue. He was back to treading lightly. "There was a Nocturian attack. We followed—"

"The attackers are back there," Raygo said, pointing over his shoulder, yet maintaining eye contact.

Roschek didn't appreciate being cut off, but he thought it best to ignore the slight, at least until he had more information.

"We caught them trying to use the lab," Raygo continued. "When we interfered, the situation turned deadly."

Roschek nodded his head, although he was extremely disappointed. He wanted to be the one to capture the bandits alive. "Veruna is dead," he blurted dumbly. "We found her in her office."

The BAIs showed no physical response. Either they already knew or were not capable of those type of emotions. Raygo placed a hand on the commander's decorated shoulder.

"Thank you," Raygo said flatly. "We appreciate the effort from you and your men." He nodded at the clusters of marines.

Roschek felt robbed, his illusions of praise and glory crashing down. He looked past these VOrg creations, down the hall at the lab beyond. A body lay sprawled along the entrance threshold. He licked his lips, uncertain.

"I would like to take a look at the bodies. We'll have to conduct an official investigation here. However, it appears that war with the Nocturians is inevitable."

Raygo squeezed the commander's shoulder.

"Of course. Anything you need, you have free reign of the complex. Now, if you'll excuse us, we have rather urgent matters to attend to."

Roschek turned as the four BAIs strode past him.

"But you will be around . . . in case I have any questions, right?" He felt like he was being pushy even though it was standard procedure. These *beings* made him uncomfortable.

The lift doors closed before he received a response.

Roschek spun on his heels and led his men down the long stretch of hall as he struggled to make sense of the situation. The building didn't seem big enough from the outside to accommodate such a long walk. He eventually reached the body, barely glimpsing at the mech as he stepped over it and into the lab. More bodies were scattered about inside.

He could not make heads nor tails of the scene. Why did they attack this particular lab? There were plenty of other more-accessible labs leading up to this one. With a critical eye the commander slowly examined the bodies and equipment. Two tables sat dead center of the room, a network of cables, monitors, and tubes linking them together.

The team leaders left a few men behind to guard the lobby and hallway, fanning the rest of the marines around the perimeter of the lab. A few of these marines thought it wise to search some of the nearby invaders' bodies. It would not be the first time an enemy combatant pretended to be dead; besides, there was always the possibility of answers hidden inside pockets.

The mystery started to take shape inside Roschek's head. He wondered if the others could hear the gears of his mind turning. The term BAI had finally come back to him, striking him like a stroke. He remembered a Sega City summit, years ago, where VOrg had paraded them around as the future of humanity.

He didn't think much of it, or *them*, at the time. Like most others at the summit, he figured they were nothing more than glorified mechs. He was taking them a little more serious now. How did these four unarmed beings take out a team of heavily armed bandits? His finger tapped against his dimpled chin.

"Sir, we have a female human over here," a marine said while rolling the woman's body over. Even in death this human was striking.

The plot thickened.

"She looks familiar," Roschek mused aloud, then immediately after, realized who she was. His face dropped. It was the woman with the crazy-high bounty. "That's Captain Joxy," he said softly.

Roschek scanned her body in search of her cause of death. His face contorted with confusion. Kneeling down he conducted a more thorough search, his hands frantically patting along her body. There was no blood or evidence of broken bones. No indication at all.

He scooted over to a mech, rolling his body around to do a quick search. Nothing. Roschek was panting, his mind racing. Pieces of the puzzle slid together. Anger flared across his eyes, veins bulging as realization dawned. They were standing in the midst of an emulation lab. He'd been duped.

"Get them," he screamed, spittle flying from his mouth. "Apprehend those BAIs, now!" As an afterthought, and before all of his men stormed from the room, he shouted, "And put her body in the cooler." He pointed at Joxy's corpse, his lip curled.

He backed away from the bandit captain to reel in his anger at being duped. After a few deep breaths, he got on the comms to his fleet officers in orbit.

"Surround the planet. No ship is to leave our system."

* * *

By the time Raygo and Joxy made it to the lab, Tano and the others had already emulated. Bobby and Marlow were hovering off to the side, wide-eyed. April was standing over the monitors, her fingers flying across their screens.

"Three each," she said. It took a moment for Joxy to understand what she'd meant. Tano, Brigs, and the crew had split themselves between Bobby and Marlow. "We're up next," April continued, patting the floating table closest to her.

Joxy's breath caught. She fought against the knot building in her stomach. This was the moment of truth. The part of this wild adventure that she'd been dreading most. She was genuinely surprised to have made it this far, the odds stacked against them as they were. The idea that fate had a hand in this flashed across her mind. No, not fate. Nostic. She didn't want to do this. She had to.

The fact that her men had left April solely for Joxy did not escape her or Raygo. He was already watching her with a smirk when she tilted her head up to look at him.

"We've made it this far," he said, shrugging. "I'll be here waiting for you on the other side."

She took a hesitant step toward the table, afraid to say anything lest she back out. She hopped onto its floating surface, her eyes darting over to where Bobby and Marlow stood still wearing far-off gazes. A shiver ran through her body.

Inhaling a deep breath, she lay down. Raygo walked over, taking April's place at the monitors as she lay on the opposite table. April turned her head to face Joxy and smiled reassuringly. Joxy flashed a nervous smile in return. She wanted this to be over already.

Raygo stepped up behind each of them, securing a headset to their heads. Wires and tubes connected to the prongs that prodded their skin, creating a tingling sensation that hugged the skull. Joxy closed her eyes tightly, tears escaping the corners and rolling down her cheeks. April was the definition of calm, familiar with the process, eager for her new member.

Back at the monitor Raygo moved the procedure forward. As the emulation machine powered up, a faint whine descended upon the lab. The edges of Joxy's view began to cloud, but she noticed that Raygo was by her side. Almost unconscious, she thought she heard him whisper, "I love you." Maybe it had been a dream.

What occurred next was a horrific nightmare. Even without the sensory input of a body, Joxy's consciousness experienced a pain unlike any other, inside of a darkness so deep in silence that she imagined it had to exist outside of time and space. It was the epitome of experiencing your own death. Joxy was completely aware the moment her mind was snatched from her body. What was in reality only seconds seemed to last an eternity. Fully conscious, her mind found itself trapped in a void similar to the one on the fringes of the known universe.

It was in this void that she panicked.

Had the procedure failed somehow? Maybe she and April weren't compatible. In her hysteria she raced to come up with the worst-case scenarios. But in the midst of this impenetrable darkness, there came a light. Her consciousness raced toward it like a fish returning to water, her mind gasping for air. Then, she was in a room, a room with other "people." She could not see them, but rather sensed their presence. Yet even that wasn't quite right.

Joxy felt her consciousness melding with the others inside the room. She was frightened, and they soothed her. A wave of calmness washed over her. They spoke to her, though not with words. They embraced her, though not with arms. She became them while they became her, yet her mind remained her own. Unanimously, they decided to allow Joxy majority control. They were aware that it was up to her to complete this journey, to save what would remain of humanity.

April sat up, her eyes blinking open. Raygo watched her intently as he propped a supporting hand against her back.

"Are you okay?" he asked.

She raised her eyes to meet his, her hand brushing against his cheek. His touch no longer felt cool and foreign. April winked, then hopped off the table and kissed him. Raygo stood there, stunned. So much so that April laughed into his unmoving mouth.

"I've waited a long time to do that again," she said breathless.

"Me too," he snorted.

Bobby came up and clapped the two of them on their backs.

"We did it," he said with surprise. "I'm still finding it hard to believe, but damn if we didn't pull it off."

Tano clearly seemed happy inside his new body.

"I hate to cut the party short," Marlow added, "but we still need to make it back to Nostic if this is going to mean anything."

April knew this wasn't over yet, not by a long shot. They still needed to get off the planet and make it back to the wormhole.

"Let's move the bodies around real quick," Raygo suggested, "to cover up what we were doing. The Segan Military is likely to wonder why VOrg was targeted."

It was a good idea that might even buy them some time. Their presence was detected entering Sega City atmosphere, so they knew it was likely the Segans would give chase. April was dragging Brigs's body out of the lab and into the hall when she heard the distinct ping of the lift. She dropped him and dashed back inside to the others.

"We've got company," she hissed.

It was time to go.

* * *

Raygo led them down the hallway with authority. Head up, chest out, that whole thing, but he was nervous inside. His body almost involuntarily broke stride as Segan Marines rounded the corner from the lobby, guns up. Fortunately, his legs did not betray him, and he strode right up to the armored troops. Lucky for them, the marines didn't decide to shoot first and ask questions later. Probably because they knew to be extra cautious on VOrg property; one mistake and their careers as marines would be over, not to mention the high likelihood of becoming part of the corporation's next experiment.

The Segans glanced at each other questioningly, seeming not to know how to handle such an encounter. VOrg was a notoriously unpredictable company, and surely none of them felt comfortable here. One of the marines spoke into his comm, probably reaching out to his superior. Another one kept adjusting his grip on his rifle, his fingers dancing along the edges of its trigger.

"Whoa," Raygo said. "We're unarmed. Be cool." He was trying to be cool himself.

The jumpy marine lowered the barrel of his rifle slightly, then removed one of his hands to wipe the sweat from across his brow. He looked beyond their small party and Raygo noticed his eyes narrow, then widen.

"Body down the hall," the jumpy marine shouted, bringing his rifle back to bear, his fingers trembling above the trigger.

Raygo raised both his hands in a disarming gesture, about to assure them of some fabricated story when the lift pinged once again. Sliding open, the doors revealed another contingent of marines. These were accompanied by an ornately decorated suit who yelled at his men to put their fucking guns down. Raygo worried that in their uneasiness they might unleash some friendly fire.

The decorated suit looked pissed, chewing his men out for everything they were worth before noticing him and his siblings. The marines parted as their superior approached, eyeing Raygo and the others warily. In an effort to disarm the man, Raygo extended his hand in greeting.

Staring at his hand suspiciously, the man eventually grabbed it and gave a firm shake. "Who are you?" he asked.

"My name is Raygo." He put a hand to his chest, then removed it and swept his arm out behind him to indicate the others. "And these are my siblings. We are BAIs, VOrg property." He tried not to cringe at that last part. "We took down the attackers."

The looks of awe and fear were plastered all over the marines' faces. Confident they wouldn't risk questioning too much of what he was telling them, he took their stunned silence as an opportunity to ease through the crowded hallway toward the lift. No one tried to stop them, but they all watched with their mouths hung open as they shifted out of their way. Raygo laughed on the inside, all he had to say was "VOrg property" and watch the sea part. The superior must have regained his wits, because right as the lift's doors began to close, he spit out something or another about wanting to question them further.

"Well, that went better than anticipated," Raygo said, pleased with himself.

"I think they were surprised to have run into us," Marlow said. "Let alone inform them that we had taken down the assailants."

"Yeah, those guys were a real dangerous bunch," Bobby said with a laugh.

All of them busted out laughing.

They reached the bottom floor and stepped into the lobby. Exiting the serenity of the lobby, they walked back into the carnage. Segan marines ran in and out of the buildings ahead. Soot continued to rain down, coating mounds in and along the streets. Raygo's mouth tightened at the sight of the destruction, their success so far had been very hard fought.

A strong breeze swept between the labs, stirring up small black cyclones. Soot shed from some of the body-sized mounds not far in front of them. His heart lurched as he caught a glimpse of Jones's face before it was quickly covered again.

Tears turned to ink as they streamed down his cheeks. He knew Joxy had seen him as well when she grabbed his hand and entwined her fingers in his.

"We saw them too," Bobby and Marlow said to him telepathically.

Raygo gathered himself; he would mourn the loss of his friends, his family, later. For now he led them to the far side of the road, skirting the buildings and maneuvering around the countless other mounds along the sidewalk. Word that VOrg property, four BAIs, were wandering around the complex must have spread like wildfire, because of all the marines rushing past, only a few dared to glance at them. Their passage through the streets went unencumbered, and it wasn't long before they spotted *The Legacy*. He let a breath out that he didn't realize he'd been holding. Their ship was still in one piece.

* * *

No marines were on this stretch of road, so they rushed to reach the ship. They were making their way up the ramp when gunfire opened up behind them. Without warning, a barrage of projectiles dinked off the ship's metal. Raygo dropped to his knees, gritting his teeth in pain as he grabbed a calf.

April grabbed the collar of his suit and effortlessly dragged him into the cargo hold. Joxy had a flashback of being a kid and helping her father up the ramp. This caused April's feet to stumble. She and Raygo fell to the floor of the cargo hold just in time as bullets raced by overhead. Bobby continued past them, running further into the ship. Marlow was at a nearby holo panel, tapping away, trying to get the door to close. The cargo door shook the hold as it started to shut, the ramp already retracting itself. April looked up just in time to see Segan Marines pouring down the streets, descending upon them.

The Legacy's shields prevented any real damage from being done. It would take substantially more firepower than what the marines had. April and Marlow were under each of Raygo's arms, helping him up to the bridge. She could hear Bobby firing up the fission thrusters and feel the slight vibrations from the ship's smaller cannons as they fired at the enemy.

The ship lurched sideways, sending the three of them crashing into a wall. Raygo groaned as April helped him stand up. Bobby came over the ship's comms.

"Segan shuttles are trying to box us in."

"Get us out of here," April shouted back. "Go through them if you have to!"

Tano's new body, Bobby, no longer had the advantage of being linked to *The Legacy's* systems, but his memory still took over. Sliding a finger steadily over a holo, he brought the thrusters up to full power. In the planet's atmosphere, their burn was almost deafening. Bobby banked right, aligning the ship with the largest gap between the wall of shuttles.

April strapped herself into the captain's chair, but not before donning the black-and-lime jacket that hung on its back. Raygo and Marlow strapped themselves into a couch. Right as the last buckle clipped into place, Bobby accelerated full throttle, throwing them all backward in their seats.

All but one of the Segan shuttles had the sense to evade. It bounced off *The Legacy's* shields, which sent it spiraling madly to the surface and crashing into one of the labs. The Sega City ground defense cannons took aim at them as they climbed higher and higher toward space. April took over the controls, weaving and bobbing the ship to avoid incoming rounds. Clouds of smoke reduced visibility as explosive rounds detonated all around them, rocking the ship. Scanners showed that a few dozen shuttles were trying to nip at their heels.

Abruptly, they transitioned to the ship's artificial gravity, their propulsion changing over to the G-drives as they reached space.

Floating along in front of them was what looked to be the entirety of Sega City's home guard armada. Their numbers stretched impressively along the window's horizon. Commander Roschek had set a blockade. April knew her ship was fast, but Nostic's wormhole was close to a week away and the G-drives would not be able to sustain the power needed to outrun the Segans for that long.

With the odds stacked against them, the bridge was eerily quiet. April sat there fondling a leather seam on her armrest.

"All right guys," she said, swiveling her chair around to face them. "The best I can come up with is that we try to catch up with the Nocturian warship."

"They'll kill us," Bobby stated matter-of-factly.

"Yeah," added Marlow, "we stole their ship, and more or less, left them for dead."

Raygo sat on the couch in numbing pain, listening, his wound already healing.

"The Nocturians might kill us, but they also might not," replied April. "The Segans will for sure. Captain Richards's pride is probably hurt but between our recent transformations and knowledge of the portal, we may have some leverage. It's our best chance as long as they don't dust us on sight."

"I don't—" Marlow started, but then Raygo spoke up.

"Let's try it," he said. "We won't be able to outrun the Segans for long. The protection of the warship might just buy us the time we need to figure something else out."

Bobby sat back, exhaling loudly. "All right. I'm down for it."

Marlow still didn't look convinced. "I'm not psyched about it, but I can't come up with a better idea, so . . . "

April clapped her hands, the sound echoing through the bridge. "Good we'll be cutting this one dangerously close," she said. "I'm already picking up multiple targeting indicators. Bobby, get to engineering. If any of our systems go down, I need you there ready to fix them."

Bobby unharnessed himself from his seat and jumped up. "Aye, aye, Captain." Then he bolted from the bridge.

"I'm setting our smaller arms on auto. Marlow, I want you to man the big guns. Keep these bastards off our tail."

Marlow stood and looked down at Raygo. "You going to be all right, brother?"

"Just a flesh wound. It'll heal in a few hours. Go."

Marlow saluted them, then headed off the bridge toward his assigned post, in the opposite direction Bobby had gone.

Raygo limped over to Bobby's station, taking a seat in the vacated chair. He manipulated a holo until it popped up a tactical layout of all the ships in the area. April already had a similar screen pulled up.

"It's going to be a squeeze," Raygo said. "The Segans have us locked down pretty tight."

"I know. We're going to exhaust a lot of power to get by them." April patted her armrest. "If my baby here makes it through intact, then it's going to take everything she has to stay in front of them until hopefully we can reach the Nocturians."

"Well... ," Raygo let the word hang in the air for a moment. "So many times I thought it was all over, yet look at us, we still manage to put on a show."

April laughed. She looked over and saw the bright gleam in Raygo's eyes. He was right. It was as though destiny truly played a role in their lives. If not Nostic, then maybe it would be destiny that got them through this next leg of their journey.

"It's always one hell of a show too, isn't it?" she quipped.

They both bathed in each other's laughter, the love.

"We're in position, Captain," both Bobby and Marlow said telepathically.

"Everything looks solid down here," Bobby added.

"Guns are hot," said Marlow.

Let's show these Segans why we're the greatest bandits in the universe!" April roared.

She dumped more dark matter into the drives, stoking the fire. After triple checking shields, power, and weapons, she aimed for the weakest link in the Segan's chain. Raygo confirmed her decision, an area with the widest gap between their battleships that contained mostly stardusters.

April took a deep breath as she settled deeper into her seat, the harness hugging her tight. They would be running the gauntlet on this one. She piloted *The Legacy's* approach at a reasonable speed. She wouldn't be able to fully crank the drives until they had a clear lane.

They were quickly closing in on the armada. Now in range of the Segan's larger ships, they began to open fire. Laser munitions whizzed by, sometimes flashing when striking their shields. While the light show continued, one of the battleships attempted to hail them. April accepted the connection. Commander Roschek materialized on the bridge. "Captain Joxy, we are aware of what you and your crew have done. Surrender to me now, and you have my word that you will receive a fair trial."

"Ooh, that is tempting," she scoffed. "Would you give me a few minutes to think it over?" She needed to buy some time.

"I won't ask again," Roschek said. "Surrender this instant, or I will turn your ship to slag."

"There's something weird happening with the scanners." Raygo slid the data feeds over to one of April's holos. "The feeds are going haywire."

The anomaly looked familiar. "Oh, shit," April gasped.

"I need an answer, now!" Roschek barked.

"Probably not this time," she said, "but maybe the next. We'll catch you later, big guy."

With that, April dropped the connection. An angry Roschek faded away.

The Legacy made a sharp maneuver to its right. A swirl of black and gray was taking shape in front of them, a flurry of light flashing inside.

Guess Nostic decided to give us a little help, she thought.

* * *

Roschek was furious. How dare these bandits take his mercy for granted. He could not believe the audacity of such a woman. Such recklessness. Did she not value their lives at all? The thought worried him.

"Commander."

"What?" he shouted, then cleared his throat and collected himself. "Yes, what is it?"

"Sir, there is something forming to our left. *The Legacy* has just changed course and is headed straight for it. What are your orders, sir?"

Roschek's legs faltered. Zooming in on the bandit ship's trajectory, there appeared to be something of a spatial tumor pulsing to life, and his prey were headed right for it.

Commander Roschek set his jaw.

"Follow them."

CHAPTER 13
CHAOS

"**Y**our eminence." A Nocturian soldier bowed. "The Lord Emperor approaches. He requests your presence aboard the *Warmonger*. Shall I ready the skiff, sir?"

Kurd waved a hand dismissively. "As the emperor wishes."

The emissary watched from the window in his cabin as fleet upon fleet made their way through the wormhole. Command back at Nocturne had received their messages. It was no surprise the emperor had decided to come along himself. This was an historic moment, and the possibilities were endless.

As soon as the NGVI had crossed through themselves, they spotted the shimmering anomaly out there in the darkness. Alone. It's what they had anxiously sent Captain Joxy to examine, but now Kurd was here, and he didn't know what to make of it. While waiting for the NGV2 to come through the wormhole, he'd experienced some rather odd visions. Images so vivid at times he would have sworn he was a part of a completely different reality. Some of those visions terrified him to his meaty core. Perhaps that was why Joxy had fled. His unease grew worse as time stretched on without Captain Richards's arrival.

Their last update came from Captain Richards stating *The Legacy* had just docked inside of his ship's hangar and that he personally would oversee their boarding. That was almost a week ago. And the lack of further communications left Kurd feeling uneasy. What was *The Legacy* fleeing from, and what happened to his other warship? Too many questions were left unanswered, and now he was having to answer to the emperor.

Though stress from the past week left Kurd paler and a fraction thinner, he still remained a large and imposing figure. Spinning on his heels, he made his way through what was once Long's cabin, and now his. The captain offered it up without protest. Kurd knew it wounded the man's ego. He didn't care.

Kurd's skiff was ready and waiting for him when he reached the hangar. It was a sleek vessel that would never do anything more than shuttle VIPs around. He plopped down, taking up a row of seats that typically held three people. A simple AI could have piloted such a craft, but luxury would not allow it. Positioned up front in a crisp leather seat, the pilot—a distinguished gentleman who kept his eyes forward and both hands on the controls at all times—radiated professionalism.

Without a word, the pilot performed his disembarking procedures. Soon after, they pulled away from their dock and moved into the open hangar. The skiff's thrust gently nudged Kurd into his couch. A sea of darkness opened up as they pulled out from the relative safety of the hangar. On this side of the warship, the only contrast to the darkness was the anomaly. So much nothingness was disorienting.

They made their approach to the emperor's ship, *Warmonger*. The towering vessel was a dreadnaught class; bigger and badder than anything most other galaxies could conjure up. From where he sat, Kurd could see fleets of battleships and warships spread out to encircle the anomaly before being cut from view by the massive ship's bow.

Access tunnels dotted the hull of the dreadnaught, allowing warships and smaller vessels to easily come and go. A hangar door was unrealistic for such mammoth proportions. Kurd's skiff was relative in size to a gnat hovering around an elephant's ass. Giant rail guns hugged the outer layer of thickly coated armor, flanked by smaller-though-still-huge plasma and laser cannons. Vast clusters of shield arrays distorted its silhouette like tumors.

The pilot directed the luxury transport into one of the tunnels. Dark metal walls enveloped them, their craft illuminating only a small bubble of light. Kurd spotted large sections of conduit crawling along the tunnel walls like vines, access panels and doors stenciled with charade-like characters of warning, and flashing lights staggered at intervals to assumably help guide them.

The emissary was for the most part relaxed, having done his job well. He'd gone above and beyond simply executing his orders by exceeding all expectations and reaching the anomaly himself. They could fabricate, if need be, how they were in pursuit of a bandit vessel when a wormhole mysteriously appeared. It was a reasonable story, not far from the truth, that should prevent any political rifts.

Kurd was on his way to receive just praise from the higher-ups. He felt his name would be added to the history books, his legacy set.

Docking clamps clanged loudly in place, snapping him from his reverie. The pilot tapped a holo, and the side of the transport hinged open. Stepping into the air-lock, Kurd grunted to himself, acknowledging how the pilot had not uttered a single word during their flight. A sign of respect he imagined.

A welcoming group of delegates awaited Kurd on the other side of the air-lock door. Outfitted in vibrantly colored dresses, they carried small wicker baskets filled with lotus flower petals. One of the delegates gestured for him to follow. With an amused smile and slight bow, he obliged her.

The other women fell into place beside him as they tossed petals at his feet. He wasn't sure if it was the petals or the delegates whose aroma seemed to hypnotize him. This was too much. For the emperor to have done this showed just how thankful he was, but Kurd didn't let it go to his head. The emperor was known to destroy those he deemed a threat to his throne.

The procession weaved its way through the ship's endless passages. People stopped to watch, some even clapped and celebrated as they paraded by. It felt like they were taking the long route, with Kurd struggling to breathe and keep up. Just when he felt certain his legs would give out and collapse him to the floor, they rounded a corner and he found himself miraculously on the bridge. He braced himself against a wall, sweat trickling down his forehead and into his eyes, stinging.

A deadly thought flashed across Kurd's mind. Had this exertion been the emperor's plan? He caught his breath and erected himself, wiping the sweat from his face with the sleeve of his Eskin. He could feel the moisture clinging to him and hated to think what he smelled like, hoping the flowers masked his odor.

"Please," his guide said softly in a sweet voice, "the Lord Emperor eagerly awaits your arrival."

He followed her through the massive bridge, itself half the size of a warship. Terraces looped around overhead, filled with even more stations and their operators. It took a small army to oversee such a vessel. Outside of Hawaii 5, this was the emperor's home away from home; he managed an entire galaxy from this mobile command center.

Holos flashed across the faces of soldiers at their stations, too preoccupied to take notice of Kurd's eccentric entrance. For once he was thankful of that. All that was about to change, though, as he reached the front of the bridge.

"Ahoy, and there he is now, everyone," a loud, jovial voice pointed out. "My emissary has arrived."

The Lord Emperor stood surrounded by his generals, gesturing for Kurd to join them. Where Kurd was round, the emperor was tall, his white hair pulled back into a fashionable man bun that allowed his sharp, pale features and dark-gray eyes to impress upon their target. The old ruler carried himself in a carefree manner, as if his muscles still rippled beneath his skin, indicating that there was still plenty of fight left in him. The emissary knew this fact all too well and would not allow himself to be fooled by the friendly welcome. Still, he played along. Politics was the name of the game even though they were all supposed to be on the same side.

Kurd dropped to both of his knees and bowed his head to the floor. "My Lord Emperor."

The emperor lifted a hand, palm up. "Rise and join us in our celebrations. We are here because of you, after all."

The emissary struggled to his feet, using both hands to push off on one knee to raise his bulk. The generals watched, each with an apparent varying degree of amusement.

"If I may, your highness, what are we celebrating? We're not exactly sure what that thing out there is, yet." Kurd's eyes flickered to outside the bridge's massive observation window.

"You have done well, risking your life to travel through that wormhole." The emperor pointed over his shoulder, out the window. "And now you have summoned us all out here to bear witness to a shiny circle that does nothing."

Kurd thought he picked up a mocking ring in the emperor's voice. The generals to either side chuckled softly.

"But you see," the emperor continued, "this is very significant. An oddity such as this, way out here in the Void. So, what does it mean?"

He paused for a moment to see if Kurd would attempt to answer the rhetorical question.

Kurd knew to stay silent.

"It means that it was put out here, by someone or some being— and recently. It means we're not as alone as we once thought."

For the past week Kurd had gnawed on that very same thought. It's what they had all hoped for in the beginning yet didn't dare to think it true. Now, here they were, way out in the middle of nowhere. So where were these mysterious beings?

"What's it doing out here?" Kurd asked, wishing he had something better to say.

One of the generals spoke up: "We believe the anomaly is a portal. A more intricate version of the wormhole we all came through. If our theory is correct, then it's a doorway to our neighbor's house."

The emperor nodded his head in vigorous agreement. "We'll be testing that theory shortly," he said.

"How do you mean?" Kurd asked, his tone sour.

This was his discovery, and he had assumed he would have a seat at the table, that his opinion would be valued. Apparently, the important decisions, or at least some of them, were already being made without him. The emperor approached the observation window. For Kurd, the window inspired anxiety—it felt as though it were too big for space, that the pressure of vacuum would break it.

A young servant dressed in the pearl and garnet colors of Nocturne came by with a tray and offered the emissary a glass of skid. Everyone else seemed to have indulged themselves well before his arrival. Kurd followed beside the generals as they, too, approached the thick polymer window, looking beyond to the anomaly at the left, wormhole to the right. Both features had been so unimaginable until recently, but only one garnered an abundance of curiosity at the moment.

If Kurd squinted, he could just make out a speck making its way in the direction of the portal. The rest of the specks maintained a perimeter at an arbitrary distance that someone had deemed safe. A nearby station's operator magnified the window.

"That's one of our battleships," a general explained.

"Why not send a smaller contingent?" Kurd asked. "In the case that it's not a portal."

The group turned to him as a whole, their faces lined with disgust at such a proposition.

One of the other generals cleared his throat. "And what if they do make it through, and our neighbors prove hostile? Sending a battleship is the least we can do in that eventuality."

Always thinking of war, these damn military types. Kurd wanted so badly to point out that nothing hostile has come from the anomaly as of yet. Why send an invitation if they planned to attack us? Instead he took a sip from his glass of skid. It was a strong batch from the royal stores that made his face flush and lips pucker.

All the attention was back on the battleship as it steadily approached the portal. Outside of the enhanced section of window, something caught Kurd's eye. He scanned the emptiness wondering what it could have been, perhaps just a reflection off the window from inside. Then it struck him what it was. His glass slipped through his fingers and shattered on the floor. Anywhere but the emperor's flotilla and the flute would have been plastic.

The wormhole was gone. Heads turned back to the emissary. Of the group, he was now the only one paying attention as the battleship crashed into the metallic anomaly. The explosive ball of fire that consumed the ship caused him to gasp aloud. Heads snapped back to the explosion in time to see the ship vanish. The emperor stormed from the window to his throne, where he unsheathed his family's ancient samurai sword. Swinging it wildly through the air, he cursed the mysterious beings and shouted, "I will kill the first one I see!"

The generals all stood by, speechless, their mouths slack. Kurd looked wide-eyed around the room. No one seemed to notice that their shortcut back home had disappeared. His jowls flapped in an effort to form words.

"Your highness," Kurd muttered.

No one responded, as if they hadn't heard him. The bridge buzzed with commotion. Operators at their stations tried to collect any information on survivors, while others rushed to put together a rescue attempt. One of the generals even saw fit to issue an order to put all ships on high alert in the event of a retaliatory action by the anomaly.

It was madness.

Kurd approached the emperor as he collected his wits. The older man was seated at his throne in an apparent state of meditation, his ancestral sword lay across his lap. The emissary swallowed, his eyes darting back along the window to assure himself that the wormhole had in fact disappeared.

"Emperor," Kurd said.

The leader of the Nocturian empire slowly raised his eyes. In them he saw nothing but calmness.

"Yes, Emissary. Speak."

Before Kurd could utter his next words, he watched as the emperor's eyes bulged in astonishment, all but popping from his head. He was staring beyond the giant man, out the window to something in the Void. Anxiety crept through Kurd's stomach, but when he spun around to see what was going on, he breathed a sigh of relief. Another wormhole was forming.

"What's happening?" demanded the emperor.

A hundred voices tried to answer him at once as operators scrambled through their holo feeds. Data indicated that this new anomaly was similar to the one that had just vanished. It was verified that this was in fact a new wormhole opening up.

"Zoom in," he ordered.

A section of the window magnified, enhancing the area where all the activity was taking place. Lightning flashed across the screen; gray clouds swirled through the darkness. The Nocturians waited in anticipation. Who or *what* was going to come through?

"Something's coming out," a random operator announced. Nervous murmurs spread throughout the bridge.

"It's a ship," another exclaimed in excitement.

Kurd's mouth fell, his eyes growing wide. He couldn't believe it. "That's *The Legacy*," he breathed. Kurd inhaled sharply. "That's *The Legacy*," he shouted. "Intercept that ship now!"

The group of generals echoed the orders to their men, which eventually reached the rest of the armada. A couple of the specks could be seen moving away from the perimeter line, converging on the bandit ship.

"I thought they were supposed to be aboard the NGV2," said the emperor. "Why are they not with Captain Richards, Kurd?"

Kurd was confused. What in the hell had happened with the other warship? What the hell was happening right now?

"I-I don't know," he stammered. "But I plan to get to the bottom of it."

"See that you do," the emperor grunted.

Everyone watched to see how the scene would unfold. Those standing by the window had their noses to it. Heads turned from *The Legacy* back to the wormhole, where activity was picking up.

"Another ship," someone shouted.

"And another."

"Another!"

Klaxons sprang to life all throughout the *Warmonger*. Alarms blared on the rest of the Nocturian vessels as fleet upon fleet of Segan ships poured forth. People and mechs on both sides were in a frenzy to reach their battle stations. The Nocturians were prepared to make their claim. It would be a fight, though not the one they'd been expecting.

"We've been betrayed. Bring Commander Vaughn over from the NGV1's cooler," Kurd ordered.

"Get me that ship!" the emperor roared, pointing a shaky finger to the magnified image of *The Legacy*.

* * *

Commander Roschek's voice was hoarse form shouting orders. He was in a desperate attempt to disperse his fleets as the rest of their armada came out from the wormhole. He fumed, knowing that he had been baited, then lured into this trap. He should have known better. His jaw hurt from clenching his teeth. If it was war the Nocturians wanted, then he would grant them their wish.

A bombardment of lasers, plasma, and Teflon-coated steel explosives crashed into the Segan's shields. They had successfully created a colossal shield wall over the mouth of the wormhole with their fleets. Battleships, warships, and stardusters continued to stream out, adding to the shield wall.

Roschek had asked his astros repeatedly what the giant shimmering object off in the distance was, but no one could give him an answer. *It must be the reason the Nocturians are way out here,* he thought, *but why bring us out here, too?*

The Segans returned fire and began to advance. The commander was torn between pursuing *The Legacy*, approaching the mysterious structure, and fully engaging the Nocturians. He surmised that if the Nocturians were keeping their distance from the structure, then he would too, for now.

"Head for that dreadnought," Roschek ordered. "That has to be where the emperor can be found. If we can take him out, then we can shorten this battle."

"And what of *The Legacy*, sir?" inquired an astro. "The dreadnought appears to be headed for them."

Roschek's smile almost touched his ears.

"Then we'll take them both."

* * *

The expanse of the Segan's shield wall was breathtaking. The Nocturians were undergoing a similar maneuver. Both the armadas followed the trajectory of *The Legacy*, the prize in the middle. The only question was, who would overtake them first?

"They're headed toward the anomaly, sir."

"We cannot allow them to reach it," said the emperor.

"They'll just crash into it like our battleship," assured one of the generals.

"And what if they don't?" the emperor hissed. "What if they make it through? They know something, and I want to know what it is!" He slammed his fist upon his throne.

A ragged, deranged-looking man stumbled to the front of the bridge, a soldier prodding him in the back with the barrel of his rifle. His bloodshot eyes scanned the room and its many occupants, eventually landing on the scene unfolding out in the Void. A piece of his old self slid into place as he spotted Segan ships in the distance. The man raised a hand, dragging it along the observation window.

Kurd stepped forward, addressing him in an accusatory tone. This was his moment to regain some standing among what he believed to be his peers. "Commander Vaughn, that is your armada out there. Did you not tell me once that you and your small party of stardusters were in pursuit of *The Legacy* only for her bounty?" He swept his arms to the side in a flourish, indicating the enemy ships beyond. "Yet now your entire command has followed—"

"Tell me, now. What is the meaning of this, commander?" the emperor interrupted, losing patience. "Are the Segans here to claim the portal for themselves? Answer me!"

Vaughn stood beside the window mumbling to himself. Kurd imagined the commander's mind was fuzzy and still adjusting from the cooler, having lived in his head for some time now. *Portal*, in the form of a question, was the only thing anyone gleaned from his whispered ravings.

"*The Legacy* is not with us," Vaughn croaked.

"You have told that lie once before," Kurd rebutted.

Vaughn punched the window, startling everyone.

"I have dedicated years of my life to hunting down that ship. We were the ones who put the bounty on Captain Joxy's head. That bounty is sponsored by VOrg, whose headquarters are located on Sega City."

The emperor eyed Vaughn from his throne, processing the man's argument.

"Then it should be easy, commander," the emperor said.

Vaughn looked confused. "What should?"

"Telling your ships to stand down and fall back."

Vaughn blinked.

"I can try," he said. "But they would have most likely assumed me dead by now and appointed a new commander."

The emperor let loose a throaty laugh. "I see. Well, try as though your life depended on it," he said fondling his sword.

* * *

"Commander Roschek, the dreadnought is requesting a comms link."

"This should be interesting. Accept."

A ghost materialized on the bridge. The commander stumbled backward a few steps. The room went quiet. Roschek had assumed the worst, and by the looks of the shell of a man that stood before him, he wasn't too far off.

"This is Commander Vaughn of the Segan Armada," the distraught-looking man claimed, stirring voices across the bridge. "I am ordering all Segan vessels to stand down. I repeat, stand down and return to the Sega System."

Roschek could hear the lack of confidence and desperation laced in Vaughn's voice. Were the Nocturians making him say this? If so, Vaughn was betraying them all. He approached the holo figure, and Vaughn's sad eyes met his own.

"Captain Roschek," Vaughn said. "I see that you were appointed commander during my absence."

"You were M.I.A., sir. I've been promoted to acting commander in the eventuality that you did not return."

"Well, as you can see, Captain," Vaughn cleared his throat, "I have returned."

Roschek stared at his emaciated former superior, unsure of how he should respond. If he relented, he would forfeit his position as commander.

"I see," Roschek said, unable to meet his eyes. "Sir, you are aboard an enemy vessel. Your appearance and intentions are questionable. I have no choice but to deny your request and demand that the Nocturians hand you over to us without delay."

His response and request were actually reasonable. It's how the situation was supposed to be handled and would cover Roschek either way.

Something in the holo flashed across Vaughn's throat. Roschek thought for a moment that it was either a glitch or he had imagined it. Vaughn's eyes swelled from his head, his mouth gulping like a fish out of water. His head started to tilt sideways, thin strands of skin and muscle clung desperately in a final attempt to hang on.

Vaughn's body somehow managed to stay upright for a few seconds after his decapitated head had fallen. The holo morbidly depicted the man's head on the floor as it rolled to a stop. Screams at both ends of the comms link erupted before the body collapsed and the link disconnected.

Roschek was disgusted, although he would be lying if he said he wasn't happy with being the undisputed commander of the Segan Armada.

* * *

April steered *The Legacy* on a direct path toward the portal. Neither side was firing at them, yet, but they sure as hell were firing at each other. She was surprised, though thankful, that the Segans had followed them through the wormhole. They appeared to be doing a great job of diverting most of the attention away from them. Unfortunately, not all of it.

"There's two Nocturian warships barreling toward us," Raygo announced.

Sandwiched between the two forces as they were, April wasn't able to use the full power of her G-drives. Somewhere along the Nocturian line, she would have to thread the needle. This was becoming a common tactic lately. First, she had to deal with the more-immediate problem.

"Bobby, Marlow, we've got two incomings. Stay strapped in, things may get a little bumpy."

The two NG-S14s dumped their fleets of Bats. These fighters would be manned, unlike the swarm they released in Sega City.

"There's a lot more than two now," she yelled, racing to come up with a solution.

The Bats positioned themselves so that they formed a barrier as wide as it was tall. There would be no crashing through them. The warships appeared on both sides. April readjusted course in an attempt to go under them, but the barrier shadowed her movements.

She growled as she pulled back the controls, then threw her hands into the air and turned to Raygo, her eyes pleading for any suggestions. Before he could say anything, Bobby came over the comm.

"Uh, Captain, are we slowing down?"

"There's a new shield wall we have to get through that's sitting in front of an even bigger shield wall, all while another shield wall closes in from behind. If anyone has any ideas, now would be the time to share."

"Oh, okay." Bobby coughed. "Take your time, then."

"Where's Nostic?" Raygo wondered aloud.

"I'm not sure, but we're running out of time."

Something on her tactical screen caught her eye.

"A dreadnought is breaking away from the rest of the Nocturian forces. That's got to be their emperor's ride. Wonder what he's thinking about all this."

In answer, the comms system lit up indicating that a ship called *Warmonger* wished to connect. *Bet I know who that is,* April thought. She pressed connect. The holo of a tall man of Asiatic descent materialized between Raygo and herself. His confusion was not well hidden as he stared at the woman in the captain's chair.

A flabby man peeked around the tall man's side. Kurd. April recognized him instantly.

"You're not Captain Joxy," Kurd said stating the obvious. "Who are you?"

"That would take a lot of explaining," April said. "For the sake of time, can you just believe me when I say that I am the rightful captain of this vessel?"

The two men in the holo glanced at each other. "Why have you brought the Segans here? What do you want? Why are you headed for that portal? One of my battleships has already crashed into it," the tall one demanded.

> *"How do they know it's a portal?"* Raygo said to her telepathically.
>
> *"I don't know. Do you think they actually know what's going on?"*
>
> *"It doesn't sound like they know much of anything."*

"You must be the emperor," April said, with a smile. The tall man tilted his head in confirmation. "Tell Kurd that it's nice to see him, too." Kurd ducked from view. "You see, it's very important that we make it to what you are calling a 'portal.'"

"Is it not a portal then?" The emperor sounded desperate to know.

"We believe it is, and we believe we may have a way to open it for everyone," April lied.

The emperor seemed to ponder that statement. "I would love nothing more than to believe that. To put it simply, however, I don't trust you. Allow me to place some of my men on your ship to ensure you hold up your end of the bargain, and we may just have a deal."

"All right," April agreed.

Raygo shifted from one foot to the other, and April knew right away that he couldn't understand why she would agree to that. Surely he assumed the emperor was plotting something.

And just as she finished that thought, Raygo spoke into her mind, *"Are you sure that's a good idea?"*

"Trust me. I have a plan."

"Do not attempt anything funny, Captain," the emperor warned. "I've dealt with enough lies today."

"Part the Bats. We don't have time to distrust one another."

"We'll hold the Segans off."

The connection ended.

"Guys, meet us in the cargo hold, and hurry." April handed over controls to the ship's AI. She gave *The Legacy* one last directive.

* * *

"Tell those S-14s to disperse their fighters and allow *The Legacy* through," ordered the emperor. "Advance our forces. We have to buy some time."

Kurd hovered behind the throne, downing abandoned glasses of skid to alleviate his ailing nerves. He wondered if they were making the right decision. What happened with Captain Joxy? He knew she wasn't easy to dispose of. And this new woman, this April person, where had she come from, and how did she manage to wrangle command of *The Legacy* from a captain like Joxy?

A thought struck him. Could April be a BAI? It was doubtful, but if she was, it explained a lot. They'd been cautioned prior to hiring Joxy that a BAI may be part of her crew, though their scans had never picked anything up. Was that the reason the Segans were pursuing them?

Kurd tried to keep his eyes from involuntarily flicking over to Captain Vaughn's pale corpse. The former Segan commander lay in a viscous pool of his own congealing blood. Kurd gagged at every glance, throwing another glass back every time. He knew the emperor had left his body there as a message: betrayal wasn't tolerated, and failure wasn't an option.

The emperor called his name, summoning the emissary to the window. When had he left his throne? Kurd had a strong buzz going, realizing at this moment that he had made the mistake of overdoing it. He tried to gather himself on wobbly legs. Fortunately for him, he always wobbled.

A hand clapped down on Kurd's shoulder, the shock sobering him up slightly. He tried hard to grasp the fuzzy, far-off words the emperor was saying to him.

" . . . want you to take a team onto that ship and make sure everything goes accordingly."

Kurd's pulse quickened. Had he understood correctly? He panicked, unable to bring himself to say anything. He nodded dumbly. *I never should have drunk all that—*

A loud slap caused everyone on the bridge to pause what they were doing. Tears welled at the corners of Kurd's eyes as he willed them not to burst. His face stung, and he could feel the outline of each long, individual finger pulsing on his skin. His extra meat and blood alcohol level dulled the worst of it—but he was sober now.

The emperor was breathing hard. "I am relying on you Kurd." He thumbed his sword. "Do not fail me."

Kurd bowed. "Yes, Lord Emperor. I will see that your will is carried out."

A station operator broke the tension. "*The Legacy* approaches."

Another operator frantically repeated for someone to "Slow down!"

Shouts and screams erupted throughout the bridge as more and more station operators became hysterical, some of them even abandoning their posts.

Kurd and the Emperor spun around in time to see a ship rapidly growing in size. Before anyone had a chance to react further, the hull of the ship tore through the observation window, plummeted across the bridge, and smeared countless bodies across the command deck.

* * *

In the wake of the destruction, debris scattered into the Void. From Roschek's view he was able to witness *The Legacy* scalp the *Warmonger*. It was an impressive sight. The bandit ship had almost cut through the entire level, until massive carbon polymer girders eventually brought it to a halt. A second later *The Legacy* had exploded, vaporizing a huge chunk in the dreadnought's hull.

Seals clamped into place all around the *Warmonger*, cutting off entire sections in an effort to retain the ship's atmosphere. It would have taken a lot more to destroy such a beast, but for now, it was taken out of the fight. The Segans pressed forward.

* * *

April had just thrown back the tarp on the *Wasp* when Bobby and Marlow ran into the hold.

"What's going on?" Marlow asked, eyeing the tiny vessel.

"Hop in, we don't have time," April demanded as she opened the side hatch.

All four of them crawled in, basically sitting on top of one another. She reached out and pulled the hatch closed.

"You know this thing doesn't have weapons, right?" Bobby said. "Yeah, but it's fast."

Bobby and Marlow exchanged glances in the back seat, shrugging at each other's unspoken questions. A track system built into the floor moved the *Wasp* into position. The cargo door slid open, its vibrations creeping into their small vessel. Off in the distance, they watched as the Bats shrunk in size.

Marlow cocked his head to the side. "Is *The Legacy* speeding—"

The *Wasp* launched from the hold; its passengers thrown back into their seats. Compact drives propelled it swiftly away from *The Legacy*. They watched in solemn silence as the distance between their home and themselves grew. They grasped what April had done. Their ship was a last-ditch effort, a sacrifice.

April cringed as her baby made its final leap into the *Warmonger*.

She maneuvered the controls gently in her hands, aligning the vessel between two warships in the oncoming shield wall. The Wasp XX9 was tiny, so small that scanners might even misidentify them as debris from the wreckage. That's what April hoped for; she knew they needed a distraction in order to slip on by.

The hole she had to thread quickly approached. It was no larger than three of her current vessel. It would be tight, and at the speeds they were going it would be a challenge for any experienced captain.

Everyone onboard held their breath as the tiny ship banked, then drifted a few degrees starboard. April managed to skirt them through with only inches to spare. Raygo could have stuck his hand out and brushed the warship's hull. They each let out a loud sigh of relief.

Explosions boomed on both sides, blowing the *Wasp* off course. The Segans fully engaged the Nocturians. With the disabled *Warmonger*, they must have decided now was the time to pounce. As close as the two factions were, each side's heavier munitions were able to penetrate the other's shields.

Bobby turned in his seat to see what was happening behind them. The warship they had just passed was now floating in large chunks. He bounced in his seat as he blindly stretched out a hand toward April, his eyes glued to the destruction. He found her headrest and patted it excitedly.

"Oh shit! Go faster. Go faster," he shouted in the cramped cabin.

Raygo and Marlow slid around, repositioning their bodies so that their knees anchored their seats as they watched in awe. The Segan Armada was tearing a hole through the Nocturians. Shields flickered before going out, balls of fire flashed along the sides of ships as they crumbled apart.

Debris filled this part of the Void like a tornado had just spun through, the battlefield and its casualties forever destined to float in an unmoored grave.

A breach loomed in the Nocturian line. A swarm of stardusters pushed through it. April didn't dare take her eyes off of the portal ahead. Although Raygo was giving her a play by play, she couldn't get stuck on anything that was going on behind them.

"Here they come," Raygo announced. "Stardusters by the thousands."

She slid a finger along a holo screen to throttle their drives to full power, but they were already there. Compact drives tended to overheat quicker and were more likely to implode, but there wasn't another option. It was a calculated gamble, one that she was desperately hoping would pay off.

The Segans fired at them relentlessly. With the *Wasp*'s lack of shields, even a close hit could spell doom. The stardusters gained on them as their own power levels depleted. A laser round grazed the side of one of the *Wasp*'s drives and sent them into a dizzying spin. April's hands nimbly moved across the controls, as she maneuvered small thrusters to correct their spin.

An alarm escalated in the back of her head. They weren't going to make it. She snatched a quick glimpse of Raygo, worry etched into the crevices of his face. He met her eyes.

"I love you." His words came filled with emotion.

"'Til the end and beyond." She swallowed back the tears.

Another round hit the rear of the *Wasp*, lifting them up and over this time; end over end they flipped uncontrollably. It was hard to make any sense of direction. They screamed in fear; there wasn't much they could do other than that. Another blow, and it would all be over.

* * *

Commander Roschek eagerly watched as his ships tore through the Nocturian line. Both sides were taking heavy losses, the debris field itself a serious hazard at this point. He had watched *The Legacy* make its kamikaze attack, evoking mixed emotions mostly because he'd wanted to catch that ship at all costs.

The crash left him confused. Weren't the bandits working with the Nocturians? He zoomed in on the destruction, the damage devastating. A flicker of light caught his eye. Increasing the magnification of the obser-vation window, he spotted a small, fast-moving vessel. At first, he thought it was just a lifeboat from the crash, but even this was too small to be a lifeboat. His eyes narrowed. He had a good idea who might be on board.

"Concentrate fire there," he ordered, pointing to where the tiny vessel had threaded through the Nocturian line.

Segan cannons bombarded the target area, shredding Nocturian shields with an overwhelming amount of focused power. Roschek ordered a horde of his stardusters through the gaping hole. The metallic oddity was still some distance away, and he felt confident his fighters would overtake the bandits before they could reach it.

He jumped in excitement when the first hit happened, his prey spinning out of control as small plumes from the thrusters struggled to stabilize. Somehow, they managed to correct themselves but had slowed considerably. They were hobbling.

Another strike!

Roschek slammed his fist on a control panel in celebration. Watching how out of control they were, flipping end over end, made him woozy with delight. He pictured the BAIs puking all over the small cabin and actually gagged himself.

They would never make it now; the fact left him giddy. He was officially commander of the Segan Armada, defeating the Nocturian Empire, and about to collect the bounty on the most wanted person in the universe. His mouth opened to give the order for the final blow when shockingly the anomaly started to move.

The order sputtered over his lips as he watched the shimmering structure start to curve in on itself. He wanted so desperately to know what it was—he needed to know. The anomaly continued to fold, the small vessel that contained the BAIs was near enough that it would cover them. His senses rushed back to him.

"Fire!" Roschek screamed. "Fire now, everyone, fire at them!" He uploaded target coordinates to all ships.

Every ship in the Segan Armada took aim at that single location, chucking munitions through the Void. A tsunami of death was about to make landfall.

It happened fast and at the last possible moment. The portal's walls reached the *Wasp* and enveloped them. Roschek watched in disbelief as a protective bubble formed around his target; a hailstorm of munitions, a second later, crashed down upon it.

He zoomed in. No damage was apparent on this giant chrome marble.

Then his own ship pitched violently, throwing Roschek to his knees. His hands and arms stopped his upper body before his face could hit the floor.

"Direct hit," someone yelled. "Shields are down. Critical damage."

The commander swung an arm over a station's terminal, using it as leverage to pull himself up. Blood trickled down his shins. The redirection of Segan firepower had provided the Nocturians with a pivotal moment to change the tide of battle. Roschek fell apart as he watched his ships turning to slag.

Retreat was on the tip of his tongue when an explosive round lodged itself into the thick polymer of the observation window. A whiny groan escaped him. The round detonated, carving out a sizable hole. One of his arms was ripped off on his rapid exit from the ship into the Void. Globules of his own blood floated around him as the last traces of life escaped into the vacuum.

* * *

All four of them had blacked out and come to repeatedly. A strong, sour stench hung in the air. April coughed as she willed her eyelids to peel back. Odd lights shimmered throughout the cabin; it was similar to finding oneself at the bottom of a pool. Her vision was blurry and her head throbbed. She tried turning to the side, but a sharp pain radiated through her frontal lobe. Any longer on that wild ride and they might have died.

She threw her hand out, grasping for Raygo. Grabbing his harness, she shook him.

"Raygo," she whispered. "Wake up."

He didn't respond at first, and a flash of fear coursed through her. Then he groaned and inched his way back up in his seat. His eyes appeared to be unfocused.

"What happened?" he mumbled, massaging his temples. "Where are we?"

April slowly craned her neck around. Bobby and Marlow were still out, but she saw that their chests were rising and falling.

She looked out the back window. It was the same scene as the front.

"Looks like we're surrounded by the same stuff the portal was made from. I'm not sure if that's good or bad."

Raygo chuckled. "Veruna would have shit herself if she had found all this," he said, looking around in amazement.

April joined him in his laughter, but it hurt too much so she stopped. The other two stirred behind them.

"You guys okay?" she asked.

"I want my money back for that ride," Marlow quipped.

"Yeah, how about we don't ever do that again," Bobby added.

April and Raygo both agreed.

"Uh, I'm not sure where we are," Marlow said pointing a finger out a side scuttle, "but are the walls supposed to be closing in like that?"

April spun back around in her seat and swallowed a wave of nausea.

The walls were closing in! Her eyes flicked to the dash. No holo, no lights, no power. They panicked as they watched the reflection of the *Wasp* move closer. They'd either make it or they wouldn't; at least they'd be together.

There was nothing left to do, so April yelled.

"Nosticcc!"

The walls consumed them.

April's face hurt from scrunching it so hard. She expected to feel pain, but it never came. She opened one eye, then the other. Somehow they were still alive. An exhausted breath slipped out.

Their ship was gone. April didn't ponder on that confusing fact for long as her senses struggled to adjust to the surrounding stimuli of her strange new environment. Focus continued to elude her as a small delegation appeared nearby. Their bodies both shifted and strobed at once. Words, entities in their own right, were spoken by who she assumed was the group's leader. It stood slightly ahead of the others.

The Others! April remembered.

The language spoken to her was a song and dance. She could see it, feel it, and without getting too carried away, thought she could almost taste it. The leader's form grew clearer as the unintelligible words began to make sense. Nostic stepped into view in front of her, his plain, smooth humanoid form welcoming them with outstretched arms and an unnatural smile.

"Welcome, Humans," he said, "to the Eighth Realm."

His familiar form slowly melted away before her eyes. He'd once told them that he took that form for their benefit. Now she understood why. Standing before her, on four pointy stalks, was a gelatinous mass of wiry tentacles, each with their own collection of claw-like apertures at the end. The Others came into view. April's chin dropped to her throat. These creatures were eerily reminiscent of the collection VOrg once maintained before Mongrel had feasted upon them.

EPILOGUE

Captain Richards regained control of his wits and of his S-14 warship shortly after escaping the Cemetery. Fortunately for him and his crew, the Segans called off their pursuit once the Nocturians were no longer in their galaxy. He was furious that the bandit captain had made a fool of him. After taking stock of what remained of his fighter vessels, and quelling a short-lived mutiny, he turned the NGV2 around. This time he would seek vengeance upon his recent captors, at all costs.

To his surprise, they managed to make it all the way back to Sega City without incident, only to be enlightened as to why by the sight of what looked to be the Segan's entire home guard funneling into a cloudy gray mass that was streaking lightning. It looked similar on his data feeds to the one *The Legacy* had popped out of that fateful day he'd been duped.

Following behind the Segans, it was obvious that they were not concerned, or perhaps not aware of, the single warship hugging their rear. Richards puzzled over what could possibly be waiting on the other side of the anomaly that held the rapt attention of the Segans. A steady stream of vessels continued to pour into the swirling grayness and disappeared. After the very last Segan ship vanished, the Nocturian captain made his move, sending his own vessel barreling into the raging mass.

The NGV2 swooped in, then almost instantaneously popped out into a situation of complete and utter chaos. It took only a second or two for the veteran captain to grasp the situation and take evasive action. Directly in front of them lay a massive formation of Segan ships that had joined their shields. Richards watched in awe through the purplish translucence of this shield wall as his fellow Nocturians responded with similar tactics. One of his nearby station operators snapped him from his daze when they pointed out that their presence no longer registered in the known universe, and that all available data strongly indicated they had entered a location extremely far out in the Void.

Richards couldn't believe it. *Why would a war be taking place way out here?* Then he saw it. A large, shimmering object loitering in the distance. It didn't appear to him to be either a ship or a planet, but whatever it was had to be responsible for the battle taking place in front of them.

He continued to observe from behind enemy lines as the struggle unfolded, the tide shifting back and forth between one side and the other. It would be futile to attempt an attack on the Segan's rear; they would only slag him into oblivion before he even had a chance to help his comrades.

In the center of the Nocturian forces, a huge explosion erupted from atop the emperor's flagship vessel, *Warmonger*. Using the observation window, a station operator zoomed in on the destruction. Richards gasped at the extent of the destruction: nearly the entire bridge had been destroyed. Scattered thoughts ran through his mind; most importantly, *Was the emperor dead?*

Moments later, the Segans concentrated their firepower on a segment of the opposing Nocturian shield wall, decimating that entire section. The NGV2 observation window zoomed in on this new area of interest. Debris from the destroyed ships was so thick that it became more of a hazardous obstacle than any shield wall. The Segans continued their bombardment for some reason that eluded the captain.

"Zoom in further," he ordered the operator.

The debris field grew in size as a section of the window zoomed in even further. He struggled to identify what they continued to fire at.

"There," the operator pointed out. "I-it looks like it might be a Wasp XX9." The operator let loose a sharp whistle. "They've got to be experiencing some serious g's."

Captain Richards only saw a fast-moving blur. Then, what appeared to be a Segan round, clipped one of the tiny vessel's drives, sending it into a nausea-inducing spin. He thought for sure that the speeding ship was done for until it somehow managed to quickly recover and continue on its course. Curious, the captain tapped away on the holo beside him. A green line indicating the XX9's trajectory popped onto the screen, ending at the metallic curiosity off in the distance.

Fireballs burst from a throng of Segan vessels at the front of their line. Ship hulls quivered as explosions ripped at their insides. Shields flickered, then disappeared, as warships and battleships crashed into each other and disintegrated. Richards couldn't believe such stupidity. How could the Segans have made such a tactical error? Why concentrate all their firepower at one little insignificant vessel? Unless . . .

His eyes darted back to the magnified portion of his ship's observation window. More rounds appeared to have hit their target. The XX9 was dotted with holes, an entire drive missing from its port side. The tiny vessel slowly drifted, no longer maintaining its initial trajectory, and still some ways off from its destination. A swarm of stardusters were attempting to navigate the Nocturian debris field in an effort to converge on their prey.

Richards quickly got on the comms to the surviving remnants of the Nocturian armada. "This is Captain Richards of the NGV2 S-14 warship. There is a Wasp XX9 that is non-operational and adrift. It's imperative that we retrieve this vessel before the Segans do. Stardusters are already in pursuit. So move!"

For a few moments only silence answered him back. Then, excited chatter lit up the Nocturian airwaves.

"Glad to have you back," multiple fleet commanders echoed.

"Where the hell you been at?" Captain Long barked. "We could have used you, but you waited until all the action was over. Typical ole Richards."

The captain smiled at the familiar voice, happy to hear that his old friend was still alive.

The stardusters retreated from their pursuit once they realized an overwhelming force of Nocturians were headed their way. In their haste, many of the Segan fighters were destroyed from colliding debris. Those who managed to clear the wreckage were mercilessly picked apart by canons. The bridge of the NGV2 cheered in celebration as they watched what remained of Sega City's home guard flee back through the wormhole.

Captain Richards maintained his poise, refraining from celebrating just yet, while he watched patiently as a Nocturian battleship retrieved the shredded XX9. Shortly after the retrieval was complete, one of his officers, who was stationed nearby, walked up to him. The captain's heartbeat quickened. He would have his revenge on Captain Joxy and any of her remaining crew.

"Well?" Richards asked the officer.

"There were four bodies inside. One was DOA. Two were unconscious, and the fourth, a female, appeared to be stuck in some hallucinogenic state, perhaps brought on by trauma."

"The female," Richards said, "was it Captain Joxy?" If so, he wondered what happened to her ship and crew.

The officer rushed back to his terminal to extract more details. Too impatient to wait, Richards trailed him. Peering over his shoulder, the captain scanned the information as it came over the holo. Pictures of the four individuals uploaded across the screen. He recognized only one of them, the man who had escorted him from this very bridge. The man who aided Joxy in the commandeering of his ship. But where in all hells were Captain Joxy and *The Legacy*?

"What are your orders, Captain?" the officer asked.

Richards rubbed at his eyes in frustration, then peered out at the mass of destruction littered before him. He had so many issues that needed tending, most important, finding out whether or not the emperor was still alive. He let out a sigh before squaring his shoulders.

"Place them all in the cooler." He held up one hand to prevent the officer from interrupting him. "Yes, even the dead one. We'll deal with them all later. For now, take stock of our forces." He pointed to the wormhole. He didn't trust traveling through the Void. "Our way home is back through that thing, and I'd be willing to bet a round of skid for the entire crew that the Segans will be waiting for us on the other side."

He turned to assess the giant, silvery object stationed in the distance, unsure of what he should do in regards to keeping whatever it was safe from enemy hands.

He blinked twice.

It was gone.

ACKNOWLEDGMENTS

In no particular order, I'd like to thank Mom and Dad, Moni, Brandon and Scott for your commitment to me as parents and a brother. Daryl "Superman" for offering to be the book's cover model. Diane for your continued friendship and support. Thank you to Hes and Bhatti for your time and proofreads. I could not have created this version of the story without Kim, whose edits and suggestions helped take this book to the next level. Thank you to everyone who contributed financially and logistically. This was truly a team effort. I take sole credit for any mistakes. Writing and self-publishing a book from prison is no easy task.

ABOUT THE AUTHOR

Tyler Bowman is an incarcerated writer serving three consecutive sentences in the state of North Carolina. He enjoys writing fiction and nonfiction, the latter of which has been published in *Dollars & Sense* magazine. He's currently working on his next novel, which is sure to tug at your heartstrings. After that, his focus will be on the sequel to *Legacy of Stars*. Stay tuned.